LOVE & WORTH

Halley Royal Hupp

Published by

Halley Royal Hupp

2024

LOVE & WORTH

First edition. July 7, 2024.

Copyright © 2024 Halley Royal Hupp.

Written by Halley Royal Hupp

This is a work of fiction.
Names, characters, locations, and incidents either are the product
of the author's imagination or are used fictitiously, and any
resemblance to actual persons, living or dead, business
establishments, events, or locales is entirely coincidental.

To my wife, Stacy,

for her love and partnership.

To my parents, Leigh and Shirley,

for their love and encouragement.

And to my children, Reagan and Sulli,

who amaze me every day.

CHAPTER 1 - WILL

THE WHITE GLOW OF THE snowstorm broke the darkness of midnight. I locked my hands on the steering wheel, white knuckles on black leather. The dry heat in the dark gray Highlander I drove kept us protected. I glanced back at my son, who slept in his car seat. *My son.* I felt a mixture of both pride and fear. Jamison J. Monroe was about three months old. He and I were of limited acquaintance, but that was going to change. One choice had led to this and, not for the first time in the last few days, I wondered if I was prepared to be a single parent.

The wind hit the Highlander from the north, and I felt the car slide left. Electricity shot through me as fear took hold. I gripped the steering wheel harder, as if that were possible. I strained to see through the blanket of snow that reflected my headlights back at me. From the back of the car, I heard a gurgle. I held my breath for a second. *What would I do if he woke up*? I couldn't pull over in the storm to care for him. *Sleep Jamison.*

Another gust of wind hit the car, and I again squeezed the steering wheel. Through the snow I saw a green sign marking the fact that I was near the city of Ellensburg, Washington. I took half a second to review the map app on my iPhone and then scanned the road ahead. Dread hit me as I saw the warnings pop up on the phone. The raging winter storm had closed Interstate 90. The red line of taillights showed the beginning of a backup. I slowed a bit and switched to the Washington roads website, which confirmed the road closure.

"Dammit." The word was halfway out of my mouth and then I dropped my voice quickly. Jamison responded with another gurgle.

The map app redirected me to Highway 97.

Leavenworth, I thought. I whispered to myself, "I guess there's no choice." If the map app was correct, an accident or an avalanche had closed Interstate 90. Currently, my phone showed the Highway 2 pass was open. I didn't want to go backwards to Spokane. *I guess it's Leavenworth*. I readjusted my hands and dried my palms on my pants. I wasn't sure at that moment what worried me more, the thought of my childhood home or the storm. I looked back at Jamison and knew there was no other choice.

Leavenworth was home until I was eighteen. I left after high school and went off to college at the University of Washington with a full academic scholarship. A Bachelor of Science in Programing and some lucky breaks led to the creation of my software company. That company created a little app that became extremely popular. So much so that Microsoft bought it rather than creating their own. I still worked because I loved it, not because I needed to. At some point, my company went international, and my life got even busier.

What I had not done over the last twelve years was communicate often or well with my parents or old friends. Sure, I sent texts at Thanksgiving and Christmas. On their birthdays and anniversary, I called my parents. I sent them checks and tried to be a dutiful son, even if I wasn't coming home. I wasn't a jerk, and I certainly didn't try to cut them out of my life. I just didn't want to return to Leavenworth. I hadn't gone back in twelve years, and I hadn't planned on it anytime soon. The town held memories. Who was I kidding, the town held her. What do you do when an entire place is love lost, especially when she remained, and you left? I had tried to go back a few times, but I knew every conversation would be about her, about us. Everyone would ask if I had talked to her. There would be no escape from the past or the memories that every store or restaurant would bring to life. And throughout Leavenworth there would be Christmas ornaments and decorations everywhere. I was never strong enough to return, but now the weather had other ideas.

Leavenworth is beautiful, and that certainly wasn't the reason I had avoided it. It's a town that reinvigorated itself back in the sixties by turning itself into a Bavarian village. It was a success and Leavenworth became a mixture of a small town and tourist town with a Bavarian wrapper. Growing up there was confusing. While the town wrapped itself in Bavaria, it was not a German village by any means. Unfortunately, people often judge a book by the cover, which meant when playing sports and dealing with people out of town, there were always the miserable German jokes. At Christmas, Leavenworth truly came to life. It was a storybook Christmas tale. The smells of cookies, the sounds of carols, and every store, restaurant, home, and tree decked out for Christmas. It was the home for Christmas in Washington. I had missed it; I knew I had. That wasn't why I hadn't returned home. I thought about my high school girlfriend, Adi. Well, really the only girlfriend I had ever had. I wondered for a second about what she was doing. I looked back at Jamison and felt the tears well up in my eyes. *How could I have known?*

At the end of high school, I just felt like I wanted more. My parents hadn't gone to college, nor could they afford to send me to UW, but I took care of that myself. Adi just wanted to stay in Leavenworth. She loved the town and wanted to have a family in it. It felt like she loved Leavenworth more than me. We broke up. A couple of my friends went off to college, but even they returned to Leavenworth, or at least that's what I learned from social media. And then there was John Greer. He went off to Afghanistan. I almost came back to Leavenworth for his funeral. I had driven halfway, but I just couldn't do it.

Highway 97 was slow going. The snow hampered the Highlander even with all wheel drive. There were cars on the road, but it looked like I made the turn before others figured out that Interstate 90 was closed. I looked at Jamison, who slept through the storm. *Lucky kid,* I thought, and then my heart jumped and fell at the same time.

Jamison wasn't all that lucky. I had met his mother at a computer convention in Spokane about a year ago. We hit it off and one thing led to another. Unfortunately, that small percentage chance that the boxes warn you about really exists. She told me as soon as she knew, and we stayed in touch. I was there for the important doctor's appointments and Jamison's birth. His mother got a paternity test, though it wasn't necessary. Jamison in all ways was a miniature me.

I thought his mother and I were communicating well. I spent as much time in Spokane with Jamison as I could. What she didn't tell me about were the complications that followed the pregnancy. Well, she didn't tell me at first. About a week before things became fatal, she called me, and I headed out again to Spokane. At the hospital she handed me Jamison, a birth certificate with our names on it, a bag, an electric cooler, and explained that I was Jamison's only family.

I tried to console her. I felt like I barely knew her, but I spent three days with her while I cared for Jamison and remained by her side until the end. She passed on December 6th. I wasn't sure how I felt about it. I still was unsure. Fatherhood and commitment weren't a life I had chosen for myself. But sometimes God has other plans. I arranged for her burial and felt like a total outsider at the service. Every Christmas I had thought about home since I left Leavenworth. Now so close to Christmas, I had the best present in the world sleeping in my back seat and yet a part of me could only feel guilty. I felt guilt for Jamison's mother, for Adi, and for John. *So many choices made.*

I came to the Highway 2 cut off and turned left and headed west. The snow slowed a bit, and for the first time I had some hope that I might get to Edmonds, Washington. Edmonds is a medium-sized city just north of Seattle on the Puget Sound. There were many reasons it was a wonderful place to grow up. Edmonds had all the benefits of Seattle, without most of the drawbacks of the larger urban sprawl. But it was small town America as well.

Hope did not last long. The drive to Leavenworth worsened the closer I got to town. The snow picked up, as did the wind. I fought the steering wheel and the blur of snow outside my windshield as I travelled into town. I wouldn't get to Edmonds tonight. The map app gave little help. There was no way I could spend hours in the storm with Jamison in the back seat. While my luck had held so far, it was only a matter of time before he woke up.

"Siri," I said, "Call Dad." The phone dialed.

My father's voice came through the Highlander's speakers, and I turned down the volume. "William, are you alright, do you know what time it is?"

"Yes, dad," I replied, "I'm in Leavenworth."

There was a chirp of joy in his voice as he said, "Come to the house, son. It's miserable outside."

"Thank you, I'll be there soon."

Jamison and I drove farther down Highway 2 and deeper into Leavenworth. I had not told my parents about Jamison. I meant to, but the year just disappeared and then suddenly he was born. At that point, I wasn't sure of my role as father, so I was even less sure of theirs' as grandparents. How do you tell your parents about a child they might not get to see? When I discovered I would be a single parent, well, there just wasn't time to tell them, until now. *Surprise!*

Even through the snow, I could see the Christmas lights that broke through the white of the storm and decorated Leavenworth. I turned right on Ski Hill Drive and then after a while I turned left on Ranger Road. I had never been to this house, but I had bought it for my parents, and I knew where it was. A few minutes later, I turned into my parents' driveway and pulled up towards the garage. As I got close, the garage door opened, and I pulled the Highlander into the garage. My father, Harold Monroe, stood at the door between the garage and the house. Behind him, I could see my mother, Anne.

They both wore pajamas and stood in the cold doorway with huge smiles on their faces.

I turned off the engine and got out of my vehicle.

"Hello, have any luggage?" Dad's voice resonated with happiness.

"Some," I replied.

"Need any help?"

"Probably. I'll hand you a few things." I went to the back of the Highlander and opened the back. I removed my suitcases, then walked to the stairs. My father grabbed the suitcases from me. My mother stood behind him, smiling and crying.

He disappeared with the suitcases for a second and then returned. "Anything more?"

"I've got the rest." I walked back to the Highlander. I opened the door to the passenger backseat and pulled Jamison and his car seat out of the back. Holding Jamison's car seat in my left hand, I disconnected his cooler from the charger, and then shut the door. I walked around the front of the Highlander and came up the stairs. My parents both fixed their gaze on Jamison.

Dad closed the garage door.

My mother asked in the quietest of voices, "Who is this?"

I walked into the house. "This is your grandson, Jamison." The door to the house closed behind me.

We walked into the warmth of the house and Jamison adjusted himself in his car seat to the temperature change and the fresh smells.

My mother's eyes shed tears and my father just stood there, speechless. I put the bags down in the hallway and then moved to the living room followed by my parents. I sat Jamison's car seat on the couch and then excused myself. I found the kitchen and moved the frozen milk from the cooler into the freezer. I kept one bottle out and began warming it. "How's he doing?"

Dad stepped into the doorway. "He's beautiful."

"Still asleep?"

"Yes, but it looks like he might wake up soon."

I finished warming the bottle. Mom sat next to Jamison and stared at him. She heard me enter. "How old is he?"

"Three months." I handed her the bottle. "Want to feed him?"

She accepted the bottle. Tears started again as I extracted Jamison from his car seat and handed him to her. He took the bottle without opening his eyes.

Dad's hand rested on my shoulder. "So, how'd this happen?"

"I believe you were the one who gave me the birds and bees talk, Dad."

"You know that's not what I meant."

I laughed. "I met a woman about a year ago. We thought we were being safe, turned out not so much." I watched my mother feed Jamison, who still had his eyes closed and seemed blissfully focused on his bottle.

My mother asked, "Where is she?"

I sat down and my father did as well. "I learned after Jamison's birth that his mother was never supposed to get pregnant. She had some health issues. But she put Jamison's health before her own. She died a little over a week ago."

Mom adjusted herself on the couch and turned to face me. "I'm so sorry."

"We hardly knew each other. At most, we were just friends."

Dad reached out and put his hand on my knee. "Seems like she'll always be more than that." He looked at Jamison.

"True," *So true.* My mind wandered and I couldn't help but think about Adi as we sat there quietly watching Jamison eat.

CHAPTER 2 - ADI

I WHISPERED TO MYSELF, "shake it off, Adi." I stood at the huge front window of my house and watched as the snow piled up in the front yard. The lights inside were off, which allowed me to see the colorful glow of the Christmas lights outside and the swirling storm beyond. Christmas was supposed to be the most wonderful time of the year - a time for family and friends, for warmth and togetherness. But as I stood there, alone in the dark, I couldn't help but feel a pang of sadness.

Through the gently falling snow, I could see the warm glow of the Monroe's house across the street. Despite being over sixty, Mr. Monroe still decorated his house with festive cheer, lighting it up as bright as possible. They had moved in a few years before I bought my own cozy home. It felt strange to live so close to them, but their welcoming smiles and friendly waves made it impossible to hold their son's actions against them. My thoughts drifted to Will and I couldn't help but wonder what he was doing at that very moment. I almost reached for my phone to check social media, but decided to focus on the peaceful snow and the twinkling Christmas lights instead.

As I stood there, I saw a vehicle approach and then head to the Monroe's house. It disappeared into the snow. I had lived in Leavenworth my entire life, but had never seen the snow fall like this. Despite my genuine concern about the storm, I smiled at the thought of a white Christmas with trees covered in snow and families all cozy in the warmth of their homes.

I moved away from the window and turned the lights back on. The joy of Christmas was tangible and brought warmth to my heart. I sat back down at the dining room table. Right before winter break, we completed projects and exams at school. The children were on break, but I still had a lot of work to do. I knew the first day of school, Tammy Huff would ask, "Ms. Lewis, what were my grades?" That little girl stressed more than anyone I had ever met. But she did decent work, though she struggled to socialize with the other second-grade children. I had tried to help her, but so far hadn't had much success. I pulled out my notebook and wrote another note to myself to meet with Tammy's parents.

I looked away from the homework and examined my Christmas decorations. Every room in the house had a theme. I had decorated most of the doors with wrapping paper and ribbon so that each door looked like a giant Christmas present. The lights glowed with the warmth of Christmas cheer, and I had to smile at my success. The house looked magnificent. When I looked over at the fireplace, I could see the nativity scene I had set up. I focused on the family in the manger and the baby swaddled there. I felt the tears well up in my eyes. *Dammit.*

My phone buzzed, and I looked down as I wiped the tears from my eyes. I picked up the phone. The newest dating app my best friend, Clare, had installed had sent me a notification. Steven wrote he loved the name "Adi" and would really like to meet me sometime. The rest of his message was the usual nonsense, and I quickly swiped left. I hate dating apps, but the second I removed it Clare would magically know and say something like, "Adalynn Jane Lewis, you cannot simply be a wallflower. It's the 21st century, it's ok to take charge of your own dating life." Clare always did what she thought was best, whether or not we agreed. I got up and pulled a tissue out of its box. I wiped my eyes and nose then I moved into the living room.

Despite my efforts to deck the halls and fill the house with Christmas cheer, I was still alone. This wasn't the life I had planned for myself. My dream was to live in a home, not just a house. In all other ways, my life was perfect. I loved my work, my friends, my home, and my family. I hadn't planned to go to college to become a teacher, but sometimes God has his own plans for us. When I didn't leave Leavenworth with Will, my parents encouraged me to go to college. I went to Western Washington University and earned a degree that allowed me to teach. WWU was great, but the whole time I knew I would come back to Leavenworth. I didn't enjoy being away from home for even four years. I had a wonderful time at college and really enjoyed Bellingham, a city in the northwestern part of Washington State less than an hour from Vancouver, Canada. College was a wonderful experience. The degree helped a lot, and because of the degree, I was now a second-grade schoolteacher. I loved teaching. It was my calling, and I couldn't imagine my life without it. I turned off the lights in the living room and looked out again at the storm and the Christmas lights. The world simply looked better with snow and colored lights. Christmas was magical.

At college, I met Edward. He was a good man, but he was never Will. We fell in love, I guess, and spent the last two years of college together. We got married about six months after we graduated. Eventually we tried to have kids. Edward was from an enormous family. He had six siblings who lived in Spokane, Wenatchee, and really all over Washington State. We both wanted children. In hindsight, it was the one thing we truly had in common.

It was a Christmas very much like this one that we finally decided we needed help. That first doctor's appointment was terrifying. We never discussed it, but we both secretly blamed each other. In the end, I had no one to blame but myself. I had a surgery and then another. We tried calendars, temperatures, and drugs. Eventually, we drained our savings and even the doctors gave up. I tried to talk to Edward about adopting, but he had a specific definition of children and family. He said he still loved me, but he left three months later. Will had done something similar. I felt the heartache in my chest and as a burn at the back of my throat. We completed the divorce in the first week of December. I got the house and the neighbors. He got to find the mother of his children. The tears began again.

"No," I said to myself, "you won't cry for him." But I knew I wasn't. I cried for myself. I knew there was no man who could give me what I wanted. My problem wasn't my husband, it was my body. This time I let myself cry. That choice was still mine.

It took fifteen minutes for the tears to stop. A good cry was a safe release and an effective way to cleanse. I shuffled the papers. Looking down at the schoolwork, I decided to finish it all tomorrow.

I meandered over to the couch and turned on the television. I chose a Christmas show and delved into memories of Christmases' past. *I do not need a man; I can always adopt by myself.* This wasn't the first time I had considered adoption on my own, but it was feeling more right. I wanted a family. I had a lot to share. There was no reason I couldn't adopt. As I reached for my computer to do a search, my phone rang. I looked down and saw it was my mother, Joanne Lewis. I answered the phone. "It's late mom."

"Yes, dear," she said. "Do you have the news on?"

"No," I switched channels to find a news station.

"Interstate 90 is shut down, Highway 2 west is closed, and the eastern route will be closed as well. The news called this a hundred-year storm."

"Think we'll lose power?" I asked.

"When this turns into ice, we might. You check your generator?"

I answered, "Dad checked it in the Fall." My father, Lee Lewis, never stopped moving. He was a man of energy and he loved to help people.

I could hear her smile over the phone. "That doesn't surprise me. Keep warm, keep safe, and we'll see you tomorrow." She paused and then asked, "Are you all done with the decorations?"

"Just need the tree."

"It is almost time to go harvest one."

I smiled. "It is. I cannot wait."

"It will be a good tomorrow, Adi."

"I know, mom."

"You sleep well, honey."

"Will do, mom, I love you."

"I love you too."

I did a few searches on the computer and I watched television for a bit to catch up on the news about the hundred-year storm. I switched to the Hallmark channel and started midway through a Christmas Hallmark show I had seen before. As I half watched the show, I pulled up Facebook on my phone and scanned through it.

I was never a big user of social media and because of the divorce; I wished it didn't exist. It's a lot of fun to have people interested in your business when you post family shots, images of meals, or photos of trips. The situation is vastly different when people post condolences, which is no fun at all. And then there's the inevitable posts of your ex dating someone. You cannot help but rubberneck and look at those posts. You cannot help but compare yourself to her and even comment in private chats with your friends about the post. In the end, none of it is healthy or helpful. I almost removed all my social media apps, but then I decided not to. It was my choice how I would react. I wouldn't be driven offline. I was glad I hadn't left social media because in December, social media became the new Christmas Card. It was wonderful to see what people were doing and read their well wishes. I loved all the Christmas photographs and the pictures of children with Santa.

I turned off the phone and walked to my bedroom. I looked at the king-size bed, which I now got to fill with as many pillows as I wanted. I smiled at that. I went into the bathroom and stripped down. A quick shower washed away my puffy eyes and the tension in my shoulders. I slipped into my most comfortable flannel pajamas and crawled into bed. The TV remote was on my side of the bed, and I hit the power button. I tried to ignore the thought that both sides of the bed were now mine. A Christmas program came on, but within minutes sleep overcame my thoughts of a white Christmas.

CHAPTER 3 – WILL

MOVEMENT WOKE ME. I opened my eyes to see my mother pick up Jamison out of his portable bassinet. It was one of the many pieces of equipment his mother had ready for me before I came to Spokane. "Shh," my mother said. I wasn't sure if she addressed Jamison or me. Maybe it was both of us.

I stretched to show her I was awake. "You want me to handle it?"

"No dear, my pleasure. You had a rough drive. Sleep."

I wanted to argue, but I looked at the clock, which showed it was just about 5:00 a.m., I decided instead to be agreeable. "Thanks mom."

She turned, smiled at me, and walked out of the room with Jamison in her arms. I tried to go back to sleep, but couldn't. As I lay there, I took the time to carefully examine the room around me. This wasn't the home I grew up in; I knew that. I had sent my parents money for years and eventually they upgraded and bought a new house. But as I studied the room, I swear it looked almost identical to the room I had grown up in. Mom had painted the walls with the same blue-gray color. My mother moved my old posters, trophies, computers, and everything else to this room. She had laid out the room the way I had left it twelve years earlier. It was an imperfect trip back through time.

My eyes rested on the bassinet, and that shook me from the nostalgia. I knew I couldn't get back to sleep. There were things to do now that I was a father. I got up, grabbed clothes, and looked down the hallway for the bathroom. I found it a couple of doors down. Mom had a washcloth and towel ready for me. There was also, I noted, a toothbrush in its wrapper and a disposable razor. *As if I didn't have my own with me.*

I took a warm shower and allowed the water to beat on my lower back for a good long while. Limbered up and clean, I got out of the shower and dried off. I threw on my clean clothes and then reached for the right drawer. Inside it, I found a hair dryer and brush. *Mom, dependable as always.* I dried my hair and left the bathroom with the towel on the counter and the hair dryer plugged in. As I exited the bathroom, I smiled a bit. I turned off the light. There was teasing and then there was teasing, I decided.

I went down the hallway into the main part of the house. I saw my mom at a small wooden table at the edge of a beautiful modern kitchen. "How is he?"

"He's so beautiful. It's like you were born all over again."

I grabbed a cup from the cabinet left of the sink, put it in the Keurig, and searched around until I found a coffee pod. The smell of Sumatra quickly filled the kitchen. "It is strange how much he looks like me."

"Do you have a picture of his mother?"

A good question, and one that his mother had prepared for. She had downloaded her lifetime of pictures into my phone. She also supplied letters and videos for Jamison for his first eighteen birthdays. I found a recent photo and showed it to my mother.

"She was lovely," she said.

"She was," I said.

"And you two only spent that one night together?"

Leave it to mom to be blunt. I'm not sure there was anything that would embarrass her. "We spent a few days together when I was in Spokane and then we stayed in touch, and I visited once she learned she was pregnant. I was there for Jamison's birth."

"Why Jamison? And is it spelled like the whiskey?" My mother grinned at me.

I laughed. "I was never a great speller."

"No, no you were not," mother patted Jamison's back to encourage a belch.

"Well, the second night we texted, and I told her how I really enjoyed the entire bottle of 'J a m i s o n' we shared the night before."

Mom shook her head. "You named him after a misspelled bottle of Jameson."

"Seemed fair since Jameson contributed."

There was the briefest of pauses, and then she laughed just a little. "God works in mysterious ways and there's no reason that cannot include a good bottle of Irish Whiskey," she said. She moved Jamison from her shoulder and into her arms. "He's quieter than you were. And you never seemed to sleep at all. Jamison is so much calmer than you were."

"Which is a good thing." I finished my coffee. "We have enough breast milk in the freezer. She froze a couple of weeks' worth. But I need to get diapers and other supplies for Jamison." It felt so good to be home, and I realized I had no plans to leave. I hadn't even looked to see if the roads were open. *Isn't that interesting?*

Mom enjoyed every second of Jamison in her arms. "How long will you be here?"

"I'm not sure."

Dad walked in from another room and put a large hand on my shoulder. I could feel his warmth through my shirt. He gave me a firm squeeze. His workman's strength had not left him over the last twelve years. "You and Jamison are welcome here. We missed you."

I looked up and saw tears in my father's eyes. I wanted to say that I had missed them as well, but it wasn't the truth. I knew what I felt, and I told them, "I'm glad to be back. I think I'll at least stay through Christmas."

He smiled and squeezed my shoulder again. He moved over and gave my mother a kiss on her cheek. "Be careful about how attached you get there, Anne." He turned and gave me one of those dad's looks. We both knew it was too late for my mom.

"I need to go to the store. Jamison needs supplies."

Dad said, "They cleared Roads this morning. It's still snowing, but your rig should handle it fine."

Mom pointed at the counter. "I made a list."

I picked the list up and scanned it. "Didn't forget anything, did you?" I smiled. Mom didn't respond. Jamison had fallen asleep in her arms.

I picked up my jacket and donned it. I checked and found my gloves in the pockets and then went to the garage door. My father met me there and handed me a garage door opener. "We always hoped you'd come to our new home. This is yours."

I looked down at the garage door opener. "Thank you." I wanted to give him a hug. It seemed proper, but neither of us seemed comfortable at that moment. I let the door close between us and got into my Highlander. The garage door opener slid nicely onto the sun visor on the passenger side. It looked simply fine next to the one that opened the gate and doors at my home in Edmonds.

I pushed the new button, the garage door opened, and I pulled out. I closed the door and backed the rest of the way out of the driveway. Slowly, I headed down the road. I had heard there was a Safeway in town now, but I had no intention of shopping at Safeway. Instead, I travelled past the heart of town to Dan's Food Market. It was a little after 7:00 in the morning, but even on a miserable snowy day like today, I knew that Dan's opened at 5:00 a.m.

I saw that someone had shoveled the parking lot and piled up the new snow on the partially bare spaces. There were a few vehicles in the lot, but it was basically empty. I turned right and pulled into the lot. I parked right in front of the building. As I got out of the Highlander, a cold, brisk wind reminded me that there was still a storm blowing. I ducked quickly into Dan's and let the warm air surround me.

They had decorated the store with Christmas decorations and lights. I grabbed a cart, opened mom's list, and foraged through the store. I had made it from the produce aisle, through the soups, and past the juices when I ran into the first person I knew.

"William Monroe, is that you?"

"Hello Mrs. Darcy," I said.

Mrs. Darcy was that voluptuous elementary school teacher that all the boys joked about. *She had to be retired by now.* She grabbed me into an enormous hug, which took the wind out of me. "I thought you had left us for good." After a longer than comfortable hug, she let go and took a step back.

That was the plan. "I've been busy. You look wonderful," I said, "Still teaching?"

"No silly," she replied. "I retired years ago. Where are you living these days?"

"Edmonds, just a few miles north of Seattle," I said, "but right now I'm at my parents' house because of the storm."

She made herself shiver and said, "It is terrible out there. I need to stock up."

"Mom gave me a list." I grinned at her. "A list I should get back to. It was a pleasure to see you, Mrs. Darcy."

"Yes, it was. Have you seen Adi yet?"

I knew the answer, but I asked, "She is still in town?"

She shook her head. "Of course; she is, you silly man. Some people remember where they grew up." Her voice lost a bit of its mirth. "If I don't see you again, have a Merry Christmas." She walked away.

"You too, Mrs. Darcy." *First person I ran into and already they had asked the dreaded question.*

I walked through the aisles and only had to walk past Mrs. Darcy twice as our alternating paths crossed. The last time we crossed paths, she gave me a startled look as she caught sight of the diapers, wipes, formula, and bottles in my cart. I knew we had the milk in the freezer, but I wasn't going to risk Jamison's health on a power outage. She was about to say or ask something, but before she could I said, "It was lovely to see you, Mrs. Darcy." I then hustled to the checkout.

I made it out of Dan's, packed the car up, and left the parking lot about the time Mrs. Darcy exited the store. I escaped for the moment, but I knew that Mrs. Darcy was about to spread the gossip of the contents in my cart among her chatty friends and family. William Monroe, father, was about to become the news of Leavenworth.

I turned on some Christmas music and drove through town. There was nothing like small town gossip. I was deep in thought about the oncoming gossip. I was not paying attention to the road. It was only at the last minute that I realized I was about to miss my turn onto Ski Hill Drive. I hit the brakes hard, turned right, and slid a bit on the ice and new snow. I must have missed hitting another vehicle because someone laid on their horn like it was their job. The back of the Highlander was still covered in snow, so I couldn't make the vehicle out. But the trumpet of the horn was no positive affirmation.

CHAPTER 4 - ADI

I YELLED, "JERK," AND held my horn down. "What were you thinking?" The SUV had almost hit me as I turned off Ski Hill Drive east onto Highway 2. I needed to pick up some things from the store just in case the storm got worse. The SUV came out of nowhere and then did a high-speed turn. My guess was it was some Seattle skier caught in the storm. Sometimes I really didn't like the tourists that visited our town.

I travelled through the heart of the town and fought my temper down. I turned on the radio. The joy of the Christmas music immediately calmed me. I could be upset, or I could enjoy the Christmas adorned town around me. I did the latter. The tension left my shoulders and neck as I enjoyed the music. As I looked at the Christmas decorations around Front Street Park, I felt even better. I passed the McDonald's on the right and saw the line of cars of people who waited for their morning coffee and McDonald's breakfasts. That was not a line I was going to get in. Past the McDonald's was Dan's. I pulled into the parking lot that was mostly empty. As I pulled in, I saw Mrs. Darcy's truck pull out of the lot. She turned right onto Highway 2. *Must be heading home.*

I got into the store without too much snow piling up on me, grabbed a cart, and headed down the aisles. They had given Dan's a Christmas makeover and it looked wonderful. As I walked into the store, I noticed the sweet aroma of cinnamon and the pleasant sound of Christmas carols playing over the speakers. As I walked down an aisle, a memory of William came unbidden, and I remembered how he always called shopping in Dan's foraging. I smiled to myself. Leavenworth had always been too small for William. I thought he loved me more than he hated Leavenworth, but I was wrong. He had been my high school sweetheart, but he needed to leave. He became a big-time computer geek in Seattle. I followed him on social media sometimes, but it was difficult to do that and balance feelings after I met Edward. I had thought off and on about him, but it felt like I could almost feel his presence in Dan's. "Foraging," I said aloud and laughed.

William was such an unusual person. If some people, like me, felt more comfortable living within the confines of a box, Will lived outside the box. No, that wasn't quite right. More like Will wasn't even aware the box was there. That wasn't to say he didn't follow the rules or the law, he just did it the best way he understood it should be done. In the case of shopping in Dan's that meant thinking of it as foraging. I smiled again and worked my way through the store doing my own foraging. There were a couple of people shopping besides me. They were all locals and we greeted each other as we passed. Mrs. Thomas stopped long enough to say how sorry she was about Edward. I gave her a smile and then left before the conversation could be extended.

When I got to the checkout line, Rob Olson greeted me. Rob had gone to school with Will and me. "Hey Rob," I said.

"Adi Lewis." He had a Cheshire Cat grin that seemed out of place.

I asked, "What's new?"

"This and that. You heard from Will recently?"

"No," I looked hard at Rob and wondered if he had heard me say forage aloud.

"Gotcha. Miss the guy. Any idea where he is right now?"

I put my groceries up and hoped it would encourage Rob to do his job. "No Rob, we haven't spoken since just before he left."

"Ah, sorry," he said. "I wonder if he would contact any of us if he came into town?"

"I doubt it."

Rob bagged my groceries. "You don't think he would?"

I replied, "I don't think he would come back into town."

"Yep, you would think that." He took my money and finished the transaction. He still had the Cheshire Cat grin on. "Have a good one Adi, stay warm."

"You too, Rob." I left the store, got into my Forester, and pulled out onto Highway 2. "Siri, call mom, mobile." The phone dialed.

Mom answered and asked, "Adi, how are you this morning?"

I replied, "I'm fine mom. Just got some stuff from Dan's. I forgot to call and see if you needed anything. I can go back and get anything you need."

Mom laughed. "Your father was out at 5:00 this morning stocking up. We are fine."

Dad was amazing. "Sounds good. What are your plans today?"

"Your father and I are going to walk downtown a little. We want to see everything they setup yesterday. We thought about getting lunch at South. You want to join us?"

Mexican food in a snow drenched Bavarian village? I replied, "Sure, I'll be there at noon." We hung up and I kept driving.

Clare called and I answered the phone. "What's up lady?"

"It's cold, cold, and well cold."

I asked, "Furnace go out again?"

"Go out, no. Working hard to put out only a trickle of heat, yes definitely. I've called the manager."

"Good. He needs to get on that. What else is going on?"

"News says the roads in and out of town are going to be blocked for a while. There are lines of people outside of Safeway. Apparently, all the Airbnb folks think this is the end of the world."

I laughed. "You go to Dan's yet?"

"Yep, went *foraging* this morning."

"You too?" I could hear an odd edge to my voice.

"Oh crap, sorry Adi, didn't mean anything by that. I just can't help but think of foraging when I'm at Dan's."

I intentionally changed the tone of my voice and hoped Clare heard the happiness I tried to project. "No problem, I thought the same thing while I was there. Hey, did Rob check you out?"

"Rob always checks me out."

I laughed again. "That's not what I meant, and you know it. Was he your checker?"

"Yes, why?"

"Was he acting weird?" I paused then quickly interrupted her canned response. "I mean weirder than normal?"

"Nope same general level of weirdness. He give you trouble?" I could hear the protectiveness in Clare's voice. "If he did, I would go have a little conversation with him. He can't do that same BS he tried in high school. We are grown now."

"No, nothing like that. He just kept smiling at me like he knew some big secret. Was weird."

"Nope, nothing like that."

I asked, "He ask you about Will?"

"Why would he do that? I haven't heard from Will since he left. No one has heard from Will since he left except maybe his poor parents. He missed the five-year reunion, the ten-year reunion, and he didn't come here for J's funeral. I'm not sure what I would say to him if he did contact me."

"I feel you there. Our world is better without William Monroe." *I heard the words come out of my mouth and knew I didn't believe them.*

"Exactly." I heard a knock in the background behind Clare. "Manager is here. Talk later 'kay?"

"You got it," I replied. We hung up.

The trip back home was safer than the trip to the store. As I turned onto Ski Hill Drive a bit of anger worked its way back up and I had to force myself to calm down.

As I got to my house, I saw Mr. Monroe outside shoveling snow. He looked up and waved at me. I wondered when the last time Mr. Monroe had heard from his son was. I felt bad for Will's parents. When Will left Leavenworth, he really left everyone behind. I knew in my heart he would never return. I paused for a second as I pulled into the garage and thought about how different our goals had been at the end of high school. Life, God, Fate, or whatever had an ironic way of reminding us how little we controlled our own lives. As the door to the garage closed sealing me back into my empty house, I felt the tears start again.

CHAPTER 5 – WILL

I EXITED THE HOUSE and approached my father who was still shoveling the driveway in the falling snow. He had asked for help earlier and had a shovel all ready for me. "Who was that?"

"Oh, right," he said, "you don't know."

"Don't know what?" I picked up the second shovel on the ground and shoveled snow.

"Adi and her husband, Edward, bought that house after we moved in." He kept his head down, didn't look at me, and his shovel picked up a bit of ferocity.

I asked, "You mean my Adi?"

"Not sure you can really call her that son, after all, you left her."

I kept shoveling. "Fair, but still, you are talking about Adi Lewis. She's still Adi Lewis or does she have a different name?"

"Never changed it. A good thing too," father threw another shovel full of snow onto the already buried lawn.

"What do you mean?"

I heard the sigh even though my father didn't make the sound. Also knew it was a bunch of BS because while my Dad pretended not to like gossip, he actually loved it. "Look, your mom can give you all the details, but I'll give you the basics, ok?"

"Sure Dad, just what you are comfortable with."

He nodded his head and kept shoveling. "So, you left, and Adi was aimless for a couple of years. Her folks kept trying to get her to go off to college. We know all this because she would visit your mom and me. After a couple of years her parents finally succeeded, and she went off to Western Washington University. That was about two years after you left. Two years after that you graduated and started that company. About the time you sold your app, Adi had graduated from Western. She came back home with a guy named Edward. It was around that time that we bought that house." He looked up at the house and then went back to shoveling. "Anyway, they got married quickly. Adi started teaching at the school and Edward traveled doing sales."

I threw more snow onto the pile. "What industry?"

"There were a lot of different companies. He never kept a job for very long." He looked back down and continued shoveling.

"Did they know you lived here?"

"If they didn't know when they came up here, they found out when your mom charged across the street and greeted them."

"She didn't."

"Of course, she did."

I laughed. "I can picture that happening."

"Your mother has never stopped thinking of Adi as a daughter. She loved the idea of Adi being across the street with her family."

"Hoping for grandchildren by proxy?"

"Something like that." He paused, then continued, "Things were good for a while and then things changed. Well, let's just say the arguments could be loud. We heard some rumors. It seems they were having a tough time having children."

"Oh," I heard myself utter. Dad looked up at me. I asked, "Him, her, or both?"

"Her. She spent a lot of time with doctors. People talk. She had a few surgeries even."

"Well, isn't that crazy?" I said.

"I thought the same thing when I heard about it. That girl lived for children and having a family of her own."

I discovered I had stopped shoveling and stared at Adi's house. "So, what happened?"

His chest heaved for a second. "They tried for a long time. At the beginning of the year, he moved out. After that, well, things progressed."

"Damn Dad, that's terrible." I looked at my father, who had also stopped shoveling and was watching me. "What?"

"Son, it's been twelve years since you've been here. Why did you come back?" He tried to show me a smile. "Don't get me wrong, I'm glad you are home. I am very pleased to have the chance to meet Jamison. But, why?"

"The hundred-year storm," I answered.

"You could've turned back to Spokane. You could've headed south. You could've done a million different things. You didn't come back for John Greer's funeral. Why did you come back now?"

I started shoveling again and heard him begin as well. He wasn't wrong. There had been choices. But I hadn't even considered them. I had Jamison in the car. The weather was dangerous, and I had come home. "I think," I said, "because for the first time it wasn't about me."

"Explain."

I sighed. "I enjoy living in Edmonds. I made a life for myself. I am successful, secure, and content. Had it just been me in the storm, I'm not sure I would have come here?"

"Honest."

"But it wasn't just me. I had to make a choice for Jamison. I might not have loved growing up here, but I was always safe. I wanted Jamison to be safe."

He smiled, turned his head away, and seemed to wipe a tear. "Sounds like you made an excellent decision, Dad. Now give me your coat. That's too light for this weather."

He was correct. I was ignoring the cold, but my jacket was not meant for this level of cold. My father switched jackets with me and plopped his hat on the top of my head. "I'm going to go spend some quality time with my grandson. Finish shoveling for me, will you?"

"I will." He walked into the house.

I wondered when my dad had become an amateur psychologist. Our conversations growing up revolved more around sports, the weather, and stories about their lives when they were young. My father had never been a deep thinker. He was a smart man, but never a complex one. I thought long about that and realized that I had never tried to have more complex conversations with my father. I was eighteen when I left. Having a man to man with him at age thirty was a novel experience. I shouldn't be so surprised.

It took me a while to finish the driveway. The work was pleasant, and I took my time enjoying the manual labor and the quiet. I focused on the ice, since the falling snow was clearly going to win the ultimate battle. I thought a bit about Adi and Jamison, but mostly I just enjoyed the work.

My father opened the garage after I called him. As I was moving towards the opening door, I heard a car. I turned to see a vehicle backing out of Adi's garage. Her garage door closed, and she backed up, turned, and then headed forward. She saw me and waved and then headed out.

She waved at me. I looked down at the shovels and my father's coat. "No, you idiot," I said to myself, "she waved to your father." Shaking my head, I put the shovels away, closed the garage, and went back into the house.

As I entered the house, I heard Jamison giggling, and my thoughts turned to him. I took off Dad's jacket and kicked out of my boots. Jamison was wrapped in my father's arms when I walked into the living room. Dad looked up. His eyes sparkled with love and happiness. "He is truly a blessing, son."

Mom was tickling Jamison's feet and he responded with more giggles. "He's such a cheerful boy, aren't you a cheerful boy." Jamison responded with more giggles.

I sat in a chair and took in the room. I watched my son surrounded by the love of my parents. The room was lit up with the light of the fire and the Christmas tree. I thought again about Adi being across the street. *What do you know, I am home.*

CHAPTER 6 – ADI

I LEFT MY HOUSE EARLY to meet my parents at a Mexican restaurant called South, which was nestled in the center of town. I was only a little hungry for food. What I really wanted was to be with my family.

I pulled out of the garage and as I did, I considered for the first time if I should add more Christmas lights to the roof. I looked back and saw that Mr. Monroe was still shoveling the driveway. He had been out there for hours but was walking quickly and smoothly as he approached the garage. He was an amazing man. I waved to him, and he waved back. I smiled as I headed down the street.

The drive to South was slower than normal because of the snow. It was so quiet I could hear the whisper of sound that meant my radio was on but turned nearly to silent. There was a flood of memories, and I turned the music up. Our song was playing on the radio. Somehow part of my mind must have heard it. The rhythm of the music jostled old recollections like a scrapbook of my life flooding me with thoughts of William. We had dated throughout high school but had been friends for years before that. Even after twelve years, it still felt odd knowing he was gone. *How could I still miss someone I hadn't seen in twelve years?*

I got to the end of the road and turned left heading into town. I travelled past a couple of stalled cars. People were outside their vehicles helping the stranded drivers. I turned right and then left until I finally passed through town to the south. I slowed down and looked for a parking spot. There were many people walking through downtown. The storm had reduced the road traffic and ensured that

I found a close parking spot. As I cracked open the car door, the smells of Leavenworth and Christmas music greeted me.

Locking my car, I headed to the front door of the small little house that was actually the restaurant, South. I opened the door and stomped my feet on the ground before entering the building. To my left, near the door to the patio were my parents. I waved and headed towards them. They had decorated South for Christmas, without totally giving up on the normal Mexican theme. There was Spanish Christmas music playing and the staff were all dressed in Christmas colors.

Both my parents stood as I came to the table. My mother gave me a hug and a kiss on the cheek and then sat back down. Her legs had been hurting her lately and I was sure the cold wasn't helping. I noticed her cane was hidden behind her booth in the restaurant's corner. Dad gave me a hug next and for a moment I felt surrounded by love, safety, and everything that was my father. After a moment, he let me go and looked into my eyes. "Having a good day?"

"Yes dad, it's a good day." I scooted onto the bench and my father followed me. He and my mother always sat across from one another. Mom slid the menu towards me, although I already knew what I wanted.

Amber Gonzalez came up to the table. "Welcome, Adi. What can I get you to drink?"

"A warm cup of coffee with two sugars, please, Amber."

"My pleasure. Do you need a minute with the menu? Your parents have already ordered."

"The usual, the chicken enchiladas, please." She winked at me and walked away.

My mother tapped on the table, and I looked at her. "Finish those papers you were working on?"

"Almost, just a couple more to go through."

Dad asked, "Dinner at your house or ours for Christmas?"

"Yours," I replied, "I'll come over early and help with dinner."

Mom grabbed my father's hand. "You can spend the night before, if you want."

"I'll think about it. Might be nice."

"Good, it'll be fun having a sleepover."

Amber came back and dropped off my coffee, a basket of chips, and two bowls. One bowl had red salsa and the other was green. The warmth of the cup made me conscious of how cold my hands were. The heat that filled me as I consumed it was nothing short of glorious. "I cannot believe this weather." I scooped up a heaping of green salsa on a chip and ate it.

Dad shivered. "The news says it's going to last through Christmas. I kind of like it. Everything feels slowed down."

I laughed a little at that. Leavenworth was not a high paced city, but most people weren't my father. "It is very pleasant." I picked up another chip.

Mom let go of Dad's hand and adjusted her place setting and then grabbed a chip for herself. "It's going to cost a fortune. It's so cold, our furnace is running overtime."

I put a hand on hers. "It might be because you like it sauna hot." This reminded me why I might not want to sleep over the night before

Christmas. My mother and I had vastly different temperature settings.

The door opened and I saw my mother lock eyes with someone who was entering South. "Lucy Darcy," my mother whispered. I could almost hear Mrs. Darcy waving her hand at the door. Mom smiled and waved back. There were multiple footsteps towards our table, followed by a loud greeting. We didn't get up.

"The Lewis', well, it's like Back to the Future or one of those reunion movies today. Not the Hot Tub Time Machine movie, which was just not funny, but you know what I mean."

The look on my mother's face made it clear she did not. My father was staring into his coffee, avoiding looking directly at Mrs. Darcy. It became clear it was up to me. "Mrs. Darcy, what are you talking about?"

"My dear, I'm talking about William Monroe finally coming home."

"Excuse me? What did you say?" My heart had stopped and then tried to burst out of my chest. My skin felt flushed, and I was fairly sure the room was spinning.

"Are you alright, dear?" Ms. Darcy spoke louder. "I said that William Monroe came home."

Words stumbled from my mouth. "Where did you hear that?" Mom was staring at me. Dad had moved a hand onto my knee.

"Hear about it. I saw him this morning at Dan's." Her voice continued to be uncomfortably loud.

I dipped my head and thought back. There was an internal click and suddenly Rob's weirdness made total sense. He must have seen Will before I came in. "Did you speak with him?"

"Oh, yes, we had a pleasant conversation. He asked if you were still in Leavenworth?"

He asked about me. My heart was still beating hard. "Where is he staying?"

"His parents."

I thought back about the man I saw with the shovel when I left to come to lunch. *He had moved quickly and with the ease of youth. The man was firm. It was Will.* I felt like I was breathing too much and not enough at the same time.

Mrs. Darcy asked, "Is she alright dear?"

Mom stood up and put herself between me and Mrs. Darcy. "This weather is such a burden. We were just discussing it when you came in."

"It is a real shock, isn't it? But not as big a shock as Will and his baby."

"His what?!" I stuck my head around my mother so I could see Mrs. Darcy. My skin was burning with tingles. I couldn't catch my breath.

"I said his baby. Are you sure you are all right? You look flushed."

"Yes, Mrs. Darcy, I'm fine." I could hear the tone in my voice, but there was no help for it. "You saw Will with a baby?"

"No dear, I saw him buying diapers and baby supplies at Dan's. You need to keep up." Mr. Darcy began pulling Mrs. Darcy towards their table. "I have to go. See you all later." Mr. Darcy pulled his wife across the restaurant, and they sat in a seat in the corner near the bar.

Mom sat back down with a sigh.

"How are you doing, kiddo?" My father was looking at me.

Mom reached out and took each of our hands. I gave her hand a squeeze.

"A baby." I could feel anger pushing away the shock.

"She saw him getting diapers. That doesn't mean it's his baby." Mom patted my hand.

"Well, it sure isn't his mothers." Mom's face reflected the heat in my words. "Sorry mom." She squeezed my hand.

Amber came over and served us our lunch. I didn't eat much of it. *William Monroe was a father. How was that fair? What did that mean? What does that say about me?*

Mom kept looking at me as we sat there. Dad was quiet, but he kept giving me reassuring pats on the back and squeezes to my shoulder. *A baby.*

The last straw was when mom's phone began blowing up with social media posts. She looked through them, then up at me. "I'm so sorry Adi."

"Not your fault," I replied. *Was it Will's fault? Was it mine?* I could feel the anger flare up inside of me. "It's not fair!"

Dad got the bill from Amber. "It's not fair honey, life is not fair, but God isn't going to give you something you cannot handle."

"I'm not feeling that today, Dad."

He gave me a one arm hug. "I know sweetie. But if William is back, it is a bit of a Christmas miracle, no? As for the rest, well, let's just wait and see."

"He left. He never wanted to have children. He's been gone for twelve years. Why is he back now? Why does he have a baby?" In my head, I heard myself say, *my baby.*

Mom stood up and we followed her. I know we walked out and that my mom said something to Mrs. Darcy, but I don't really remember it. I vaguely remember giving my parents hugs. After I got in my car, it was all a bit of a blur.

CHAPTER 7 – WILL

MY MOTHER ASKED, "Will, who did you see when you were out shopping?"

The serious tone of my mother's voice caught my attention. I answered, "Mrs. Darcy and Rob, why?"

She handed me her phone and I scrolled through the Facebook posts. People in Leavenworth were on Facebook and the posts were about me and the possibility that I had a baby. I scanned through the comments. "I guess it was inevitable." She stared at me. "Ok mom, what am I missing?"

"Social media, this story is spreading all over Leavenworth. That means Adi and her family as well. Have you thought about her?"

I hadn't. *Dammit.* "This is not good!" My words punctuated my realization and disturbed Jamison, who was sleeping on a blanket on the living room floor. I scooped him up and held him tight. "Mind getting him a bottle, mom?" That broke through her serious mood, and she smiled. She went into the kitchen. I bounced Jamison and tried to settle him as I watched the comments fly through the Leavenworth local group chat. My concern for Adi grew. I realized I should have reached out and told her myself. But it'd been twelve years. I had no clue how to tell her. But anything would've been better than social media.

My parents knew the scoop. Back when I lived at home, I hid nothing from my parents. They knew why we broke up. They knew I hadn't wanted children. I looked down at my son and smiled at him. They had dressed him in a little blue onesie. I had heard about the smell of babies, but I had never understood it. I leaned in and kissed

Jamison on the forehead, inhaling his scent as I did so. In that moment, I couldn't recall why I had not wanted to have children. I closed my eyes and enjoyed the warmth and scent of the child in my arms.

Jamison had drifted into half sleep about the time my mother appeared with a bottle. As she approached us, my phone rang. I looked down at the phone. "Work," I whispered. I handed Jamison to mom and I walked into the living room. "Jim, what's up?"

Jim did not sound happy. "I thought we were keeping the baby thing on the down low until we completed the contracts on the new consulting project."

"We are."

"Well, your fatherhood appears to be going viral," he said. "We have already gotten calls from the Seattle Times and KIRO news."

I mentally kicked myself. I was losing it. Not only had I forgotten Adi, I had also forgotten how the internet and social media worked. I went quiet and I could hear Jim patiently waiting on the other side of the phone. We had known each other since college, and he knew my process. After about five minutes of running the options through my head, I said, "I think this is something we need to own. You received any calls from the vendors?"

"Yes, a couple, but they are trying to be PC and not ask too many questions."

"Well, re-assure them I will be available to oversee all our consulting projects, ok?"

"Will do. How are you going to 'own' this?"

"Leave that to me." I hung up. "Mom and Dad, I need a favor, please." I walked into the room and found my mother sitting on the couch feeding Jamison. My father walked into the room.

He asked, "What do you need?"

"Have a seat next to mom, Dad. Mom, turn Jamison so it's obvious you are feeding a baby, but so I can take a picture without capturing his face." Dad sat down next to mom. "Put your arm around her." He did. I stood in front of the three of them and took a few pictures. I then sat in front of them and took a few selfies. A couple of texts later and the photos were off to the company's media team with instructions. Less than five minutes later, the pictures showed up on all my social media accounts. I watched them appear and then showed them to my folks.

"Why?" my father asked.

"Because he cannot be a father ashamed of his child," my mother said.

"Mom's not wrong. It's about perceptions for sure. I want to clarify that I'm a proud father, that I'm not hiding anything, and that my family is happy for me. That should stop an avalanche of negative posts. It should also reduce my company's customers' fears that I will not be around by making it upfront and normal. Perceptions based on possibilities and hidden truths are usually worse than the reality. I need to control the perceptions."

"Makes sense," mom said, "but I do not believe this is going to make Miss Adi feel any better about all of this."

I wanted to tell myself I wasn't being selfish again and that I was putting my son's needs over Adi's, but I knew better. "I have to agree with you, mom. I'll be right back."

I grabbed a sticky note pad off the fridge along with the sharpie that had been next to it. Pulling on my jacket, I went through the front door and headed across the street to Adi's house. The storm outside had slowed but had not stopped. I skidded a couple times on the ice but made it to Adi's door and the beautiful wreath that decorated it. I knocked twice before I thought too long about what I was doing. There was no answer. I stood in front of her door for a good five minutes, trying to think about what I should write. The first note was nonsense and was too embarrassing to think about. I ripped the note up into pieces and stuffed them into my jacket pocket with a plan to throw them in the fire when I got back to the house. None of the drafts that I wrote conveyed my feelings. I thought some more and realized there was no way for me to write an actually thoughtful note when I did not know what I was feeling at that moment. My entire life had changed and learning how Adi's life had gone was making me feel guilty. I don't like to feel guilty. Guilt and anger are emotions I don't handle well. The frustration over feeling guilty moved me towards anger with myself. The entire experience was not helpful nor fun. So, I just wrote:

Adi, I'm home. We need to talk.
Sorry about the social media.

Will

I put the note on her door and worked my way back to the house. As the entry door closed behind me and I stamped my boots in the entry, my mother asked, "What did you do?"

I looked up and replied, "I left her a note."

"Do I want to know what you wrote, son? You were gone a long time for just writing a note."

I walked over to the fire and threw my first draft into it. "It was difficult to find the exact words to express what I wanted to say. I decided it was impossible. So, I just let her know I was home and that I wanted to talk. I also apologized for the social media."

Dad walked in. "It's the thought that counts, Anne."

"Harold, he should've thought more about this before putting himself in this type of situation."

"Mom, are you talking about Adi or Jamison?" I asked.

"William, you were always the smartest child in your class. You challenged your father and me with questions the second you were speaking. I didn't always understand how you saw the world, but you always seemed so many steps ahead of the rest of us." She paused and stared at me. "Where is that side of you?"

I laughed. I laughed hard. It took me a few minutes to stop laughing. And at some point, my parents joined in, and we all had a very cathartic group laugh. After the laughter finally ceased, I answered her. "Mom, I have had my life planned out since I can remember. I carried out each step on time and, as expected. Then twelve months ago, that all changed. I thought I adapted and rolled with the changes, but when the snowstorm hit and I realized I was heading to Leavenworth, it wasn't only Jamison I wanted to be safe here. I truly do not know what I am doing anymore."

My mom dashed forward and wrapped me in her arms. I felt the burn of tears in my eyes and fought them back. "Welcome to the world of us normal people, William." She hugged me harder.

"Son?" I looked up at my father, who had a huge smile on his face. "Where did you put the note?"

"On the front door," I replied.

CHAPTER 8 – ADI

THE DRIVE HOME WAS not great. I focused on the music that played on the radio and calmed down. After that, I attempted to make sense of the emotions that were swirling in my head and my heart, but the jumble of thoughts, feelings, and emotions were too overwhelming to decipher. My heart was pounding in my chest so hard that I thought it was going to break through my ribs. I had not had an anxiety attack since middle school, but I remembered what they were like and knew I had just experienced a significant one. That made me remember Will and how he had cared for me at school when I had my first attack, which made me smile, then cry, and then scream.

I made it home, though honestly, I do not remember the entire drive. As I drove towards my house, I opened the garage. I didn't look around. I did not look at the Monroe house. I entered the garage, closed the door, and then made my way into the house throwing off boots, jacket, and clothes as I made a beeline for my bedroom. I threw my phone onto my bed and marched into the bathroom. My flannels were still on the counter, and I grabbed them and put them on. My heart was still racing.

I went back into my room and moved the phone to my side table. That made me remember both tables were now mine and the tears flowed. I jumped under the covers and spun wrapping myself tightly in the heavy blankets and comforters. I needed to be confined. I needed to be wrapped tightly in my safe bed. I buried my head under my pillows and let myself breathe.

I laid there for a while. I do not know how much time passed. The longer I was there, the safer I felt. My heart slowed. I gained focus. My phone beeped. The text messages seemed to be endless. Then my phone started ringing. My mother had her own ringtone and it played repeatedly. I was cocooned in my covers, feeling the warmth radiating around me. I could think. I just needed to think and figure out what I was feeling and why I was feeling it. *It's all right. You'll be all right. You are safe.* I pulled the covers tighter. *This is just another challenge. You'll be all right.* "Why this challenge God?"

"That is a foolish question," my mother said. I pulled my head out from under the pillows and bent myself so I could look at my mother in the doorway. She was holding my spare key in her hand. "God only gives us the challenges we can handle, honey, nothing more, and nothing less." She took off her boots and jacket and crawled next to me in the bed. I collapsed against the softness of the pillow.

"I'm not sure I want to handle all of this, mom."

"Darling, I understand it can be challenging, but things seem to work out in the end."

"Mom, what if I knew I couldn't have children before Will left? Would I have gone with him? Would we be together today?"

"We cannot know that."

"But I might not have lost Will."

She asked, "Would you have wanted Will to adopt children?"

"Yes," I answered without a second's thought.

"So, would it have been any different?"

I thought long and hard about her question. "No, no, it wouldn't have been different."

"So, eighteen-year-old Adi and eighteen-year-old Will made the right choices for them. You cannot go back, honey. It is not helpful to second guess yourself. Those decisions made you who you are, and I love that woman very much. You are an amazing teacher. You change children's lives every day. Imagine if you changed that. Imagine how many children's lives would be impacted by that change."

Mom wasn't wrong. I was an excellent teacher, and I loved the children and being a teacher. I took a deep breath. "Today has been just so much, mom."

"I know. And of course, Mrs. Darcy only exasperated the situation, like she always does."

I rolled over and faced my mother. "Why didn't he tell me himself?"

"When did you two chat last?"

I rolled out of the cloth that was confining me and sat up in bed. My mother sat up as well and looked at me. "We haven't spoken since we said goodbye." *Since you said, "No,"* echoed silently in my head.

"Then I cannot imagine it would be easy to even come back and say 'hi' to you, let alone tell you he has a child."

I knew she was right, but it didn't make me any happier. "I get it. Mom, I really do. I mean, there's a lot of things we don't know, right? For instance, he could have gone through the same emotional turmoil I had just been through when he discovered he was a father. The Will I knew would not have been happy."

"I could see that."

"Maybe he's home because he is trying to dump the baby on his parents." I heard a little excitement in my voice.

"Adalynn Jane Lewis, that is not the daughter I raised. Don't you go looking for other's hardships." I wasn't. I knew I wasn't. My thoughts were centered on Will's parents and how they may need help with Will's baby. I could help them. I could help raise Will's baby. A giggle escaped me. Mom's eyes squinted. "Adalynn, what are you concocting?"

"Nothing, really mom, nothing. I just realized that Will wasn't attacking me personally. His having a child wasn't an attack on me or my inability to have a baby." I heard the catch in my throat as I said the last few words. "All these emotions I'm going through, he's probably going through as well. I just need to take it less personally. Look at the positives."

"That's quite the change of emotions."

I stood up. "How long did you expect me to fall apart over all of this?"

She smiled and rubbed my back. "I was thinking a good twenty-four hours of self-pity and recriminations were a possibility. I told your father I would spend the night here in this freezer of a house."

I had to laugh at that. The house was a cozy 68 degrees, which was just right. Any warmer and I couldn't sleep under my heavy blankets. "I appreciate it, mom, but I think it was just too much information too fast. And gossip coming from Mrs. Darcy and her friends always feels rawer anyway."

"She does like to goose up the drama, doesn't she?"

"I do not know what that means, but sure."

Mom headed out of the room. "Want to make cookies?"

"Yes, mom, I'd love that."

We headed into the kitchen. Cooking was a comfort thing for mom, and she always thought it helped me as well. I also knew she wanted to get the oven heated, so the house would warm up. I smiled at that thought. As I joined her in the kitchen, she said, "Oh, I completely forgot." She reached into her pant pocket and pulled out a yellow sticky note. She handed me the note. I folded it open. It read:

Adi, I'm home. We need to talk.

Sorry about the social media.

Will

"Well, what do you think about that?"

CHAPTER 9 – WILL

DAD WAS CORRECT ABOUT the note. I watched Adi's car fly into the garage and the door close. I stood at the window with Jamison in my arms and looked at her house. As I stood there, I thought about what I should do next. Those thoughts were about Adi, but they were also about the amazing child in my arms. *What life was I going to give him?* I looked at his little nose and felt the insatiable urge to kiss it, so I did. Becoming a parent was more gratifying than I could have ever imagined. I stood there terrified of the future and my responsibilities as a parent, but I knew instinctively that every moment would be worth it.

I focused back outside when another car pulled up. A woman got out. I couldn't be sure, but I was guessing it was Adi's mother. She made her way through the snow and unlocked Adi's front door. Before going inside, she found my note, read it, and then pulled it off the door and went in, closing the door behind her.

I went back to the living room. My mom had set up the bassinet near the couch. I kissed Jamison again and laid him gently in the bassinet. I wrapped him tight in his blankets and another sense of pure joy washed over me.

Mom sat on the couch, smiling and looking at me. I walked into the kitchen and found my father drinking a cup of coffee as he leaned up against the counter. "Hi," he said.

"Hey."

"Figure out what you are going to do about the note?"

"Took care of itself. Looks like Adi's mother found it."

"Ahh. I'm sure she will give it to Adi. She is a good woman Mrs. Lewis. Did I ever tell you about the time they came over when you and Adi were in high school, and she and your mother drank too much glug?"

"Yes, Dad, pretty much every Christmas after that happened."

"Oh, yes, well, it was hilarious. I had never heard two people sing so many Christmas carols off key."

The house phone rang at that moment, and I grabbed it quickly to prevent it from disturbing Jamison. And yes, I hoped it was Adi. "Monroe's," I said in a relatively faint voice.

A musical female voice said, "I heard you were back in town, William Monroe."

It took me a second, but then I recognized who it was. "Felicia?"

"Yes, it is. How are you doing, William? How is that baby of yours?"

Felicia D'Angelo had been the most popular girl in school. Our interests had few overlaps. Much of my focus was computers, D&D, and other similar high school activities. I also played soccer and was a member of the popular kids' groups. Felicia was "the" popular kid. She was a cheerleader, played soccer and volleyball. And, of course, year after year, the town ranked her the most beautiful person in Leavenworth. I lost track of how many times she was a princess in a Leavenworth parade. We had one common interest, which resulted in our chats about the future during high school. We both unabashedly wanted to get out of Leavenworth. She left the same time I did. "You're in Leavenworth?" I asked.

I heard the disappointment in her voice. "Not following all of us on social media? We sure all follow you."

"Don't believe everything you read. I rarely post anything myself these days."

"Oh, you bigwigs hire people for that, don't you?"

I didn't answer that question. "When did you come back to Leavenworth, and why?"

"Those are some immense questions for a phone call. What are you doing tonight?"

"No plans," I replied.

"Want to take me to dinner?"

"Sure, where?"

"Where what?" my father mouthed.

I clicked the phone on mute. "Felicia is on the phone. She wants to meet for dinner."

Mom said from the living room, "I have dinner halfway made already, fried chicken and mashed potatoes. Those are still some of your favorites, right?"

They were still on my top ten list for sure. "Yes, of course." I unmuted the phone. "Felicia, I forgot I have dinner plans with my folks tonight. What about lunch tomorrow if the storm is not too bad?"

I could hear her pout on the other end of the phone. "Fine, but you'll just have to wait then for my story. I'll meet you at Gustav's at noon, ok?"

"Sure, noon at Gustav's."

"And you are welcome to bring that beautiful baby of yours." She ended the call. I put the phone down and stared at it.

Mom walked into the kitchen. "Didn't you have a crush on her in middle school?

"Everyone had a crush on her, mom." I paused and thought a bit about Felicia and my past conversations. I had not, in fact, kept track of her. *Why was she back?* "When did she come back to Leavenworth?"

Mom walked back into the living room and Dad and I followed her in. She sat down on the couch near Jamison. My dad scooted over so that he could put his arm around her. I sat down in a comfortable leather chair across from the two of them. Mom made a sigh and then said, "Ok, Harold, give it to him."

My father's eyes sparkled. He said, "She left the same year you did. I only know what I know from Mrs. Darcy and some of Felicia 's mother's friends." He looked down, covering a smile, and then looked back up, meeting my eyes. "Felicia went to a small college on the East Coast. The rumors were her parents paid to get her in, but Felicia was always a rather talented student and an incredibly determined young woman. My assumption is she worked hard and went to the school she wanted to go to. Other rumors were that she went to college to meet the right type of man more than to get a college degree and there, the rumors are unfortunately true." He said, "Mrs. Darcy referred to it as a M.R.S. degree, which I found fairly offensive, and your mother wouldn't talk to me for a day when I referred to it as that."

Mom nudged him, and he gave her a squeeze. "It's not a politically correct term now, is it, Harold?"

"No ma'am,"

"Agreed," I said, "but if it makes you feel any better, I'm pretty sure there are both men and women that go to college just to meet someone that will take care of them."

My father nodded his head. "It's sad how many people are afraid of a little hard work." My mother patted his knee.

I nodded my agreement. "Dad, did she meet someone in college?"

"So, I'm told. I can tell you she never brought him to Leavenworth and when she came back a couple of years ago, she was alone with neither type of degree." He snickered a little at his joke. I saw my mother elbow him. "Ouch."

"Don't be an ass."

"Yes, dear."

I laughed a little. "Stop it, you two. Now Dad, you must have gotten more scoop than that."

Mom nodded. "Yes, yes, he did. Tell it Harold."

"Well, it seems she met a young man with family living in the Hamptons. You know where that is, right?"

"Ritzy area in Long Island, New York."

"Right. Anyway, she moved to New York with her man, and they got married. They traveled the world and had just a grand time. Felicia's mother posted a new picture daily in our group chats. She was immensely proud of her daughter." I could hear his own thoughts about the matter in the tone of my father's voice.

"Ok, so they lived it up and traveled. Sounds great. What happened?"

He looked at my mom and then back at me. "This is how her mother tells it, so don't go thinking I would say things like this." I nodded my response. "Her mother told us that to secure her M.R.S. Degree, Felicia wanted to have a baby. Her husband didn't like that idea."

"He divorced her because she said she wanted to have a baby?"

Dad shook his head. "No, he divorced her because he told her he didn't want to have children and her response was to go off the pill without telling him."

"Oh shit," I heard myself whisper. Mom's face got taut. "Sorry mom." She stared at me for a moment, then dropped her eyes. Just the slightest smile broke her lips.

Dad spoke again. "I do not know how her husband found out. I don't really know if the story is true. But I know she got divorced and has been living with her parents for the last two years."

I asked, "Is she working?"

"There was a prenuptial agreement, but from what I understand, she is financially secure."

Dad went silent and we all sat in the living room enjoying the fire and watching Jamison.

I said, "he should wake up soon."

Dad smiled. Mom said, "I'll get a bottle ready for you. After that, let's get to that dinner."

"Sounds great, mom." I scooped Jamison up in my arms and held him tight against my chest. He stirred lightly and then snuggled in against me. I went into the kitchen. As I joined my mother in the kitchen and inhaled the delicious aroma of the food cooking, it reminded once again me of how much I loved being home. I was glad I turned down dinner with Felicia. I looked forward to a quiet night with my family. A little peace before I tackled the storm and the outside world again tomorrow.

CHAPTER 10 – ADI

I WOKE UP AND IMMEDIATELY thought about Will's note. My mother was in the guest room bundled under a hundred blankets. I tucked her into bed after she finished a bottle of wine at dinner. She had collapsed in the huge pink chair in the corner of my living room and when I went to bed; I had to half carry her to the guest room. Mom was an immense support, and I loved the fact she stayed with me. The note, however, was something else. It meant Will after twelve years had reached out. Sure, none of this was ideal, but it was better than the alternative. *Maybe we'll talk again.*

I thought about twelve years ago and the William I loved then. We had dated for most of high school and in a truly cliché move took each other's virginities during our senior year. I remembered Will finding a pharmacy outside of town to buy condoms. We were being responsible, neither of us knew how unnecessary that was. That year for me was full of love and positive emotions. It was about Will, and it was about us living in Leavenworth. I wanted to get married, have children, and live in Leavenworth forever with my family and friends. That life was supposed to never end. I couldn't fathom a future that was different. I was naïve and romantic, but it was an amazing time.

The first shadows appeared in my perfect world when Will got acceptance letters from every college and university he applied to around the country. I knew his parents couldn't afford any of them, so I secretly hoped he would stay home. The scholarships followed the acceptance letters and my hopes of a simple life with Will ended. I loved Will, but I came to realize that I did not know what his actual dream was. My love, my passion, and my own goals blinded me. Like I did not know that he had a 4.0 or that he got a near perfect SAT score. I didn't even know he was basically a computer genius. What I knew was he was kind, he loved me, and I loved nothing more than laying in the grass with him and talking about, well, everything or anything.

I sighed and got out of bed. I walked into the bathroom, closed the door, and stripped out of my flannels. As I stepped into the shower, I welcomed the warmth of the water cascading over my body. I leaned back and allowed the warm water to massage my shoulders and neck, relieving the tension. Thoughts of Will continued as my hands moved the water around my body. I found memories of high school push old passions to the surface. We had never questioned the fact that we were deeply in love and it was never in doubt. He was always amazing and was always there for me. And the sex, I mean for two inexperienced kids it was just special. Sometimes it truly felt like we became one person. I pushed the shower handle, turning down the temperature and cooling myself off. "Damn," I said out loud, "who knew I still felt that strongly?" *I did.*

People's general belief regarding our breakup was mostly correct, but there were minor aspects that neither Will nor I ever mentioned to people. I didn't because I wasn't comfortable with the truth. Took me several sessions with a counselor during college to admit that to myself. My guess is he didn't because he still loved me and he didn't want to hurt me, which was perhaps a romantic dream, but why not? I knew no better.

It's true that I wanted to get married, stay in Leavenworth, and have children. It's true we discussed this, and Will made it clear he didn't want children and he needed to get out of Leavenworth. I mean, that's the story everyone knows, and it works, right? I turned the heat back up, as I could feel the tension grow in my neck and shoulders. *The memory was so hard to deal with.* I ducked my head under the stream of water and let my tears join with the shower's flow.

People believe Will left me because he left Leavenworth and because, to be fair, I've never corrected them. The reality of the situation differed from what most people were aware of. Will loved me and he wanted me to come with him. Thanks to his scholarship, he could locate an apartment that was suitable for married couples and he had the financial means to pay for it. He saved up money and bought a ring. He turned down Harvard, Stanford, and even MIT to remain in Washington, so we were at least relatively close to home. Once he had his entire plan put together, he invited me out on a hike and as we stood near a river in the middle of the forest; he proposed. He told me his dreams, his plan, and what he had chosen so we could stay together. I asked him if he wanted children. He said he didn't. I said "no." There was no discussions of possibilities or thoughts that things might change. I demanded that eighteen-year-old William commit to having children when he clearly wasn't ready to do so. I said, "no." I turned the water off and shook the water from my head and then grabbed a towel. I had to be honest with myself and I knew since I was 12 years old that I have been dreaming of the day when I would become a parent and have children of my own. I had no siblings or even cousins, but I had worked at a daycare and Boys and Girls Club, and I knew children were my life. If I knew that at eighteen years old, wasn't it fair that Will knew he didn't want kids at that age? So, I said, "no."

We walked out of the forest together. Both of us cried the entire way. We got into my car without talking. We drove into town and then I dropped him off at his home. He said goodbye and I said goodbye as well. That was the last time we spoke. I mean, what do you say after that?

I went into my room and threw on some blue jeans and a nice thick pullover. I looked out the back into the yard and saw even higher piles of snow on the ground, though the new snow seemed to have slowed.

My phone rang. "Hey Clare, what's up?"

"Do you know what time it is?"

I looked over at the clock. "Little after 10:00 a.m." There was silence. "What?"

"Do you know what day it is, Ms. Adi?"

I thought about the last day of school and then counted forward. "Oh, crap."

"Oh, crap indeed, you are late."

"How are the roads?"

"They plowed them again this morning. You should be able to make it here without too much effort."

"Be there as soon as I can." I hung up and pulled on a pair of boots. I walked to the dresser and picked up the coat I had laid there the night before.

"Mom!"

My mother came out of the kitchen. She showed no signs of last night's wine. "Why are you yelling?"

"Sorry, thought you might still be in the guest room. I'm late. I'm supposed to meet Clare and some teachers to help with baking cookies in town."

"I know, honey, but you really cannot be late for that. It is going on all day." She handed me a cup of coffee. "You needed sleep. How do you feel?"

I thought about the question and realized my cathartic daydreaming had been helpful. I picked up Will's note again and smiled.

"Are you going to talk to him?" Mom's voice had an edge.

"Mom, so I kind of didn't tell you all the details of our breakup."

Mom's head cocked a bit to the left. "I didn't want to pry, honey; still don't."

"I know, but you've always been pretty angry with Will."

Her eyes went wide. "He hurt my child. Why shouldn't I be upset? He left you, honey. He left all of us."

The last sentence surprised me. "Look mom, I never told you, but he asked me to marry him."

"He what?" Her face mirrored the emotions I felt.

"Yep, surprised me too."

Mom's voice became a whisper. "When did he ask you?"

"End of the Summer. He had a plan to get married and live together at UW. He even turned down a bunch of other colleges to stay in Washington with me."

"And he made all those plans without discussing them with you?"

I nodded. "I mean, we discussed marriage, kids, all that, but I just thought it wasn't going to work out. I never thought he was going to propose and ask me to go to college with him."

"Clearly you said 'no' at some point."

"Right away. He didn't want to have children."

Mom's face suggested she did not agree with how I handled that, but she said nothing negative. After a bit of a pause, "Well honey, I'm glad you finally told me, but it's all water under the bridge now, isn't it?"

"I guess." I picked up my car keys and finished my coffee. "I'm heading down to Front Street. We're decorating cookies with the kids at The Gingerbread Factory this year. They offered to help."

"I'm going to stay here for a bit and clean up, and then I'll head home. Talk to you tonight?"

I gave mom an enormous hug. "I love you. Thank you for coming over."

She smiled. "My pleasure, honey."

I left the house and headed to downtown Leavenworth.

CHAPTER 11 – WILL

IT WAS AFTER 10:00 a.m. when I heard the car. I ran to the front window like a teenager. I had heard the snowplows around 5:00 a.m. while feeding Jamison. As I stared out of the window, I could see Adi's Forester making its way down the plowed road. Her mother's vehicle was still at the house. *Maybe they are going out for breakfast.*

"What are you doing?" my mother asked.

"Looks like a nice day, mom." I turned away from the window and headed towards her. "I'm meeting with Felicia for lunch today. I need to go get ready. Would you be willing to babysit?" Her face lit up. "I will take that as a yes." I walked down the hall and into my room. After collecting some clothes, I had a thought. "Hey mom."

"Yes?" she walked to the door of my room.

"I need to wash some of Jamison and my clothes."

"I already started the first load, don't worry about it Will."

"Thanks mom." I went to the bathroom. Mom's help was nice and made me feel loved. At home, I had a couple that ran the house for me there. I realized as I stood in the bathroom that I hadn't experienced someone helping me just because they wanted to in what seemed a lifetime. I have no idea why I didn't recognize that until now. It never seemed to make a difference before, but as the water poured over my head and the warmth softened the muscles in my back, I realized it made a huge difference. *Had I shut down every emotion so I could leave Leavenworth without any regrets? Or was it just that I tried to leave the Leavenworth Will behind? Neither of those seemed to fit. Probably, the reality was like many people I got too rich too fast and didn't handle it well. At least, I didn't burn up my money on drugs and other addictions. I hadn't really spent my money at all. Most of the time, I just kept working. It was the life I had chosen and enjoyed. But Jamison was going to change all of that.*

I got out of the shower and toweled off. I texted my personal assistant and asked her to investigate nannies for Jamison. After a shower full of questioning thoughts, I laughed at myself. Within moments, she responded and let me know she had already done so and had interviews setup. She also told me she'd been shopping and had prepared a room for Jamison in my house.

She's amazing, simply amazing. But do I want her setting up Jamison's room for me? Shouldn't I be doing that myself? I picked up the phone and called her.

A confident female voice answered, "hello."

I said, "Hi Hannah," and before she could follow up, I continued, "first, I would like to thank you and ask you send me some pictures of the room. But also, let's hold off buying anything more for Jamison. I would like to do that shopping myself."

"I'm sorry, Will." Hannah's voice sounded hurt and concerned.

"You are marvelous, as usual. It's great you think of things I need before I do. With Jamison, I feel like it requires a personal touch from me."

I heard the "oh-that's-so-cute," tone in her voice when she replied, "I understand." There was a pause and then she said, "I have been watching the roads. Unfortunately, it appears that you will be snowed in and unable to leave until after Christmas. I've investigated some alternatives. We might hire a helicopter, but even that is dicey right now with the storm."

"Thank you, Hannah, keep an eye out, but it's not urgent. Things are going well here."

"Yes sir. Also, we have received all the purchases made for your parents for Christmas, but I don't have a way to get them to you. I'm sorry about that."

I'd forgotten I had her do that. "No problem. I'll see what I can do locally. We'll save those for an after Christmas surprise." I strained my brain to remember what Hannah and I had talked about concerning the gifts, but I was drawing a blank. "What else is going on?"

"The office is slow with the holidays. Your social media accounts have been receiving many well wishes for the birth of Jamison." There were a few seconds of quiet, then she said, "I spoke with Mr. Barkley a couple of hours ago and his impression was you were coming back sooner."

"Understood." I switched screens and sent Jim a text. **Hold down the fort. I'll get on my laptop today and see what fires I can put out.**

Hanna asked, "is there anything else you need?"

"I think I'm good for now. Thank you for everything you've done. Are you taking time off for Christmas?"

"I had planned to, but with you trapped in Leavenworth, I figured I'd cancel my plans and stay here."

"No!" I shifted the phone to my other ear. "When is your flight to Utah?"

"At 7:30 p.m. tonight."

"Then be on it. We can survive without you for a few days." I made sure my voice had a positive tone. "If worse comes to worst, Jim will have to do some double duty."

"Are you sure?"

She truly was amazing. How'd I get so lucky? "I am, have a Merry Christmas."

"You have a Merry Christmas as well, Will. I'm looking forward to meeting Jamison when you two get back home." The phone disconnected.

I sent another text to Jim to make sure he let Hanna leave without a conversation about her leaving. Jim would mean no harm, but his filter was not always corporate grade.

My father walked up with Jamison in his arms. "Going to get ready for your date?"

"It's not a date." I put the phone down and looked at my father, who stood in the doorway to the kitchen smiling at me. He was feeding Jamison, who was content in his arms.

"For you it's not a date, but for Felicia, well, I think she might want something else." He got a bigger smile on his face.

"Nice dad." I walked over to my father and looked at Jamison in his arms. He was back to sleep and looked very peaceful. I let the little curls wrap around my fingers, feeling the warmth of his scalp. I bent over and kissed him gently on the forehead, inhaling the smell of baby. There was a smile on my face. "I love you, Jamison." I pulled myself away and went into my room and got ready for my not-date.

I took some time to get ready and I will confess I changed my shirt a few times before I was content with my decision. I had to be creative with the limited contents of my suitcase to put together a nice outfit. As I walked into the living room, my father whistled, and mother nudged him with the back of her hand on his shoulder. She then pointed at Jamison. I walked over to Jamison and tucked his blanket in. He was deep in sleep and didn't react when I gave him another kiss on the forehead. He still smelled wonderful, and I felt a tremendous urge to cancel lunch and just pick Jamison up and hold him. I fought the urge, though it was a close call. "Be back soon." I moved away from Jamison, opened the door, and walked into the garage. I got into the Highlander and pushed the garage door button. Driving into the street, I saw that Adi's mother's car was still there. I closed my folks' garage and headed to downtown and Gustav's.

Gustav's was a Bavarian restaurant downtown with a variety of sausage options. It was a tourist attraction, but it also was a fun place to meet and had great German food. I travelled down the snow-covered streets to downtown. I took my time because although they had plowed the streets, the new snowfall had completely covered up all the freshly cleared asphalt.

It was daytime, but the decorations and lights strung out between the trees and around the buildings still conveyed the atmosphere of Christmas. I thought about Jamison at home tucked in his bassinet and the urge to turn around hit me. It felt like a part of me was missing.

I rolled my window down a bit and listened to the Christmas carols that blasted from the speakers around downtown. As the snow fell on my windshield, I could not help but smile at the white Christmas laid out around me. I drove the Highlander to Gustav's and, thanks to the weather, found a parking space with little to no trouble. Well, to be frank, I believed it was a parking space, and that's exactly what I'm going to tell any parking patrols that might question it. The fact is, the space might have been two spaces reduced by the mounds of snow at the back and front. I really did not know because the snow had long ago covered the lines on the street.

I left the warmth of the Highlander, and the cold of the storm surrounded me. Snow blew into the vehicle before I could close the door. I shook off the snow already piling up on my hair and pulled my hood up. Bundled up and ready to race to Gustav's, I pushed the button on my fob, locking the vehicle and began walking through the snow.

I walked towards Gustav's and felt the powdery snow crunch beneath my boots. Cold made its way through the soles of my boots and even through my father's jacket. I shook the snow off my coat as I entered the restaurant. Gustav's was warm and full of cheerful voices. The lunch hour appeared busy, and there were very few seats available. *People must have walked.*

I looked around through the gaggle of patrons and saw Felicia in the corner. She stood up and waved. I walked over to her, and she wrapped me in a hug, which caught me a bit off guard. She was still lovely. She was 5' 7" with gorgeous blonde hair, blue eyes, and the curves that supported all the parades she had been in. I was fairly sure that she could still wear the old cheerleader outfit from high school. Physically speaking, Felicia had been fortunate in life. I patted her on the back and said, "hi." The pat seemed to surprise her, and she disconnected. The feeling of the hug was so different from the ones I got in high school, and I couldn't help but note the difference.

"It's so good to see you." Felicia stepped back and sat down in her chair.

As I sat down, I pulled out my seat and sank into the plush fabric. I leaned forward and grabbed the glass of water, waiting for me. I took a big swig and then sat the glass down. "Good to see you as well." After looking around a bit, I saw a couple of phones pointing my way. I had a variety of projects I was currently working on, including a social media app. I realized I was becoming less and less interested in the world of social media. Until this moment, I had always found it to be a tool. Now I found it enormously intrusive.

"Do you want a drink?" Felicia waved a server over.

"They have a good IPA?"

"Hoppy, citrus, or both?" she asked.

"Hoppy."

"Hi Amy," Felicia said to the server that approached us, "could we please get a Boundary Bay IPA."

"We are serving their Northwest Original IPA right now."

"That'll work and I'll have another Irish Coffee." Amy smiled and headed off to the bar. "Now, where did we end that phone call?"

I tapped my finger for a moment in thought. "I was asking how Felicia, who wanted nothing more than to get out of Leavenworth, found herself back in town."

"Well," she started and then continued to tell me the drama that was her life for the last twelve years.

CHAPTER 12 – ADI

I ARRIVED AT THE GINGERBREAD Factory closer to eleven than to ten. The smell of the warm sugar cookies drifted out of the restaurant and reminded me I hadn't had breakfast. Clare met me at the door with a hot croissant and a cup of coffee.

"Bless you," I said as I accepted the food and shook the snow from my shoulders and head. "I'm so sorry I'm late."

"No problem." She guided me with croissant in mouth into the bakery. "They shut down for the day to host the event."

I listened to the conversations flowing out of the bakery. There were squeals of the cheerful children cutting through adult voices. As I moved farther into the bakery, the smell of freshly baked cookies filled the air, and I saw the joy on the faces of the children decorating their Christmas treats. While the smell of cookies was strong at the door, the sugary aroma of Christmas joy was tangible in the air within the bakery. I breathed in that joy and felt it surround me with warmth and happiness. The spirit of Christmas enveloped me. It was nearly equal to the chorus of joyful children that rose as I approached. "Ms. Lewis is here! Ms. Lewis is here!" They engulfed me in hugs and frosting coated hands. They encircled me with love. I felt my heart beating in my chest. These children were mine because I taught them. *I have the best job in the world.*

"Ms. Lewis," Tina Lane came up and pulled on my shirt.

"Yes, Tina?" I asked as I disengaged her hand from my shirt and gave her hand a gentle, friendly squeeze.

"Would you help me make a Santa Claus, please?"

"Sure," she pulled me over to her table. There was a pile of Santa Claus cookies already half decorated on her workstation. There were also white sugar cookies, gingerbread cookies, and a variety of other beautiful cookies piled up and waiting for frosting. An assortment of colored frostings and various candies for eyes, noses, and buttons were on the table. I sat down and helped Tina. The children were having a wonderful time as they created every Christmas character imaginable. I inhaled again and felt the warmth of Christmas spread through my senses.

Clare put her hand on my shoulder and gave it a squeeze. "Pretty awesome, isn't it?"

"Couldn't be better." I rolled up my sleeves and started working on a Santa cookie. "It was a stroke of genius to have this here."

"I know, right?" Clare was helping a little girl make a snowman.

I worked with the kids for a couple of hours. I would move from project to project to share my time with the children who were baking, frosting, and, yes, even eating the cookies. Christmas music played behind the sounds of the children. Happiness emanated from everywhere. I was lost in the sense of wonder and joy of childhood and the Christmas scents filling the air.

"Nice to see you smiling," Clare walked over and looked at the cookie I was decorating. She moved behind me and looked over my shoulder as I helped a young boy finish an angel cookie.

I looked up from the cookie. "I agree." As I turned my head, I noticed a couple of other teachers that were standing near us.

Ms. Peters, a fifth-grade teacher, said "I'm proud of you Adi. You've survived a tough year and come out of it with grace. You are a remarkable woman." She leaned forward and gave me a brief hug. That broke some dam of affection and with that, I received a hug of encouragement from pretty much every adult in the room.

"Thank you all. This is wonderful. But let's focus on the kids, OK?" I felt the blush as it burned its way through my cheeks.

"We love you," Clare said, as she gave me a light punch to the shoulder. "You must remember how much you've contributed to this community. I cannot image what my life would be like if you hadn't come back to Leavenworth."

"I would never stay away."

"You say that, but you never know. You could have met someone who didn't want to come back to Leavenworth."

I looked at Clare. "We still talking about college?"

Clare looked down at the cookie she was working on. "You and I both know you still have feelings for Will."

"Do we?"

Her head jerked up quickly and she brought her face close to mine. "Adalynn Jane Lewis, you might convince yourself that you stopped loving him, but" she lowered her voice to a whisper, "you and I both know the only reason you didn't say 'yes' was because of one thing and it sure the heck wasn't because you didn't love him."

"That was a long time ago. I should pine for Edward, not Will."

"Exactly! But you are not. You really do not care that Edward left, do you? It is the fact that Will came home with a child that's really got you messed up and questioning things, no? In fact, I bet you haven't shed a single tear for Edward."

"Ha," I said a bit too loud, then lowered my voice. "I'd win that wager."

"Really?" She put her mouth to my ear. "Do you miss him or just the chance to be a family?" She turned to me and looked me in the eye. "You have a family. You have children. You have all of us. We love you, Adi." Clare hugged me and as she let me go, I saw a tear in her eye. It was my turn to punch her in the shoulder, which brought a smile to her face.

"I'm not going anywhere. This is my home forever."

"Good!" Clare gave me another punch and then drifted over to help another child with a cookie.

I went over to another table and helped some more kids. I couldn't help but think about Clare. *Was she really worried I would leave? Had Will returning with a child created this much drama? I realized how little we knew. Like where was the baby's mother? Was he married? Why was he in Leavenworth?* These thoughts bounced around in my head until I realized I had stopped working on the cookie and was just staring at the unfinished cookie.

"You ok Ms. Lewis?"

"Yes." I helped finish the cookie. In my head, I told myself to focus, and I pushed aside thoughts of Will and his baby. In fact, it quite surprised me when the elementary school principal spoke up and thanked everyone.

Ms. Roberts said, "Everyone, thanks for coming. We are going to break for lunch and bring in some more students and teachers at 1:00 p.m. I want everyone to have an amazing Christmas."

There were more hugs and Christmas wishes. Eventually, Clare pulled me away from the kids and we returned to the cold of the snow falling outside the Gingerbread Factory.

Clare pulled on her gloves and then rubbed her stomach. "I'm starving."

"Me too. Where should we go?"

"I haven't been to Gustav's in a while, and I feel like a beer."

"Sure. Walking?"

"Definitely." She reached out and grabbed my hand. She nearly pulled me down as she trotted towards Gustav's.

"How hungry are you?"

"Very. I avoided the cookies. I was saving my carbs for a beer."

We walked down Front Street and through town. We relished in the Christmas decorations and lights as we made our way to the restaurant. Christmas carols pulsed from the hidden speakers throughout the town. They had cleared the streets and sidewalks enough to make downtown the most accessible place in Leavenworth, but the snow had not stopped.

As we walked, we passed many locals and a few folks that were staying at the B&Bs and hotels in town. We got closer to Gustav's, and I looked down Eighth Street towards the hotel. What I saw made me stop and pause.

Clare stopped next to me. "What?"

I pointed down the street. "Isn't that Edward's Range Rover?"

Clare looked where I was pointing. "I'm not sure."

As we stood there and stared at the vehicle, Edward and a woman I did not know came out of the Post hotel and got into Edward's Range Rover.

"What is he doing back in town?"

"I don't have a clue." I pulled my phone out and dialed Edward.

He answered on the third ring. "Hello Adi."

"Edward, you are in town."

"Not a question, so I would assume you know I am."

"Yes, I just saw you coming out of the Post Hotel."

I heard him cover the phone and say something to the person he was with. The phone became clear again and he said, "I came back to get some things I had in storage. We got caught in the storm. I was lucky enough to get a room at the hotel."

Lucky. "Who is the lady?" I could hear the possessiveness in my voice but didn't care.

"A friend." There was another long pause. "We are leaving." I watched as the Range Rover went out of sight. "But we should meet up and talk before I leave town."

"Sure."

"Good," he said and hung up.

"Did he explain?"

"He got caught in the storm." We started walking again towards Gustav's.

"Why is he back? And who was the chick?"

"He was getting something out of storage, and I do not know."

We made it to Gustav's. We left the cold of winter and entered the restaurant. The place was full of warmth and life. Voices filled the room with energy. I looked across the room and saw Felicia D'Angelo sitting at a table drinking, eating, and talking with Will Monroe. I turned around and exited Gustav's.

"What?" Clare asked.

"Look for yourself." I pointed in Will's general direction and then the door closed behind me.

CHAPTER 13 – WILL

FELICIA WENT ON AT length about the wonders and tragedies that she experienced after she left high school. From her point of view, the entire universe seemed to revolve around choices she had made. She even seemed to feel that she was the one that had encouraged me towards what she referred to as "my great success." I smiled through most of it and enjoyed the drink and the atmosphere of Gustav's.

I can't deny that I spent some time looking at Felicia. When we sat down, she took off her jacket to expose a shirt that was more pushup bra than outerwear. Her breasts were about double the size I remembered in high school. And while it had been a while, my memory was that normal breasts weren't supposed to remain stationary, the way Felicia's did when she moved. Her life before Leavenworth 2.0 had left her with some permanent alterations.

"Felicia, your ex-husband sounds terrible."

"Thank you, Will." She reached out and held my hand.

I smiled and disengaged my hand, patting hers as I did so with my other hand. "But, even with his misconduct, I'm curious. Why did you come back to Leavenworth? Why not get a job or finish college?"

Her shoulders slumped and a bit of the liveliness she had been displaying seemed to fade away. "I don't know." We sat there as she wrestled with her answer. Two young women delivered our food, and the smell of the food triggered memories of prior meals at Gustav's and, of course, reminded me of Adi. Felicia was gracious to the woman who brought her plate. She remained quiet as she picked at her food. Eventually, Felicia answered me. "Will, the answer isn't great. It just came down to feeling like I failed. I mean, I had gotten out of Leavenworth. I had most of a college education and achieved the life I always wanted with the correct husband, correct friends, correct houses, and oh my God, the travel!" Her eyes sparkled for a moment before fading. "I lost all of it."

"You gave up?"

"Pretty much. I didn't think about it. It wasn't a plan or anything. I just felt lost." She brought her glass to her mouth and sipped. She put her glass down and looked at me. "I didn't think I was doing anything irrational in the moment, however I can now see that I was feeling down when I made my choice. There was no one to look out for me. I didn't even have money for counseling. I had nowhere to go."

"So, you came back to the one place you were always safe?"

She laughed a little. "It seems so simple when you say it, but it's true. As much as I wanted to leave this place, it was always safe."

"I agree. It is a safe place. I think that's part of the reason I wanted to leave. I never felt challenged here. There were no risks. Everything always came so easy. And if there was an issue, my parents and everyone else were there to catch me."

Felicia ate some more and downed her drink. "The danger outside of Leavenworth was half the fun. But even that wore off. Life becomes normal eventually, no matter where you are."

"I guess we both figured out life away from Leavenworth doesn't guarantee fulfillment." I stopped and pondered my own words. *How long had I felt that way? I had been taking on a lot of new projects the last few years, but never thought about why. Was I getting bored?*

Did I miss the risks? My life the last few years had been the same activities on repeat. Travel, work, and everything else my money allowed me to do had stopped being a thrill years ago. I put some food in my mouth. *The last year had been different. It was a surprise and an adventure. I wasn't prepared for the roller coaster of emotions and dramas that would result from a weekend in Spokane. And now I had Jamison. Was there anything scarier than becoming a parent?*

"Where'd you go?" Felicia grabbed my hand again. Her nails were long and glossy, with a perfect French manicure that showed they were fake.

"Sorry, was thinking about life and the unimagined turns it can take."

"Which reminds me, we've been talking about me this entire time. What about you and this whole baby thing?"

"His name is Jamison." I disengaged our hands.

"How old is he?"

"About three months old."

"Oh, a little one." She moved some food around on her plate. "Where's his mother?" This wasn't the person I wanted to have this conversation with. I started thinking more about Adi. I wondered what she thought of my note or if her mother even showed her. "It's not a trick question. You didn't kidnap the kid or something?"

The anger was immediate and flooded me like a dam breaking. I almost stood. *Stop. Why are you so angry? It was a stupid question, but calm down.* I took a deep breath. I stared at Felicia. Her face was no longer a mask of beauty. She was trying to hide it, but there was a slight quiver of fear in her eyes.

"I overstepped." Her voice was silent.

The room seemed quieter as I focused on Felicia and tried to calm myself. I took another breath and forced relaxation into my body language and face. I felt no less calm, but hopefully I was radiating less anger than I had been moments before. *Why had the question done that to me? Why don't I have an answer?* Another deep breath. I said in the quietest voice I could, "No, I didn't kidnap him. Jamison is my child."

Her face was flushed, and she squirmed in her chair. "I'm sorry Will. It was a poor joke." She stared at her plate. "You are just bigger than life. I've followed your social media and the news media about you. People in town after you left talked about how you weren't the settle down type. Everyone is just surprised you have a baby with no wife or mother in tow." She paused. "I didn't mean to be a jerk."

I rested my eyes on her face and her eyes for a while as I breathed slowly in and worked to accept her apology. As I was getting ready to speak again, the door to Gustav's opened and Adi Lewis and her best friend Clare entered the restaurant. The anger in me vanished just like that. I could feel my heart catch in my chest. New stronger emotions of concern, fear, and yes, love flooded through. *Adi!*

Before I could get out of my chair, Felicia tugged at my hand, and I looked back at her. "What?"

"You disappeared again."

I disengaged myself again from Felicia and stood up to find Adi. I looked again at the door and then scanned the room. They had left. *No, no, no!* I shoveled some cash onto the table and stepped away from it. "My apologies, but something has come up. Have a wonderful lunch on me. I'm sure we'll talk another time. Have another drink and enjoy Gustav's." I rushed away from the table, heading towards the door. I bundled up on the move.

I heard behind me, "I'm sorry Will, I didn't mean to offend you."

I waved goodbye to Felicia as a reply and then opened the door. Frigid air hit me as I exited the building and searched for Adi. I looked left and then right but saw no sign of her. Right would take me up to the main street, so I turned left, hoping she had parked somewhere on Front Street. I balanced the need for speed and my desire to keep my footing as I rushed forward and continued to search for her. There were a few tourists and some locals moving up and down the street, but no Adi. *Where did you go?*

I made it further down the block with no luck and then Clare Johnson intercepted me. "Hello Clare," I became conscious of the sweat on my skin under the warm jacket.

"Mr. William Monroe, I see you have finally returned to Leavenworth. What do you want?" She had her hands on her hips and it was clear I wasn't going to get past her without having a conversation first.

"I saw Adi with you. I'd like to talk to her."

"What if she doesn't want to speak with you, William? Have you ever thought of that? I'm not saying she doesn't. But I think you should take a step back and make sure you are making the right choices for you both. We don't want another fiasco, do we?" Her eyes had locked onto mine. Clare Johnson was the enforcer on the girls' soccer team during high school. She was tough, confident, and unmovable.

"Clare, you know the complete story, right?"

"Your proposal?" she asked, "yes, I know."

"Then you know how I felt. I don't want to hurt Adi. I just want to talk to her."

Her eyes flashed with anger. "And you think appearing in Leavenworth at Christmas with your baby, posting on social media, and leaving a note on her door was taking steps not to hurt her? You are selfish, William Monroe. You always have been, and you always will be."

The wind picked up and the snow fell again. Clare's question required an honest answer. "I did not plan to bring my son here. I did not know Adi lived across from my parents, I didn't know the Leavenworth social media groups would out me. The note was my attempt at reaching out to Adi. I agree that all of those things were done without concern for Adi. I feel terrible that it hurt her. That's why I want to talk to her. I want to apologize." I felt out of breath.

"Is all of that true, William?"

"Hand to God, Clare." She thought for a moment, then nodded her head to herself. She handed me her phone.

"Put your phone number in here. I'll give it to Adi. From there it's her decision, ok? Her choice - you got me?"

I accepted the phone and typed in my personal information. "I understand. Let her know I'm sorry and..." *Please tell her how much I miss her.* "...I'll abide by her decision."

Clare said, "Good. Nice to see you, Will."

"Nice to see you too, Clare." She walked away, and I turned and headed back to the restaurant. I turned on the ringer on my phone, turned the sound up to maximum, and double checked the charge on my watch. This was not a call I was going to miss.

At the door of Gustav's, I thought for a moment about going back in and talking to Felicia. I looked through the window and saw a man sitting across from her. The two of them were drinking, talking, and clearly enjoying one another's company. The guilt I felt for leaving her sitting there disappeared. Felicia was looking for something and whatever it was, it surely wasn't me. I walked to my vehicle. *Felicia knew what she wanted. What do I want? Why did I feel so excited and why did my chest hurt so badly? Twelve years later, was I still really in love with Adi Lewis?*

CHAPTER 14 – ADI

CLARE CAME AROUND THE corner.

"Did you talk to him?"

She nodded. "I certainly did. That man is still gorgeous, and his voice is amazing." She fanned herself. "I love a deep baritone male voice."

"Hey now, I believe you contacted him for me, right?" I shoved her shoulder. "When did you get a crush on my boyfriend?"

"Your ex-boyfriend." Clare looped her arm into mine and we hiked down the sidewalk. "And truth be told, there were many of us in high school that had a bit of a crush on William Monroe. We were all a little envious of your relationship and how much that boy loved you."

A warm, genuine smile stretched across my face. "What did he say?"

"He's sorry you found out the way you did about his son. He wants to talk with you." She let go of my arm. "Let me have your phone." I gave it to her, and she typed information into it. "Ok, you have his number now. He agreed to leave you alone until you reached out to him."

"Why did he do that?"

She let out a little chuckle as she grinned. "Because I told him to."

"But that's not what I want. I don't want to call him."

"You don't have to do anything." Clare walked and I followed. "You have choices, honey. You can call him and go down that path or choose not to call him and keep going the way you've been going; your choice."

"What if I don't want the choice? What if I want him to make the choice?"

"You want him to make the choice? Really?" Clare stopped and looked at me. Our eyes met. "Adi, it seems to me you always made the calls in that relationship. I didn't know you had changed your ways."

"Hey now, he proposed to me, and he left Leavenworth."

"Yes, but you said 'no' when he proposed and you chose not to follow him to the University of Washington, right?"

"And how are my choices the one's in control?"

"Because if you said 'yes,' you'd be married now and if you had followed him to the University of Washington, he would have taken you in and you would be part of his life. You realize Will was and probably still is head over heels in love with you, right? It's not like he can control that. Twelve years later, and if social media is to be believed, he never married or had anyone significant in his life. At least he's never posted about a relationship. The media talks about his lack of social life and how he's a work-acholic. They assume he has no social life because of his work, but I think we both know the truth."

"And his baby's mother?" I asked.

"You expect him to be celibate? I have no clue who she is or where she is right now. Maybe you should call him and find out for all of us."

I processed what she had just said, and then we walked again. As I thought about her words, I brushed the snow off my shoulders. My emotions were a mess. I bounced between feelings of excitement mixed in with clear anger towards both Clare and William. "Ok, this just isn't fair. Why did you do this to me?" We turned a corner and, finally looking around at where we were at, I realized we made a big circle around downtown.

"What exactly did I do to you, Adi? How has the situation changed? Well, you have Will's cell phone number now, but besides that, how are things different from the last twelve years?"

"Let's see, I have a degree, I'm a teacher, I'm divorced, and I know I will never have children. Is that what you want to hear?" I could feel the tears as they rolled inward down my throat, but my eyes themselves were a desert dry with anger.

Clare stopped, and in a swift, agile move, wrapped me in a hug. She literally squeezed the anxiety out of me. The burn and tingles inside me died down. "Honey, you keep looking at things in such black and white terms. You not only got a degree and became a teacher, but you discovered you are a fabulous teacher. You tried marriage to someone and tried having a child with that person and discovered that wasn't going to happen. But that doesn't mean there isn't someone else you couldn't start a family with." She paused and then said, "and to be extremely blunt, you should know that none of us liked Edward."

"What?!?" I felt my heart drop.

She laughed a bit. "Do you really think he would've left you if he really loved you just because you couldn't have kids? That man had issues from day one."

"Well…"

"Shut up! I mean it, stop it." She shook me a little. "Someone doesn't leave the love of their life because there's a hiccup. Do you not remember your vows, 'until death do us part?' Do you think that was just a suggestion? He didn't have that kind of love for you, and we all knew it. It's just…" She paused and caught herself. I could see the emotions in her eyes. "It's just after Will, it was nice to see you in love again. But he did not leave you because of children. He left you because he didn't love you enough. His fault. Not your fault."

The tears were pouring from my eyes now. The moisture on my face crystalized in the cold. "Damn you for making me cry in a snowstorm." She hugged me again and then started us in a fast but safe march towards the bakery.

"You, ok?" She handed me a tissue from her pocket.

I cleaned up and blew my nose. I placed the used tissue in my pocket. "Yes, thank you. All of this is quite a challenge. This is not the Christmas I imagined." I grabbed ahold of Clare's hand and squeezed. "So, you think Will still loves me?"

"That's what you took from my little speech?" She shook her head.

"No, I'm going to accept what you said about me as the truth. I agree Edward left me because of Edward. It wasn't my fault. It was his." She smiled and nodded. We made it to the door of the bakery. "But I have no clue about how Will feels about me or really how I feel about him. I know I still feel hurt. I never thought he would actually leave. And of course, once he left, I never thought he'd come back with a baby."

"Why is it so important for you to know how he feels?" she asked.

"I'm uncertain. I mean, I've lived twelve years without him. We've never called each other, emailed, or texted. It's my fault as much as his, but if we really were meant to be, don't you think we would've reached out sooner?" The snow swirled around us, but the stir of emotions kept me warm inside. I used my glove to disengage the crystals of tears from my face. "Why twelve years?"

Clare answered, "Adi, you've spent most of your money and time the last few years trying to have a child." I nodded. "Why would you contact the man who didn't want to have children with you?"

"Ok, maybe that's true, but he didn't try to contact me either."

She sighed. "Hon, I don't pretend to understand how men think, but I have to believe it's a big deal for a man to get the courage to ask a woman to marry him. And I would guess that when the answer is no, well, how does someone come back from that?"

I let out a deep sigh and felt my lips turn down in a pout. I realized over all these years I had not once put myself in his shoes. Even though he hadn't discussed it with me, he had chosen a path he thought would keep us together. He was wrong, but that didn't mean my 'no' hadn't hurt him. "I never thought about it from his point of view."

She said, "No reason you should've until now. But he is back and it's probably the right time to think about it."

"Why?"

"Because at some point the two of you are actually going to talk to one another; and that conversation is going to go a lot better if you both have a bit of empathy for the other person."

"When did you get so smart about relationships?"

"I have four channels of Hallmark shows I watch." I could only laugh at that. When I opened the door, I felt the warmth of the room and heard the cheerful voices of the children.

Clare asked, "Are we going in for some more cathartic cookie making?"

"It would seem like a good idea, don't you think?"

"I do."

"Good." I hugged Clare and we went into the bakery.

CHAPTER 15 – WILL

STEVE GREER WAS LEANING against the front of my Highlander as I approached it.

"Been awhile, Will," he said. Steve was a year ahead of me in high school, but he really had more friends in my grade than he did his own. Steve and John had been inseparable at school, and John and my friendship had sometimes rattled Steve.

"Hi, Steve." I clicked the Highlander's fob, which unlocked the door. I climbed into the driver's seat and Steve got into the passenger's side. I turned on the vehicle and warmed it up to give us heat. "How are things?"

"Why have you come back?" To me, Steve looked like he had ten years on me. The cracks in his face documented his stress and worry. His hair, once vibrant red, had taken on a more muted silver hue with age. You could see outwardly how much the man had been broken by his brother's death. And who knows, maybe it was guilt as well, because Steve had not followed his brother into the military.

"I was heading to Edmonds from Spokane. The storm had other plans."

He said, "I heard you have a kid."

"Yes, that also wasn't planned. Life has taken some odd turns for me lately."

He said, "I will not ask you why you didn't come to the funeral. My folks and I didn't know how to reach you, but we appreciated the money you sent for the funeral costs."

I wanted to say it was the least I could do, but I knew that wasn't true. "I wasn't ready to come back, but I loved John. I wanted to help."

"Well, we appreciated it. He has one of the best plots in Mountain View Cemetery. We had a bronze covering made with images of his life. There's even a picture of the three of us engraved into it." He paused for a second, then asked, "Do you want to go with me and see it?"

The question jarred me. I knew I owed it to John. I felt terrible about not attending the funeral. But it also just felt so incredibly uncomfortable. "Sure Steve, sure." I popped the parking brake and pulled out of the parking space.

The sun could not break through the snow filled clouds above us, but the afternoon sun lit those clouds up and reflected off the surrounding snow. I put on a pair of sunglasses and drove south towards the cemetery. "What have you been up to, Steve?"

"Do you know where you are going?"

"I lived here my whole life, man, of course I do." He nodded his reply. I asked, "How's the family? How are you?" He stared out the window and we drove in silence for about 20 minutes, fighting our way through the snow and some roads that weren't plowed. Even with all wheel drive, we struggled, but in silence, we made our way to the cemetery.

The snow had covered the place in a blanket of anonymity. Only the taller signage made it clear where we were. There was no way to find an actual parking spot, so I parked close enough to the road that we wouldn't have problems leaving. Steve jumped out of the car and began hiking through the snow. He needed very few landmarks to guide him. I got out and followed the path he had cut through the snow. We stopped at a place in the middle of a cleared field covered in snow. Fir trees bound the location with a beautiful view of the surrounding mountains. Steve kneeled and cleared the snow from his brother's grave. The bronze grave marker was a couple feet wide and high and they had etched it with images of John's life. It was an amazing tribute to the man.

"I miss him so much, Will." Steve placed his hand on the center most image of his brother in his uniform.

"I do too."

We stood there quietly for five minutes, giving John his due.

"So," he asked, "why has it taken you so long to come home and see him?"

I kneeled and cleared off more of the marker. "It was never about John. I'm coming to understand that it wasn't even about Leavenworth." I traced the images of John and me. "I was just so wrapped up in escaping that I didn't realize I had escaped and could come back anytime I wanted. Call it irrational fear or maybe just stupidity."

"Will, we had a damn good childhood."

I laughed a little and patted Steve on the back. The small contact turned into a side hug, and I could feel a single sob resonate through his chest. He whispered, "You two were my best friends and neither one of you came back. At least with Johnny, I knew why."

"It wasn't you, man; it wasn't anyone other than me. It took an act of nature to make me realize I needed to come home. Call it a Christmas miracle if you'd like." He laughed at that.

Steve shifted on his knees and grasped his hands together. "Mind if I say a prayer?"

"Please," I responded.

With us kneeling before John's grave, Steve closed his eyes, and I did the same. He started with the Lord's prayer and then spoke to John. He said, "John, Will and I are here. I know you had something to do with guiding him home, and I thank you for that. Keep watching over and protecting us, my brother. We cherish your memory, and we miss you."

I added, "John, I'm sorry I wasn't here for your funeral. I'm sure you are aware I had a child recently. When we were naming him, I told his mother about you and what had happened. I told her how much I loved you and missed you. John, his middle name is John in honor of you. We named him Jamison John Monroe. I miss you, buddy." Tears erupted from my eyes and flowed down my face. The water on my face immediately chilled.

We kneeled there for as long as we could stand the cold and then trudged back to the Highlander, following the path we had cut earlier. With the heat on, we thawed. Once my teeth had stopped chattering, I said, "Thank you, Steve. Thank you for bringing me here."

"I'm glad you were able to come," he said. I was fairly sure he meant "willing," when he said "able," but I appreciated the sentiment. He said, "To answer your earlier question, the family is doing ok. My parents are retired, and my dad is carving animals and toys out of wood for the tourists. Mom helps with some charities in town, now and again, but she got kind of quiet after John."

"And you?" I asked.

"I went to a little college in New York when John went into the military. I got a B.A. in communications and came back to town. I got married a couple years ago." He held up his left hand, showing the black rubber wedding band on his hand. "We had a miscarriage the first go around, but now we have a beautiful son named John. Life's ok."

"What are you doing for work?" I asked.

He laughed. "You're going to love this. I'm the communications director for the town." He said, "I also volunteer to help with some of the cemetery's communications. Just keeps me closer to John."

"I get it," We entered the town proper. "Where should I drop you off?"

"Back where we got in your rig."

"That brings up a good question. How did you know this was my SUV?"

He laughed again. Our trip to the cemetery had been good for both of us. Steve looked years younger. "This is Leavenworth, man. Even before social media, it was a small town full of gossip. If one person saw you in this vehicle, it's genuinely nice by the way, then everyone knows it's your vehicle."

"Right, small town, silly me."

"To be honest, your company logo on the back window kind of gave it away as well."

"There is that," I said, and then we laughed together

We kept chatting as we drove. Eventually, I pulled back into the parking spot where we had left from.

"I need to get home," Steve said, "but I want to see you again before you leave. And I want you to meet my family." He stepped out of the Highlander.

"I would like that. I want you to meet Jamison as well." He stuck his hand out and I shook it.

"Twelve years was too long, Will. That cannot happen again." The pressure of his grip strengthened.

"I hear you, man. It won't. I want our sons to grow up knowing each other."

A huge smile broke Steve's face. "Johnny's two namesakes growing up together. I love that."

I didn't correct the growing up part. "Sounds great." He closed the door and I drove off, headed back for my parents' home. I had a tremendous need to hold my son.

As I drove, I thought about Adi and the fact I gave my phone number to Clare. I pulled my phone out of my pants, while stopped at a light, and scrolled quickly through the texts and calls I had received. There were lots of calls and texts from work, but none from Adi.

CHAPTER 16 – ADI

I STARED AT MY PHONE, attempting to summon the strength to either call or text him, but I just couldn't do it. I came home after finishing up at the bakery. It was just getting dark, and I had spent an unreasonable amount of time making what should be a straightforward decision. I mean really, how hard is it to send a text?

My phone rang. It was Clare. "Still staring at your phone?" she asked.

"What the hell? How did you know?"

She laughed. "Because I was there when you applied for college, your teaching job, and, well, everything else in your life. You know you overthink things, right, Adi?"

"Sure, sure," I said, "but this is different."

"How do you figure?"

I sighed. "Because in all those situations, I knew the right thing to do. I was just scared that it wouldn't work out."

"And how is it different here?"

"Well," I said, "I'm still worried about what will happen if I call, but I also don't know if I should. Will and I haven't spoken in twelve years. Do I want to open myself up for that kind of hurt? I mean, I just got divorced and my old high school boyfriend is in town with his child. What kind of choice am I making by calling him? And I know nothing about the child's mother. Maybe they are still together, maybe they're getting married. Why would I call him?"

"Take a breath," Clare said. I did. "Now listen to me. I've done some digging on social media and I cannot find anyone claiming to date Mr. Monroe. There is scant information about his son and none about his son's mother. I do not know what's going on, but I think it is significant that he's at his parent's house with a very young baby and no 'mother' for that child."

"That is an educated guess," I said.

"Yes, but all it takes is a text for you to find out more. He left a note on your door after all. It's clear he wants to talk to you. And if that's not enough for you, he gave me his phone number so you could reach out. Doesn't sound like someone who doesn't want to talk with you."

"Why is it me that has to call?"

"What do you mean?" I heard her sigh at the end of my question. She paused, then asked, "Oh, your goal; your purpose?"

"Yes, that's exactly it."

She laughed and said, "How about you don't have a goal, don't have a plan, and just reach out to your old friend?"

"Is that what I am about to do?"

"For now, yes," she said, "I think that's enough, don't you? Or do you expect more?"

"I don't know what I want. That's my point. Every time I think about calling him, I think about his son. Then I ask myself a thousand questions that have no answers. It's frustrating."

"I get that, Adi, but there will never be answers to those thousands of questions if you do not make the call. There's a lot of information you could get in the first couple of minutes of a conversation with Will that will answer many of those questions."

"Like he's about to get married," I said.

"Right, or he's living with his son's mother, or a host of other answers. Right now, all you know is he's here, he has a son, and he wants to talk with you."

"Did I screw up twelve years ago, Clare?"

"I can't answer that for you, Adi, especially in hindsight, given what we now know. But let's forget children for a second. Would you give up teaching or the last six years living in Leavenworth?"

I immediately knew the answer was no. "Being me required that."

Clare said, "These are the days that must happen to you."

"A Walt Whitman quote," I stated.

"Very good," she replied. I laughed. "See, look at that college education at work."

"You are so funny. I have to say this is the first time I really thought about how that quote applies to my life."

"It's an interesting way of looking at fate, right?" she said, "it's not about a predestined future as much as our past and present that makes us the person we are." I looked at my phone and considered what Clare was saying. "What are you thinking?"

"I'm thinking you could be one hundred percent correct, but that still doesn't help me decide what to do."

"Ok," she said, "let's look at this another way." She then asked, "What's the worst that could happen?"

"Oh no, don't get me going down that road or I'll never call, text, or even answer my phone."

"Seriously?" She sounded a little angry.

"You really underestimate my ability to worry about things."

Clare made a humming sound. "Yes, perhaps that wasn't the smartest suggestion. So let me just say that the worst-case scenario is that Will is not in your life for the next twelve plus years, and the only thing that guarantees that is if the two of you don't communicate." Agitation was apparent in her voice. "You know you have an account setup on my Mac, right?"

"So?" I asked with more confidence than I felt.

"So, I can login to your iMessage account and text him anytime I feel like it. Don't make me have to do it." She hung up.

I almost changed my password, but after a bit of thought, decided against it. Clare wasn't wrong. I went into the kitchen and cooked myself a grilled cheese sandwich and a very vanilla milk shake. I knew that if Will and I didn't make contact while he was in Leavenworth that it was unlikely we ever would. Neither one of us took the initiative over the last twelve years. Clare had already started the process by getting Will to give her his phone number. And it was true that Will had left a note on my door. It was clear he had reached out first either way, right? So, was I too scared to respond?

The grilled cheese was good, but the vanilla shake was cold-vanilla-gloriousness. I enjoyed the touch of freeze brain it gave me as I drank it. It was worth the pain. Thoughts of Will and his son stayed with me as I ate. I'd like to say that I had stopped thinking about them as I did the dishes and cleaned up the kitchen, but no, I kept thinking about them. I needed to figure out what I was going to do and what I wanted from Will.

I shut the lights off in the kitchen and headed for my bedroom. I stripped out of all my warm clothes and headed into the bathroom.

I turned the shower on and let it warm up and then jumped quickly into the comforting water. Fifteen minutes into a warm shower and my mind was clear and focused on little other than the pleasure of the water.

A text on my phone ruined the clarity as I wondered if Will was texting. I opened the door to the shower and looked down at the phone. Clare had sent me a message telling me to get out of the shower and text or call Will.

"Ok," I said out loud, "Adi Lewis, you just must be the most predictable person in the world."

There was another text. I looked at it again. This time Clare wrote, "I just know you really well and stop talking to yourself in the shower."

I sighed. No answer for that, outwardly or inwardly.

I enjoyed the shower for another 25 minutes because it broke my normal cycle and because I wasn't going to do what Clare was telling me to do. *She's not the boss of me.*

When I got out of the shower, I took my time to primp myself and enjoy the warmth of the blow dryer as I dried my hair. My long brown curls spun tightly in the water but loosened as the dryer warmed them. I stood in front of the mirror and admired how my hair gently framed my face.

I then did my toenails, and once they looked fantastic realized I had to do my fingernails as well. The entire process took quite some time. At some point, I realized my thoughts had cleared. I smiled and looked down at my phone. I was so focused that I had even missed some texts. It's hard to move or even pick up a phone when all your nails are wet.

Eventually, when I was dry, I read the missed texts from Clare, who thankfully had not predicted what I was doing. She did, however, seem a bit miffed I hadn't responded to her. I quickly wrote, **Had a bit of a personal spa experience. Going to bed. Talk tomorrow**. I ended it with a heart emoji.

As I got into bed, I looked at Will's number one more time and then delicately, with my freshly painted fingers, put the charger in the phone. Then I heard the ringing. I saw I had accidentally dialed Will. Cancel or not? Choice made; I canceled the call. "Oh, shit!"

CHAPTER 17 – WILL

I YELLED OVER THE PHONE, "I don't care." The chair in my father's study was not comfortable, and I had spent the entire call pacing around his desk. I was trying to keep my voice down, so I didn't disturb Jamison. In the middle of my tirade, a call came in and then immediately disconnected. The phone number was from Leavenworth. Adi, I thought, but she disconnected, so I continued with my call.

"Sir, they want you in Japan by New Year to complete the deal. I don't think they'll take 'no' for an answer."

I slammed the phone in my hand twice and then took a deep breath. "Put Jim on," I said through an exhale of breath. There was a long pause, and I heard the call transfer. Jim picked up.

"You know, Will," he said with a bit of laughter in his voice, "you really shouldn't yell at the messenger. Frank is just relaying what he was told when he stood in for you at that meeting."

"First, I do not know when I'm going to get out of Leavenworth," I ticked off on my finger. "Second, even when I get to Edmonds, I have to think of Jamison and get him settled." I put up the third finger and said, "And I don't like to be told where and when I'm going to be somewhere. They want our involvement. They don't get to set terms."

He replied, "This is a multi-million-dollar international deal, Will. You have employees and a company that needs this contract."

"Remind me why I run this company in the first place? I mean, after selling that app, it's not like I needed money."

"First," I heard him snicker, "you get bored easy. Second, and yes, I'm ticking these off on my fingers just like you did. You enjoy being the boss. And third, while you never talk about family, you like having a work family that depends on and is loyal to you."

"Thanks, Freud."

Jim said, "Not the correct discipline, but you are welcome. So, what are you going to do?"

"For now, tell them I'm stuck in Leavenworth for the near future and have no way to predict the weather. Let them know at the very worst, I'll appear live via computer. They want to create the world's best integrated conferencing software; we might as well show them what we've put together so far."

"Turn it into a beta test of sorts?"

"Sure. Even if it doesn't work 100%, it'll still turn heads. Work with Tokyo and make sure there are enough VR headsets for the key people. Are they close with the holo-projector?"

"Not close enough for actual marketing, but under a staged, controlled environment for a bit of a show, I bet they could get something to work."

"Great," I said, "put them to work on that. At the very least, they'll be too busy to be worried about me."

"How are things in Leavenworth?"

"Enjoyable," I said. "Jamison has really taken to my mom. He lets me hold and feed him for a while, but eventually he always wants to go back to her."

"What are you going to do with him in Edmonds?"

I sighed. "I'm not sure. A nanny would make sense, but that's going to take time to find the right one."

"Trying to hire Mary Poppins?"

"Not quite what the doctor ordered," I replied. "Honestly, I'm not sure anyone could top what my mom's doing right now."

"So, bring your parents to Edmonds? Your place is enormous. Or they could live in the mother-in-law house in your backyard."

"I have thought about it," I said, "but I know they do not want to leave Leavenworth."

Jim asked, "You know that for certain?"

"They have lived nearly their entire lives here. Their friends are here. Why would they leave? I mean, they never tried to follow me to Edmonds, right?"

"Did you really want them to?" There was a pause and he said quickly, "Dumb question, sorry. But, Will, a grandson changes everything, right? From the way it sounds, your mother has become quite attached. Will she be able to let go?"

"Good point. You might be right that they would move Edmonds for Jamison, but it doesn't seem fair to have them make that choice."

"So, what's the option?"

"I don't know Jim, I'm playing this all by ear. For now, the snowstorm continues to limit my options."

"Not going to last, buddy."

"No, it won't, but for now."

"Gotcha," he said, "ok, new topic. How was lunch with the high school hottie?"

"She is searching for a replacement husband with the 'right' credentials."

"Meaning the correct bank account?"

"Probably," I replied, "the conversation didn't last long. While we were eating, Adi came into the restaurant, saw me, and bailed."

"Oh shit, did you chase after her?"

"Yes."

"And?" Jim asked.

"I caught her friend Clare, well no, more like Clare caught me."

"Oh, tell. This is better than the shows Jason makes me watch."

I laughed. "He still making you watch those on the weekend?"

"Hey man, love is love. We do dumb things for love."

"Fair enough." I thought back to my proposal to Adi and my choices that led me to the University of Washington. "But remember, there's no guarantee those choices will always bear fruit." I heard the snicker and before Jim could say something, I said, "no, stop there. I know where you're going with that joke. I apologize for using those words in the same sentence." I could almost hear the jokes in Jim's head trying to get out. There was a long pause, and then the sound of stifled mirth on the other end of the phone.

"You know you tee up the best jokes, boss."

"Yes, and as boss I get to knock the ball off too." He snickered. "My God man, stop it. Go home, it's late and clearly you can think of nothing else."

"You're the boss," he said, and hung up the phone. Jim was a funny guy, but his humor was often better for the bar than the workplace. It was just safer to stop him before the thread of jokes got started.

I had hopefully found at least a temporary solution to the Tokyo problem in the short-term. They really didn't need me there for New Year's Eve, but the publicity would be good, and they would have the face of the company committed to the deal. I understood why they wanted me there, but the more I thought about it, the less I felt like I wanted to attend.

I wondered again if it was Adi that called.

I opened the door of the study and walked into the living room. Jamison was in my mother's arms. He had just finished a bottle. I scooped him out of her arms and began patting his back until a couple of good burps erupted.

I held him for a while. As I looked at my son, I couldn't help but make quiet cooing sounds as I cradled him in my arms. I smiled as I rocked him and enjoyed the warmth of his body against my chest and arms. He had a smell to him that seemed better than any of the smells of Christmas. Well, most of the time, that is. After about twenty minutes of rocking him, the smell that flowed from him was nothing pleasant. I took him into my bedroom and changed his diaper. It was a bit of a fight. I'm not sure why he got so agitated when his diaper was removed. Perhaps he was just shy, but the second that diaper was off, the struggle began. After the initial struggle, I managed to change the diaper and he settled into my arms.

Eventually, sleep won out and I placed Jamison in his bassinet.

"You're a wonderful father," I heard my mom say in a whisper behind me.

"I didn't hear you come in," I whispered.

"I was watching you. I've missed you and now you have brought me such a treasure." The emotion in her voice was audible to me. "Sorry," she whispered, and left the room.

I sat down in a chair and texted the number that had called.

CHAPTER 18 – ADI

WILL: WHO IS THIS?

Great, now what do I do? The walls of anxiety crashed down on me as my heart rate picked up. I hadn't meant to dial him. *I wasn't ready for this*. As my heart raced, I felt a headache begin.

I crawled into my bed and pulled my weighted blanket on top of me. The weight was an immediate comfort, and my heart slowed a bit as my bed hugged me with weighted comfort. I stared at the phone. *Do I text him back? What if I don't? I knew I wanted to, but what would I say?*

Will: Adi, is that you?

I texted Clare and sent her a screen shot of Will's texts.

Clare: He texted you. How'd he get your number?

Adi: I butt dialed him.

Clare: OMG you hung up?

Adi: Of course.

Clare: Why?

Adi: Because

Clare: Did you text him back?

Adi: No, I texted you.

Clare: Well, stop texting me and text him. Simple advice that didn't feel simple at all.

Adi: Are you sure? I'm fairly sure I'm about to have a heart attack.

Clare: Shut up, woman up, text him.

I lay there wrapped in warmth and security. I felt like a thirteen-year-old girl worrying about calling the boy she likes. *Do I still like him? Is that the problem? Of course, I still like him. Love, like, or friendship, whatever you want to call it, was never the issue between us. So, why am I so nervous?* As I stared at my phone, I thought about what was happening. I typed a message and then deleted it. I typed another and deleted that one as well. *Why am I so damn anxious about this?* Then I realized he was seeing the three dots on his phone because I was typing. *Oh no.*

Adi: Hi, yes, it's Adi. I paused over the send button. *It's a nothing text. No harm no foul. Push the button.* I didn't push it. I just laid there looking at my phone and the send button.

Clare: Have you texted him? The incoming text scared me, and I almost pushed the send button. I switched to her text thread.

Adi: Almost.

Clare: Almost? WTH does almost mean?

Adi: I've written it.

Clare: Push Send! and she finished the text with an angry emoji face. I switched back to my text thread with Will, as limited as it was. I took a deep breath, clicked send, and then closed my eyes as my heart rate doubled again.

Will: Hi, sorry I missed your call.

Do I admit it was a butt dial? I thought. **Adi: No problem.** There was no response for a while. The lack of texting was now making me uncomfortable. **Adi: OK with just texting?**

I saw the three dots of the iPhone's typing awareness indicator showing me that Will was typing. The text then popped up on my phone. **Will: Sure, whatever works. You got my note?**

Adi: Yes, thanks. Social media sucks.

Will: It does. Again, Sorry.

Adi: You didn't expect it?

Will: Forgot small town gossip has a worldwide platform now.

Adi: Tech CEO forgot about tech?

Will: Had a lot on my mind.

I wanted to ask him about his son, about his life, but it didn't feel right doing all that by text. **Adi: I understand. All OK at your parents' house?**

Will: Yes. Feels strange being here.

Adi: I bet, but it's a new house.

Will: Mom decorated my room to look like it did in HS.

Adi: Seriously? I hadn't ever been in the Monroe's new house. I couldn't help but laugh at his mother decorating her missing son's room the way it used to look.

Will: It's weird. This conversation was weird, I thought. It had been twelve years and we were talking about his bedroom instead of important things. I thought about him and his high school bedroom, which brought up old memories, and suddenly I was flushing from head to foot. **Will: Why'd you run off at lunch?**

That was a straightforward question. Will had always been a straight to the point guy. I had forgotten that. Best thing was to be equally blunt and honest. **Adi: Didn't want to talk to you in the middle of a restaurant. Knew you'd make us talk if I remained.**

Will: Fair. We should talk.

Adi: Agreed. This is ok though, isn't it?

Will: Sure, I guess.

I knew what he meant. As I read his texts, I heard them in my head in his voice from high school. *Did he sound like that now? He couldn't, right? I meant it has been twelve years. We've both gotten so much older.* **Adi: Let's catch up. You graduated UW and started a business.**

Will: I did and sold an app and made a bunch of money. I hear you got a teaching degree from Western and now teach 2nd grade.

Adi: Have you been asking around about me?

Will: My parents filled me in.

Adi: On everything?

Will: I heard about your ex-husband. I read the words and felt the pain of them; the stain of them.

Adi: Yes, the big D, that's me. How about you? There was a long pause. Then I saw the three dots appear again.

Will: Marriage, no. Long-term relationship, no. Mostly just work.

Adi: It may be just the texting, but you don't seem happy about that.

Will: I was fine with it. Jamison has changed things.

Adi: Your son?

Will: Yes.

Adi: Jami will make a nice nickname.

CHAPTER 19 – WILL

THAT WASN'T THE NICKNAME I had thought of, but then Adi didn't know the entire story. **Will: I guess that would be ok. His middle name is John.**

Adi: After John Greer?

Will: Yes.

Adi: So J.J.?

Will: Thought about it. I thought about John a lot since being at his grave. I missed my friend more than I realized. Being back in Leavenworth was opening doors in my heart and mind that I hadn't realized I had locked. Life really had been all about work and success since leaving Leavenworth.

Adi: J.J. is nice.

Will: Jamison seems to fit him right now. I added a smiley face to the end of the line.

She started her text with a smiley face. **Adi: Sounds right.**

I changed the subject. I didn't want to discuss my son with Adi over text. I realized I wanted to discuss him with her but face to face. **Will: Switching topics. Why Western?**

Adi: Clare was in her third year there when I started. It was nice having a friend.

Will: At least at the beginning.

Adi: No, Clare turned my arrival at Western into an excuse for a double major and two minors; the six-year plan.

Will: No surprise. She was always there for you. She responded with another smiley face emoji. **Will: Teaching satisfying?**

Adi: Mostly. I love the kids and I'm good at it.

A smile crossed my face. *I knew that she loved the children and that she was good at teaching. When we were growing up, Adi always worked at daycares, camps, and even in the hospital, so she could work with children. I had never understood it. I mean, being a kid was being a kid, but I never really enjoyed it and I couldn't imagine being stuck with kids.* I looked over at Jamison sleeping in his bassinet. *Well, until recently.* **Will: I'm glad.**

Adi: So, Mr. Social Media tech CEO what's the limelight like?

I laughed out loud. Jamison stirred but didn't wake up. **Will: You made me LOL and I almost woke him up.**

Adi: Sorry. Well?

Will: Success is fine. The limelight, as you call it, is meh. And is no fun when your son becomes part of it.

There was no response at first. Eventually, the three dots showed Adi was writing. **Adi: I assumed you were used to it. I didn't like it.**

Will: I don't blame you and I'm sorry you learned about Jamison that way. Once the Leavenworth gossip started, I had to respond, but I didn't mean to hurt you.

Adi: I get that. I do. But you came home with a baby. It's all just a lot.

Will: Right. I mean we haven't communicated in 12 years, which is stupid and I'm sorry about that, really sorry. *Should I say how I felt? Texting sucked, but would I get another chance? I wanted to suggest I walk over to her house, but that seemed inappropriate.*

It was never hard to talk to Adi. It shouldn't be this hard. **I hate having this conversation by text.**

Adi: I know, but for now.

Will: Ok, then you should know I was angry when you said no. She started to respond; I could see the dots. **Will: Angry and hurt, probably more hurt. It got pretty mixed up.**

There was a long pause. I assumed she was deleting what she first wrote. **Adi: We were both hurt and angry. We were eighteen, making life-changing adult decisions.**

Will: True and we made a fair mess of it.

Adi: I never got to thank you for not telling the story to everyone. I only just told my mom when you got back into town.

Will: Really?

Adi: Yes, I was too embarrassed, and I felt like it would disappoint my mom.

Will: Why would she be disappointed? She didn't respond to my question. After a couple of minutes of no response. **Will: Sorry, prying too much by text. I'm glad you told her. I always figured she hated me for leaving. Figured everyone did.**

Adi: Is that why you didn't come back at all? Why didn't you call or email us?

Will: Not at first. Especially not in school. I was just so busy. And then, my third year in school, I started designing the code that ended up being the app I sold.

Adi: Did you date in college?

I felt like responding and asking who is prying now? **Will: I saw women, I wouldn't call it dating. I had a lot of friends. My best** friends from college are all in my company. You met your husband in college?

Adi: Yes. But tell me, after college, why didn't you come home?

Will: You mean why didn't I come home for John's funeral? There was a brief delay. Adi: Yes.

Will: I wanted to. Was halfway here. But by then I was already in the news and in social media. I didn't want to bring that to the funeral. I knew there was more and given how this discussion was going; I wasn't going to stop now. Will: I was, like I said, fairly sure everyone hated me because I left. Also, if I'm honest, I didn't know how I would handle seeing you again. I guess I just didn't want to cause drama.

Adi: You cause drama... She ended the text with a smiley face with the tongue sticking out.

Will: Nice emoji use. She replied with a thumbs up. Will: Yes, maybe I do. I certainly have the last few days. But I didn't mean to.

Adi: Larger than Leavenworth William Monroe.

Will: Is that my nickname?

Adi: More or less. But you have done amazing things in the world.

Will: My contributions all feel relatively small these days. Life is funny.

Adi: Good with the bad.

Will: Yes, but sometimes it's hard to know which is which, or even if there is an obvious difference at all.

Adi: Maybe. My focus leaned towards the bad lately.

Will: Sorry about your troubles. You, ok?

Adi: Yes, I think so. Still a bit raw.

Will: I get it, kind of going day by day myself.

Adi: Yes, but your change is such a wonderful one.

I could hear the energy and smile through the texted words. It reminded me just how much Adi loved children. She truly envied what I was experiencing. **Will: No argument. Still a huge change.**

Adi: I would like to meet Jamison.

Will: Sounds like a plan. What are you doing tomorrow?

Adi: No plans. Just getting ready for Christmas.

Will: How about Visconti's at noon?

Adi: Feeling like Italian?

Will: It tends to be a bit quieter. Maybe we'll get a little privacy.

Adi: I'm not sure about bringing a new baby out in the cold.

Will: Fair point. Just you and me tomorrow. We can stop by the house after.

Adi: Texting not enough for you?

I wanted to respond in so many ways. Texting with her was driving me crazy. All I could think about was the Adi of twelve years ago. There was a reason I had never dated seriously. I found I always compared everyone to Adi, which wasn't helpful. But also, I was so hurt by her saying "no" that I never really risked those feelings again. If nothing else, I needed closure and texting wasn't getting me there. **Will: There's nothing like face to face in person communication.**

Adi: Somehow, I have to think that goes against your company's motto.

I sent her a laughing emoji. **Will: Our goal is to get as close as possible to face to face as you can without being live.**

Adi: Sure, sure, she texted. Adi was never one to let me get away with anything.

Will: See you tomorrow at noon?

Adi: Pick me up. Two cars are a waste.

Willliam: Fair enough. See you tomorrow just before noon.

CHAPTER 20 – ADI

NOT ONLY COULD I NOT SLEEP, but when I did, I would wake up every half hour to check the clock. I couldn't stop thinking about Will. At around 5:30 a.m., I stopped trying to sleep and started wandering around the house. First, I started straightening things up. After a while, I just mindlessly cleaned. The last straw was when I vacuumed my bedroom.

What the heck are you doing? I had become my father. When he couldn't sleep, we would always find him somewhere in the house doing a project. Sometimes it was cleaning. Other times, he went out into the garage and built something. Garage projects usually ended fairly quickly because the sound of power tools was not a popular early morning treat. I hoped the sound of my vacuum remained in the house but given that it was still only 6:30 a.m. and I didn't want to disturb my neighbors, I stopped and made myself breakfast.

These childish nerves. Was I really this excited about seeing Will again? Or were these nerves of concern? I stopped and thought silently for a long time before coming to the conclusion that I didn't have an answer. I also decided that was alright.

I went over to the fridge and pulled out a couple of eggs, some nice parmesan cheese, butter, ham, and some green onions. Fifteen minutes later, I was sitting at my kitchen table eating a more than passable omelet. *Will loved my eggs.* I choked a little and then laughed as I thought of the double meaning of "my eggs." *Was this going to be a reoccurring issue? Was it really that simple? Will had the baby I always wanted.* "Are you jealous of Will?" I asked out loud.

I felt jealous of anyone and everyone who had a child. I wanted a baby so badly. Tears crept into my eyes. I stood up, forced them back, and cleaned the kitchen. After burning another fifteen minutes, I headed to the bathroom for a nice long shower and a good cry. That took another fifteen minutes. *I seemed to be in a temporal rut.*

I gave into the weird timing and took fifteen minutes to dry off and do my makeup. Another fifteen minutes got me dressed and ready for the day. I walked into the living room and turned on the news. I let it play in the background as I cleaned again. This time I didn't overthink it. The projects helped whittle away the time, but I still kept thinking about Will. I had dressed, so I was ready. The house was immaculate. I was ready for this. Right?

Just before noon, my doorbell rang and shook me out of my internal dialogues. My heart raced and a light sweat started, which, of course, challenged the foundation on my face. I went into the hallway and as I passed the thermostat; I reached out and turned it down ten degrees. *Great, now I'm having hot flashes.* Moving to the door, I could see Will standing outside my house.

I opened the door and Will Monroe stood in front of me with a huge grin on his face and twelve years between us. He looked older, but not because of anything obvious. There might have been a bit of a crease between his eyes, but there was no sign of wrinkles or loss of hair. His brown-black curly hair seemed unchanged. His eyes held the same sparkle of excitement and fun that they always had. But there was a strength and confidence built over time that showed his age. His cheeks showed stubble, even though he had clearly shaved this morning. And, of course, the acne of youth no longer dotted his face. *What has changed?* I realized after asking myself the question that I knew the answer. He wasn't the scrawny, nerdy boy of high school. As I looked at him, I realized he was thick with muscle and success. He stood six foot three and looked down at me at five foot three. As I looked at Will with his handsome grin and strong shoulders, I had an overwhelming desire to wrap myself in everything William.

"Hi," he said.

"Hi yourself," I heard myself say. *Oh my God, the first words out and I'm already flirting.*

"You ready to go?"

"Yes, let me grab my jacket." I walked into the dining room and picked up the jacket I had hanging on a chair. He stepped in behind me and as I turned around, I watched him look over my home.

"Nice place. I like the modern esthetic."

I smiled and felt a bit of blush. "Modern feels clean."

"You've created a beautiful home for yourself, Adi."

"Thank you," I replied as I walked towards him, and he stepped back through the door in response. I closed the door and locked it. "Let's go."

We walked to the vehicle in silence. He was gentlemanly and held open my door for me. I smiled and blushed. We were standing out in the cold, but I felt entirely too hot.

He then got in the driver's seat and closed the door. "Still feeling like Visconti's?"

"Sounds wonderful. I haven't eaten there in a long time."

"We had a couple anniversary dinners there if memory serves."

"And a couple prom dinners too."

He laughed. "That's right. I remember a particular fetching white prom dress that didn't survive dinner."

"Oh my God, junior prom! That was terrible. I couldn't stop crying."

"It all worked out."

"Yes, after you rescued me by taking me home and letting me change."

"Good thing you hadn't taken that other dress back."

I felt myself frown. "Mom was not pleased about paying for two dresses."

"Would've been difficult to take the white one back given it was no longer very white." A chuckle began in his chest and then turned into robust laughter. His laughter was contagious, and I laughed wholeheartedly with him. "Simpler times," I mumbled.

We quieted down just about the time we made it to the bottom of the hill. "Sure, didn't seem that way."

"I agree. Funny how distance and time can change your perspective."

"Agreed." He turned left onto Highway 2.

"It was you!" I stared at him.

"It was me what?"

"The crazy guy who almost hit me turning into that very intersection."

"Oh, that was you blowing on your horn? I didn't realize you'd become such a horny driver."

The growl started in my chest. "Not funny and I hope you didn't have Jamison in the car driving like that!"

His voice dropped a bit. "No, I didn't. I'm sorry about that. My timing was off on that turn, totally my fault."

He just simply apologized, no defensiveness, no argument. Was this really the Will I had known so long ago? I dropped my voice as well and said, "Apology accepted. Just make sure you drive safe from now on."

"Yes, ma'am," he replied. We pulled off the highway and drove onto Front Street. We drove behind Visconti's and found a parking spot. There were people milling around town, but it seemed most people were not braving the frozen Leavenworth roads.

"How long have you had the Highlander?"

"A few years now. I really like it."

"I'm surprised you don't have something fancy, like a BMW or a Mercedes."

"Oh, I do, both actually. I drive them to meetings and dinners for appearances. But for a reliable and comfortable drive, my Highlander is perfect. Though I have to admit, I do like the Limited edition's features." He got out of the vehicle, closed his door, and then came around to help me out. After locking the Highlander, we walked slowly over the ice. At one point, I slipped and before I could get off balance, he was next to me with his arm under my arm, supporting me.

"Thanks!"

"No problem. Let's get to lunch in one piece."

We made our way through the snow and ice into Visconti's. The restaurant was not busy. The aroma brought back an immediate flash of old memories. Will and I removed our coats and hung them. Then we walked into the restaurant and took a table, looking out the window near the fireplace. He pulled my seat out for me, and I sat. He went to the seat across from me and sat down. When we dated, he always sat across from me. He had explained it was because he wanted to see me. The first time he told me that, I felt like the most beautiful girl in the world.

I looked at Will sitting across from me. "Penny for your thoughts."

CHAPTER 21 – WILL

SINCE THE DOOR OPENED, all I thought about was how beautiful Adi was. She was short, but not too short. She hadn't gained a pound since high school. If anything, she was fitter. Her hair was a beautiful brown mixed with some hints of light red that gave depth and body to her natural waves. Her eyes had not changed, they were still the color of rich topaz. There were no signs of age around her eyes, but this was not the girl I had grown up with. There was strength in those gorgeous eyes, which shone with knowledge and experience. The girl was gone. Now she was a woman, and an amazing one at that. I counted the dark freckles that broke through the almond-colored skin of her nose.

"What? Seriously, what are you thinking?"

"Daydreaming about the past, Adi. It's hard to believe it was twelve years ago." I laughed. "I almost said 'just twelve years ago,' but I guess a decade doesn't really warrant a 'just.'"

"I don't know. In some ways it feels like we just jumped twelve years and we're eating at Visconti's again for some school event. In other ways, this is simply weird, and something out of the Twilight Zone."

"You used to love those marathons."

"I did, but I never wished to be a part of one…"

I lifted my glass of water, and she lifted hers. We tapped them together and I said, "Well, here's to our personal Twilight Zone in Leavenworth locked in by a snowstorm at Christmas time." The glasses clinked, we smiled, and then we set them down. "What's your thoughts about lunch?"

"Changing the subject, huh?" She looked over the menu and said, "Well, let's see, if it was twelve years ago, I would get the Spaghetti and you'd get the Spaghetti & Meatballs."

I looked through the menu, which hadn't changed much in twelve years. "If I recall, we chose those because we didn't want to spend money on the more expensive meals."

"That had something to do with it." She smiled and looked over the menu some more. "If you are treating, think you can handle the $15.00 Tortellini Pesto & Spinach and a $7.00 Caesar?"

"Hmm, yes, my treat. You really are trying to spend me out of house and home? You know I'm a father. Now I have to watch my money." I watched her closely. She laughed a little at the joke and didn't appear to tense up.

"We could always get the Spaghetti."

"Did I ever tell you how much I don't care for Spaghetti."

"No," she laughed, "you never mentioned that."

"I'm thinking about the Veal Piccata and we could start with some of the amazing looking Fried Calamari I see over there. Would you help me with them?"

"Sure."

Our server approached our table with a friendly smile, ready to take our orders. I listed our choices and ordered a nice bottle of red wine. As she left, I realized I could not stop smiling. I was having a wonderful time. It also surprised me at how relaxed I was. I had told the office not to disturb me and had even put my phone on do not disturb. I had explained to my parents if they called twice, it would override the do not disturb function. Wanted to make sure they could reach me if Jamison needed something. "I'm looking forward to lunch."

"Me too," she said. She adjusted her silverware and plates and then asked, "Where's Jamison today?"

"With my parents. My mother has barely let me feed him or even change him. I think she's trying to get every minute in, dreading when we will leave."

"So, you are really going to raise him in the big emerald city?"

"Actually, no. I only lived in Seattle for a pretty short time."

Her frown started at her eyebrows and then worked its way to her mouth. "What?" she asked.

"That's right, you don't know where I live. When I talk about living in 'Seattle,' I generalize the greater Puget Sound area. I moved out of King County as soon as I realized the tax consequences. My company started in Seattle, but we moved the company to Everett. It was cheaper not to deal with Seattle taxes and ultimately, we took great advantage of the new Everett airport. Even before I moved the company, I had moved to Edmonds's years earlier. Just made sense. I have property in King County, of course, but it's mostly rental. Though I have a nice summer house on Lake Washington and an apartment I keep in Seattle for meetings, sporting events, and the occasional concert." After saying all of that, I realized how crazy rich that all sounded. But how to make up for that protracted line of unfortunate bragging? "It sounds all TV cool, but really, I just like to hang out in Edmonds. There are wonderful schools for Jamison. It'll be a wonderful place for him to grow up."

"But not Leavenworth."

"No, nothing is quite like Leavenworth."

She asked, "Don't you miss your family and friends?"

Before I could answer, the server brought our calamari. She served the plate in the middle and gave us each small plates with our own small bowls of aioli.

"Looks good, dive in." She did and I followed. There were many minutes of quiet between us as we enjoyed the food. Between bites, I would look up and watch her.

"So," she said as she gave her fork a rest, "family and friends?"

"Do I miss them? Well, that's not as simple a question to answer as you might think."

She watched me with hard eyes. "Why? Seems like the answer would be a simple yes or no?"

"The first month of school was a struggle for me. My entire life had been in Leavenworth. I had no friends, and I was reluctant to reach out to anyone at home. Then school started getting busy, and then I added a couple of jobs into the mix. I was lucky to get five hours of sleep. Later, there were work projects and I started the business. As my company grew and I just got busier and busier. Success seemed to just mean hard work and little time for a life outside of work. I talked about the house on Lake Washington, but I've only spent a couple of days there. The apartment in Seattle would be great fun, but I haven't gone to a baseball game in years. I'm sure if at any point in the last twelve years I stopped and thought about Leavenworth, I would have missed you all, but I just never stopped."

"That's crazy."

"It kind of is, I agree."

She said, "But you are back now. You brought your son home. Won't you miss your parents if you leave?"

"Yes, I'm sure I will. But now I must figure out how to keep my company going while still being a good father. I need to find balance."

"Think you can do it?" she asked.

"I honestly have no clue. You've found balance in your life. How have you done it?"

She frowned and tapped the end of her fork on the table. "I'm not sure I really found any more balance than you did. I went to college because my parents pushed me to, but once there, I liked it. And when I worked hard, it allowed me to lose myself and forget. It made me forget how badly I wanted to have a baby. Then I met Edward, and the dreams of an enormous family became a reality. Well, at least I thought it had become a reality. I forgot my old plans and tried to focus on the hope of a new future. From there it was getting married, working, buying a home, with the plan to have children. But in the end, that was also just a distraction. Like you, I'm in Leavenworth in the middle of a snowstorm trying to figure out how to balance the priorities of my life."

"I always figured we would meet again. I did not dream it would be like this. I imagined myself meeting your husband and your family and I wondered how that would make me feel."

"Did you ever reach any conclusions?"

"I knew I'd be jealous. I knew I would wonder what if? But I figured we both made our choices and that was that."

"Twelve years. We aren't the same people we were."

"It's cliché, but you are as beautiful as I remember." I paused.

"What?"

"I don't know how to say it other than you are now truly a beautiful woman. My memories are all of the girl."

She laughed. "Eighteen to thirty were some significant twelve years."

"Truly, and clearly not wasted on either of us." I became more aware of the old attraction between us.

We both reached for the last piece of bread, and I raised my hands in surrender. She laughed, tore the bread in half, and handed me my half. "We can share."

We had shared so much, so long ago. "Yes, we can. And I'd like to hear more about Western."

Adi smiled and began telling me about her four years at college. The conversation became easier and easier as the tension of our meeting vanished. And just as the ease of our connection reached its peak, the server arrived with our main courses. We savored the delicious flavors of the dish, and a tranquil silence filled the air. The plate emptied as we swapped bites, savoring the flavors that mingled between us. *She was so beautiful.*

I watched her as I listened to her speak. My gaze became a stare and then I realized just how long I was staring at her. My heart raced as I met her eyes, and there was a shocked recognition of mutual old feelings. With a smile, I looked away, but it was too late. She had noticed as well, and in that moment, I knew things had the potential for getting complicated. It was a spark, but was I going to let it catch fire?

We finished talking about her college and she asked me about my business and the places I had traveled to. As I told her about England, Ireland, Germany, and Turkey, brief glimmers of memories came back to me. I remembered sitting in hotels around the world and wondering what Adi was up to. I also remember just as quickly pushing those thoughts aside. *I guess she had always been on my mind. But how could she not be? She was my love.*

We talked for a while more about smaller things, and then the server brought us our desserts. There was a calm silence as we dug in. We kept talking between bites. We even shared some with each other and I reflected on how the little things between us hadn't changed. At some point I realized I was staring at her again and before I could stop, she noticed it as well.

"Counting freckles?" she asked.

"You caught me." I laughed and sat back away from my plate. "Twelve years really doesn't feel that long as I sit here and at the same time it feels like centuries. It is strange how time works. I have to say, Addi, the twelve years have only made you a better person. A brilliant woman and, from what I hear, a fantastic teacher." She smiled.

I said, "To return to our earlier conversation, I have wondered where I should raise Jamison. Part of it is memories of Leavenworth. The other part is being aware that he's not going to have a mother and then thinking how amazing my mom was growing up. I'm considering whether he should stay with my parents or if I can persuade them to move to Edmonds." I took a couple more bites and then swallowed. Adi was staring at me. "What?" I asked. "I know I don't have any freckles." She laughed. "What do you think about the idea of moving my parents west? Think they'd do it for Jamison?"

CHAPTER 22 – ADI

THE QUESTION, *think they'd do it for Jamison?* kept repeating in my head. The little voice in my head said *I would*, but I never once considered uttering the words myself. Instead, I replied, "I'm sure they'll want to. It's going to be tough to choose between the place they've lived their entire life and their grandson. This is also so new to them. They went from not having their son around for twelve years to suddenly not only having you back but having a grandson as well. Imagine the emotions they must be feeling." She paused and then said, "but ultimately everyone wants to do what's best for Jamison, right?"

"Sure, but I've tried to get them to move before and it was a no go."

"You know Jamison makes it different." I paused for a moment and then asked, "Could you live here? I mean, could you run your business from here?" He thought about what I asked, and I felt a brief spike in my heartbeat. *This is dangerous Adi, what are you doing?*

"It wouldn't be ideal, but with technology these days, I probably could do a fair amount of my job remotely. Wenatchee airport is small, but it's only 45 minutes away...well on a normal day without holiday or summer traffic."

"How many times did we get home later than curfew because of traffic?"

"Well, we at least blamed it on traffic." He laughed.

"Do you think they believed us?"

"You ever ask your parents?"

"No, did you?"

"God, no. Think of the field day my mother would have with that conversation." We both laughed. He continued, "so, I could fly from Wenatchee to Seattle and then off to wherever I need to go."

I said, "And your parents could take care of Jamison while you travel for business."

"True." He stopped and thought for a while. His eyes became sad, and I reached out and held his hand. Will said, "I'm not sure I want to be gone from him. It's been great having my mom bond with Jamison, but at the end of each day I like the fact that I'm in the house with Jamison and he's asleep next to me at night. It's odd, but I even miss him right now."

I squeezed his hand and then let go. His words tugged at my heart. I felt myself flush not from lust, but just from Will being an example of a good father. *What is going on here, Adi? Get a hold of yourself. He will just leave again. He's in Leavenworth just because of the storm. Once the snow clears up, he's out of your life again. Stop it!* "You're going to be a wonderful father." *I always knew you would be. My heart hurt.* I picked up my glass and finished the wine that was in it.

Will picked up the bottle and poured me some more. "I hope so. I am learning how to do this day by day. This wasn't the way I had pictured things would turn out." He dug back into the food in front of him.

I knew this wasn't his plan, oh how I knew it. I wonder if Jamison looks like him. What did Jamison's mother look like? Was she like me? Did Will have a type? "Would you mind telling me about Jamison's mother?"

Will smiled, but the sadness shadowed the happiness in his amazing smile. There was a hint of pain in his eyes as he thought of her. "Sure." He paused, drank some water, and then began. "We met at a computer convention about a year ago. I really didn't date much after I left Leavenworth, but when I saw her, I was...well...smitten. Her hair was jet black and straight. And her eyes kind of reminded me of yours, if I'm going to be honest. Her skin was like the color of deep adobe. When our eyes caught, we just kind of locked on one another. One thing led to another after that." He paused and seemed to drift into his memories. After a short while he continued. "I learned recently when she provided me with information for Jamison that her mother's family had ties to the Colville and Yakima tribes. Her father's side was Cuban, Irish, and Portuguese."

I tried to push back the feelings of jealousy that I realized were overshadowing everything else I was feeling. *Stop it, Adi. Will was not mine. We hadn't dated for over eleven years when he hooked up with Jamison's mother. Why do you feel this way?* "What was her name?"

"Koyoty. I called her Koy." The focus of his eyes faded again and I saw the sadness fall over him.

"What happened to her?"

"Something to do with her heart caused by the pregnancy. I wasn't family, so the doctors didn't give me all the details."

I said, "But not right after Jamison's birth?"

"No," he said. His voice was flat, and I could see that he was struggling to block his emotions. Will was good at hiding his feelings, but at that moment, his emotions were quite visible. I could feel the pain. It broke my heart to hear him tell the story. The Will I knew could always have hope. He always had a plan or a goal. He was an optimist. Some of that seemed broken now.

"I'm sorry," I said.

He smiled and held my hand for a second. "Nothing to be sorry for. I was incredibly lucky to meet her and spend time with her. I wasn't sure how I felt when she told me she was pregnant, but I knew I was in love the second I saw Jamison's face. Koy's dying wasn't so much a loss to me as it was to Jamison. I hurt for him."

"Will, that's empathy and it's great you have it. You have a bond with your son, as it should be."

"It's strange to hurt for someone else. Seems like my whole life has been about me. Now I must consider him."

"And again, we come back to finding balance." We both laughed a little at that.

We continued to eat, but our conversation moved more into small talk. I kept wanting to divert the conversation to Jamison. I had so many questions. But there didn't seem to be an appropriate way to switch topics. At some point, I stopped worrying about Jamison and enjoyed dinner and Will's company. *It's so good to have him home.*

Will asked for the bill and paid for it with a credit card after quickly reviewing the bill.

"I can pay my share."

He looked up and smiled. "My treat, you know that."

And I appreciated it.

We got up and put our jackets on in preparation for the voyage back into the weather. "What now?" I asked.

"Walk some of this food off and look around Leavenworth."

"Sounds like a grand plan." I grabbed Will's hand. "Where shall we go?"

In a quieter than normal voice, Will said, "I'm not all that great at path selection for us, remember?"

"Being snarky?"

Will shrugged his shoulders. "Maybe a little." We walked north up the shoveled sidewalks that were being covered by new snow. "I always thought you'd follow me to college."

"Even after our last conversation?" *This is insane.* He *actually thought I was going to follow him.* Then I thought, *and why hadn't I? Sure, I wanted to have children, but looking back in hindsight, why hadn't I followed Will? I know I had loved him. Why?*

"Conversation? My proposal was a conversation?" he laughed, but there was no mirth in it.

"You know that's not fair," I replied. "We had discussed marriage many times and always arrived at the same roadblock. Let's be real. Going to UW and proposing in the woods was your choice, not ours. You surprised me. What did you expect me to do?" I paused, stopped, and looked at him. "Let me rephrase that because I know you expected me to say 'yes.' A better question would be, weren't you at all prepared for me to say 'no'?" We looked at each other for a moment, and I could see the wheels of his mind as they turned. We walked again, but in silence, and he had let go of my hand. As we turned a corner and then another and I realized he was silently guiding us back to the car. "Well?" I asked in a quieter voice that I hoped conveyed softness as well.

"The answer is embarrassing."

"Why?"

"Because the answer is simple, but the reason behind it confuses me."

I shook my head. "You're going to have to explain that."

"The honest answer is I never once thought you'd say 'no.'" I stopped. He stopped a few steps past me and then turned and walked back to me. "What?"

"How...how...how...I'm just furious with you." I could feel the heat radiating from my cheeks. Suddenly, my warm clothes were becoming too hot. I could feel sweat break out everywhere.

"See," he said, "that's the problem. Looking back, I can see how that could be perceived as being arrogant, foolish, or even just inconsiderate. We had talked about marriage many times and I knew your position and that children were the issue." The snow was picking up and he pointed down the sidewalk to encourage me to move. I gave in and walked. "So, the embarrassing part is looking back and deciding why I was thinking the way I was."

"And your answer?"

"Ok, first something you don't know. I have always kept a journal."

I looked at him. "You have?"

"Yes. It was a way to direct my goals, hopes, and plans. I started in sixth grade after reading a Jack London book. Anyway, I go back periodically and look over those plans and dreams. I like to see how I used to think and how I have changed. I usually avoid senior summer, but I have read it a couple times. What I know with one hundred percent certainty was that the me back then was utterly and completely in love with you. He could not envision a life without you, but still he needed to leave Leavenworth. That led to the natural conclusion that you would follow him/me to college."

I thought about that for a bit and responded, "But in hindsight, you are not sure?"

He sighed. "In hindsight, it might simply have been the hubris of an eighteen-year-old boy with dreams of a brilliant future. But I am still very certain even with hubris he still loved you." He smiled. He grabbed my hand and gave it a little squeeze, and then let go.

"I'm still angry with you," I said. I walked away and even picked up my pace. He caught up with me.

"I know."

"What you did was not fair. It could be based on all the best reasons in the world, but it still wasn't fair."

"I was angry with you for a long time," he said. "I get it. Even after twelve years, it's hard to forget the anger."

"It's not my fault. You shouldn't have proposed."

"I loved you with all my heart. You said 'no' and then that was it. Neither of us said anything, neither of us wrote anything, but suddenly, without another word, our relationship was over."

"That's your fault too."

"How so?" He stopped next to his Highlander.

"Did you ask me out again? Did you ask me to visit you in UW? Did you ever just come home? And we both know the answer is no you didn't." I paused and then said, "You hurt my heart."

CHAPTER 23 – WILL

SHE OPENED THE DOOR of the Highlander, got in, and slammed it behind her. She wasn't wrong at all. I hadn't done any of those things. But then neither had she. I got into the vehicle and looked at her. "There is plenty of blame to go around," I said. *But why do I feel like it's all my fault? God, I never meant to hurt her.*

"You think so?" She wasn't looking at me. "I waited two years for you to come back. And not only did you not come back, but you also never even picked up the phone to call me." She wouldn't look at me. *Was she crying?* "You left without saying goodbye. How do you think that made me feel?"

I started the vehicle and we drove. "I didn't have the strength to say goodbye, Adi. Had I tried, I'm not sure I would have left."

She turned and faced me. "Are you serious?"

"Very. Leaving you for a future without you was the hardest thing I ever did. As I drove to school, there were many times I nearly stopped and turned around." I looked at her for a moment and asked, "Why didn't you call me?"

"I didn't have your number."

"You could've asked my mom for it." She sat quietly and didn't answer. "Really, are you going to give me the quiet treatment now?"

"I have nothing more to say on the subject," she replied.

We drove for a bit and then I pulled over onto a side road before hitting Highway 2. I exhaled heavily. Disappointment settled in and I felt on edge. "This isn't the way I wanted today to end." She nodded. I pulled out my phone and switched on a playlist of high school songs. We sat in the car as the music tore through space and time and brought us back to age 18.

After the third song, she said, "I know you didn't mean to hurt me. I mean, I know that in my head. It's my emotions that are still confused." She paused. "Do you know I didn't mean to hurt you?"

"Yes, I do now." I drummed my fingers to the music for a while. "This is just impossible. Fear of this conversation and the fear of feeling like this is what kept me away for so long." I felt the warmth of the tears as they welled up in the corner of my eyes.

"You blame me for that?" she asked.

"No, no," I replied, "this was just a painful conversation for both of us that we could not avoid if I came back. I have run this conversation through my head a thousand times. It was only about half as painful as I had imagined." I tried to smile a little at that.

She made a small sound and then said, "No, I get it. The first couple of years after you left, I wondered what it'd be like if you did come back. I also imagined the pain of that first conversation. However, that eventually faded from my thoughts. Instead, I became sure you'd never come back." She paused and then said, "and we both knew you wouldn't remain in Leavenworth."

I drove the Highlander back onto the main street and headed for our homes. *Our homes,* it felt odd to think that.

"What?" she asked.

"Just thinking of my parents' home. It's not our old house, but it sure still feels like it is home."

"Will, I don't know how your parents felt after you left. Did you stay in touch with them?" she asked.

"Yes, phone calls, letters, and later video calls."

"Oh, good. Your mom is such a good woman, and your dad has such an immense heart. I always wondered if you kept up a relationship with them."

We were quiet some more. The music kept pulling me back to high school and I thought about our junior year and our first physical adventure with each other.

"I've seen that lecherous look before. The party at Pete's is on your mind, isn't it?

"Got me."

"Do you remember why we didn't go further that night?"

I thought about it for a while and then laughed. "We didn't have protection."

"That's true, but I was still willing, if you remember."

"I remember. You brought up having a baby."

It sounded so cold the way he said it. "If I recall, what I said was, 'would it be the worst thing in the world if I got pregnant?'"

"And if memory serves, I said, 'yes.'" *I sure don't feel that way anymore.*

"And of course, the entire conversation ruined the mood. We spent the next few hours arguing."

I looked at her. The woman in front of me wasn't the child or even the teenager I once knew. She was so much more, so perfect. "You were seventeen years old. Getting you pregnant during our junior year in high school would've been the worst thing in the world, don't you think?"

"No doubt for you."

Does she hate me? I waited a second and tried to cool down a bit. I remembered these arguments. We hardly ever argued, but when we did, it was usually about parenthood or my plans to leave Leavenworth. Now we argued about the past and our prior arguments. But as I paid attention to her, I realized there was something else. "Look, I get it," I said. "I was blunt, unfeeling, and self-centered. You weren't asking to get pregnant at seventeen, you wanted me to commit to you. To say if you got pregnant, I would stand by you. I didn't understand that." I paused, thought about my next words, and then said, "But you know, my choice of UW and the fact I asked you to marry me was how I attempted to express that very thing."

"You are just spinning that back on me."

"I can assure you I am not. From your point of view, I realize that besides telling you I loved you; I never communicated that love properly." A small uncomfortable laugh rose out of me, and I pushed it back down. "I have an entire team at work that helps me express myself to investors and clients. Sometimes, my mind races so quickly that I just don't have the words to express what's in my head. When I was with you in high school, that also meant not having the words to express my heart." I took her hand in mine. "But to answer that old question a little differently, had we made love at Pete's and had you gotten pregnant, I would have been there for you and our child."

There was silence in the car. I put both hands on the wheel and guided us to our houses. After another song, she said in a quiet voice. "Did you really feel that way back then?"

"Yes, Adi. But I was so afraid of being tied down to Leavenworth I couldn't imagine having a child."

"I always thought you just, well, hated the idea of having children."

"It was not about children. It was not about you."

"But you were never willing to help me babysit."

I laughed. "Because I knew we would end up, you know, together in the house with the children there. I didn't want to be rude to the parents." She turned and looked at me hard. I could feel her eyes burning into the side of my head. "Ok, ok, I was afraid of getting caught, happy?"

"I thought you were afraid of nothing," she said.

Afraid of nothing? How could she think that? "I was afraid of losing you, and then I turned that fear into reality."

"We did, we did. Why didn't we talk like this when we were in high school?"

"Could we have?" I asked her.

She thought some on my question and responded, "No, no we couldn't have. You might not have expressed things well back there, but you were right. We needed to get out of Leavenworth. We needed to grow up. I learned so much about how to communicate in college." She laughed a little. "And I have to admit, I gained confidence in myself."

"Well deserved. You are even more amazing than you were back then."

"Thank you."

I pulled the Highlander into her driveway, and we sat there listening to music.

"I feel better about the past, but it doesn't really change much in the present, does it?"

"How so?" I asked.

She thought some more and said, "I'm not sure. I've been so angry with you for so long, it's like a habit. Our conversation makes my head feel better, but my heart is still kind of..."

"Broken," I finished. "I get that. It's no different for me. I think we both understand our young selves a lot better, but we've spent twelve years being hurt and, well..."

"Angry with each other. So angry that neither one of us reached out to the other. So angry that you've never come home."

"Anger with you didn't keep me away. Fear, embarrassment, and hurt played a role."

"I agree. Anger was just a feeling masking my pain and the doubt I had about my decision to say 'no' to your proposal."

I looked at her and asked, "When did you doubt that?"

She laughed and replied, "The second the word came out of my mouth and then pretty much every minute after for the next two years."

"Life is so baffling."

"Agreed. Are we going over to your parents' house now? I'd love to meet Jamison."

I thought about that for a bit and asked, "Would you mind if we waited on that? I want to get my head straight. This has been a lot."

CHAPTER 24 – ADI

I WRESTLED TO KEEP my emotions under wraps, but it felt like a lost battle. "Fine," I managed to say, but deep down, I knew there wasn't anything 'fine' about it.

Will nodded. "Tomorrow, let's plan on breakfast at my parents' around nine."

I smiled like that was a great idea, but all I felt was profound disappointment. Will got out of the car and came around to open my door. As I got out, my heart sank further as I realized that the snow had stopped, and the sky showed patches of blue. *Would he be here tomorrow?* He walked me to my door, which I opened.

"I enjoyed lunch and the conversation," he said. "I'm glad we cleared a few things up."

"Me too," I heard myself say, but felt like I was stuck in my head. We both stood there staring at each other. "I feel like we should hug or something." *No reason not to be honest at this point.*

"Me too," he said and laughed. I stepped forward and he met me, surrounding me in an enormous bear hug. At that moment, he smelled just like Will of high school, and I felt myself drift into happy memories. *Oh my God, I'm in trouble. How can I feel so disappointed and happy at the same time?*

He let go, and then I did. He stepped back. "I really am glad the storm brought me back to Leavenworth."

"I am too." I moved into the doorway of my house. "But now that the storm is ending, I cannot help but wonder how soon you will leave." I closed the door before he could answer and then I just stood there. It felt like one of those movies where the man and woman are on each side of a door, both wondering if they should do something. I let that feeling linger for a good thirty seconds, looked through the peephole, and saw he was still there.

"You still there?"

"I am," I said through the door.

"I will have to leave, but not tomorrow, probably not even the day after that. We should talk more."

"Alright." I watched him walk away from the door. I could feel my heart pumping against my chest. Once my heart settled down, I went into the kitchen and poured some sweet tea from the fridge. I then walked to the couch and sat down. *So many thoughts and feelings, how to address them all?* The answer came to me immediately and I called Clare.

"About time," she said as she answered the phone.

"Waiting with bated breath?"

"Something like that. How'd lunch go?" I could hear the eagerness in Clare's voice.

"It was not what I expected."

"You mean you didn't look into each other's eyes, realize that the two of you are still madly in love, and mourn the last twelve years of lost love?"

"Wow, you really are on a roll today, aren't you?"

"Well?"

I sighed. "More like years of psychiatric care wrapped into an incredible lunch."

I heard the energy in her voice. "Oh, no! A closure conversation?"

"Maybe. I think more healing for both of us. But I'm honestly not sure if it's the start of something new, or as you say, closure."

"Ok, lady, details, now!" I recalled and retold the story of lunch. It was, in fact, helpful going over it again. The parts that hurt, hurt less this time. My head was clearer, and it was easier to think about what we discussed without Will sitting across from me. As I got to the end of the lunch, I recalled his hug and fresh heat rose in my face and I could feel my heartrate pickup.

"I can hear it in your voice," Clare said, "That hug meant something. You felt it."

"Shut up."

"Nice comeback. You still have feelings for him."

"I don't know if I have feelings for thirty-year-old Will. I mean really, how could I? But I have lots of old feelings for eighteen-year-old Will and I have not figured those all out."

"Still angry?

"Work in progress. But I am miffed that he wouldn't let me meet Jamison today."

Clare said, "Alright, I'll play Dr. Freud for a moment. Why is waiting to meet Jamison bugging you so badly?"

I pulled a blanket over me and pushed myself into the thick cushions of the couch. "That is a damn good question."

"Meaning you don't have an answer?"

"Meaning, there could be lots of reasons, but none of them are standing out to me."

"Well, let's unpack that a bit, ok?"

"Please, that's why I called."

Clare laughed. "Sure, sure, now let's do it. Lunch didn't go the way you expected it to?"

"True."

"And by the end of the lunch, you both were feeling pretty raw with emotions?"

"Also, true."

"So, it really wasn't a good time to meet Jamison?"

I paused and thought hard on the question and then answered with over emphasized exacerbation, "I don't want to admit it, but yes, true."

"And even before I asked that question, you knew that was true, right?"

I paused and thought about her question. The answer was obvious. "Yes, mom."

She responded to my quip by saying, "That's my good little girl."

"It's a little strange how that makes me feel better."

"Because you are twisted, because we are best friends, and because I would be the first person to call you out about being stupid."

I laughed and said, "True, true, and true."

"So, again, why was not meeting Jamison today such a big deal?"

I thought some more about her question. Thought about Will and me at Pete's, the proposal, our lives in high school, and lunch today. "I don't know this Will. He might be the same guy I loved, but he might not be." I knew what I wanted to say but didn't know what it would be like to say the words; what it would be like to hear myself say them. "No surprises that I want to have children."

"True," she said.

"But that's probably too simple a statement." I sat and thought some more.

"Explain."

The tears began and I replied, "I wanted to have Will's children" and then the dam broke, and I couldn't speak for a good five minutes. Clare remained on the line, saying comforting things, but asking no questions. She knew I needed to have a good cry.

I'm so confused. My heart feels so full and so empty at the same time. It wasn't hard to fathom that somewhere in me I had always dreamed about Will and I getting back together. It had always been a silly little fantasy that I never had to really face. But now, Will back in Leavenworth, our lunch, that wall I had kept up so many years had cracks in it. What was I going to do?

I caught my breath and focused. The tears dried. I pulled out tissues and cleared my nose.

"Feel better?" Clare asked.

"Yes, damn it, I do."

"Good. So, explain to me why meeting Jamison is so important."

"Because Clare, he's Will's son. Yes, I wanted to have children. Yes, I wanted to have Will's son. But a big part of that dream was Will having a child, whether mine or not. I loved him so much. He was such a good person. Why wouldn't I want him to have children? Jamison is literally a dream realized."

"Adi, I must be honest. I'm confused. Are you saying you wanted Will to have a child more than you wanted to have a child of your own?"

"No, that's not exactly right," I replied. "Look, when we were kids, I just wanted to have children. I figured they'd be with Will. No, that's not right either. More, I couldn't imagine having children with anyone else but Will. The children I imagined raising were his kids. They had his looks, his personality. I never really focused on my contribution to the genetic mix."

There was a pause and then she said, "Look, I want to understand this, but I'm not getting there."

"I love children. I want to raise children. I love teaching children. But for me, it was never about my genes or my identity. I just wanted to be an exceptional mother."

Clare said, "Ok, I get that."

I took a deep breath and said, "But I have to admit when I daydreamed about having children, when I pictured those children in my head, they were always Will's."

"Even when you were with Edward?"

Oh my God, had I? I thought about what I had imagined back when Edward and I were together. I hadn't labeled them as Will's children, but as I thought about what I had imagined, it sure seemed like the children of my dreams were more like Will than like Edward or even me. How had I not seen that? Had I never really let go at all?

"Clare, I knew Edward and my children would be our children. Of course, I knew that. But if you are asking me whether I imagined a bunch of little Edwards running around, if I'm honest, I would have to say no. At some point, I stopped thinking about it. I even stopped imagining who the children would be like. The struggle to have a child became everything and then nothing. At some point, I just lost hope."

"Interesting. Have you considered counseling?"

"I have, I've done it. It was only moderately successful, and you know that."

"Right, I forgot for a moment. I want to understand this," Clare said.

"I think I put Will's imaginary children on a pedestal, and they have been my image of my dream children since high school."

"Probably more like elementary school," Clare chirped.

"Fair."

"So, what are you going to do about all of this?" she asked.

"I'm going to breakfast at Will's parents' tomorrow and I'm going to figure it out from there.

"That's not going to help you deal with what's going in your head and heart, Adi."

"The last twelve years haven't helped deal with my feelings. I think lunch with Will has helped. I hope to talk more with Will. And I hope those conversations lead me to a new resolve and acceptance, however things work out."

"Sounds like a plan. I'm not going to say it's a good one, too early to tell, but it's a plan, of sorts. Now tell me about how Will smelled again."

CHAPTER 25 – WILL

THE MOMENT I STEPPED into the house, the wonderful aroma of coffee and cookies hit me. Mom had baked and it smelled fantastic.

"Welcome home, Will," I heard her say from the kitchen.

"How did it turn out?" my father's voice came from the living room.

"How about we sit down with some of that coffee and those cookies, and I can tell the story once?" I laughed a bit as I went into the kitchen and gave my mom a hug. "Where's Jamison?"

"Your father insisted Jamison hang out with him while I baked."

I ambled into the living room and my father was in his favorite chair with Jamison in his arms. An empty bottle of milk and a half full coffee cup sat on the side table next to them.

"He had a good drink, a good burp, a less than stellar diaper change, and he's asleep again," my father said in a hushed voice. Even with that muted voice, Jamison stirred a bit in his arms. I stepped towards my father and gingerly scooped Jamison into my arms. My father stood up and put a blanket over my shoulder. "Just in case," he whispered.

I sat down on the couch with Jamison. *My child*, I thought as I looked down at him. He smelled like a baby, but there was something else there, too. Smell, sight, touch, all my senses kept reaffirming that this child, Jamison, was mine. I had never felt like this before, and I was finding it still overwhelming. No, not overwhelming, awe-inspiring was a better way to put it. I felt so connected to my son. I knew I would do anything for him. I felt the warmth of his body against mine and his gentle breath as it warmed my neck. The tears in my eyes matched the smile on my face. *This is happiness.*

Mom asked, "Where's Adi?"

"I dropped her off at her house."

"I thought she was coming over," my father said.

"It was a rough lunch. We didn't pull any punches and covered a lot of history. The whole thing left me feeling a little raw."

My father sat down next to me. "How bad was it?"

"Bad isn't the right word. In fact, I think it was rather good. We aired a lot of hurt feelings and learned a bit about each other's perspectives on the past. Even so, the emotions were a lot."

Mom said, "I am curious about the conversation. Honestly, I'm still a little curious about the past myself. How about you provide your parents some details?"

I laughed. "Sure mom." I detailed most of what had happened at lunch. I smoothed out a lot of the edges and dropped some details. These were my parents and while I loved them, I was never one to share too much. When I finished, I said, "I don't know whether our conversation should have occurred years ago, or if this was the perfect time for it. What I can say was the experience was cathartic."

"It sounds like it," my mother said. She paused and I could see tears creeping into her eyes as she looked at Jamison and me.

"What, mom?"

"So many things," she laughed, and the tears picked up. "I'm glad you are home. I'm so glad you brought Jamison to meet us, but well…" She sat in her chair, unable to finish the sentence.

"Son," my father said, "you were always a smart boy. You were always a hard worker. You had the amazing ability to set goals for yourself and achieve them. You remain the youngest Eagle Scout in Leavenworth history. And of course, you achieved remarkable things once you left." He paused and collected his words and then said, "It's hard to put this into words." He walked over to my mother and held her hand. "Your mother knows I love her because I show her every day. I don't mean doing things for her or even telling her I love her. It's the emotion that rises in me when I see her, when I talk to her, or when I touch her." He squeezed her hand. She looked up at him and smiled. "And that's how I know she loves me as well." He took another pause and then said, "Until just now, hearing that story and watching you with Jamison, I guess we just weren't sure you processed emotions that way...which is alright...everyone is different." He stuttered in his explanation. "We're simply happy that you found your emotional self. And yes, that sounds like something out of a self-help book, and it probably is, but still..."

"It's a wonderful thing," my mother finished.

"So let me get this right. You all thought I was a cold-hearted bastard?" I tried to put a bit of humor in the statement, but it'd been a rough day so far and I wasn't sure the humor in my voice got past the hurt.

"No son, never," my parents echoed each other.

My father let go of my mother's hand and paced a bit in front of me. "Some people are just more emotional than others. Sad movies make me cry, which amuses all my friends, but that's just how I'm wired."

"And it's not a choice your father has." My mother stood and gave my father a hug. "Since you could walk and talk, your focus was on the future. You don't dwell on the past. Even as a child, you never slowed down long enough to say you were sad. Instead, you just found ways to solve the challenge in front of you and move onto the next one."

That made sense to me. Not a cold-hearted bastard, just someone who never stopped moving long enough to recognize his own emotions. Probably meant I hadn't slowed down even long enough to think about my own emotions. "I'm so sorry."

"For what?" mom asked.

"You're correct. I can't remember a time when I wasn't going non-stop. I never stopped to express how much you two mean to me. I never stopped to think about how you would feel about me leaving Leavenworth. I haven't just ignored my own emotions, but everyone else's as well. Maybe I am cold-hearted." The pain in my chest seemed to call this into question. *Maybe I'm just so out of practice, it actually hurts to feel.*

My father walked behind me and put his hands on my shoulders. He kissed the top of my head. I was certain he went behind me because he was fighting off his own tears. "You are a fine man and a great son. You have given your mother and me a retirement free of worry. You are generous with your time and money. You have lived an amazing life. But, and I ask this from a place of love, have you slowed down enough to enjoy that life?"

As I sat there with my father's hands on my shoulders, my mother lightly crying in the chair besides me, and my son in my arms, I knew the answer was no. That's not to say I hadn't had fun or hadn't felt content. But there were very few moments like this one in my life. This was new and I really enjoyed it and realized how much I needed it. "Taking it easy every once in a while isn't a bad thing, is it?"

"Correct," my father said. He broke contact with me and went to sit in his chair next to my mother. As I sat there, I felt drained. There was a feeling of shock and of loss. *I have never really stopped long enough to think about my feelings, let alone express them to someone else. My God, talking about my feelings, what a strange concept. But, talking with Adi and now my parents were wonderful experiences. And as wonderful as they were, I still felt completely drained by the experiences. Am I just out of practice? Is this how I'm supposed to feel? And why do I feel like Adi should be here, too?*

"Are you alright?" my mother asked.

"I'm not sure. I just realized that for the first time in my life, I'm completely uncertain of the future. I honestly don't know what I want to do." *And why does that feel so good?*

"Welcome," my father said, "to what the rest of us go through."

"Stop it," my mother said to him. "It's not time for teasing."

"It's the perfect time for teasing," he replied, "now that I know he can actually appreciate it."

"Funny." A wave of heat flooded my face as my father's words provoked a bit of angst and I felt my ego kick back in. "I need to make plans, that's all. I get it."

"The snow has stopped." My mother sounded a little sad. "The passes should clear up soon. What's your plan?" Her voice then took on a tinge of fear.

"Not to leave for a bit. I need some time to think." I laughed. "For the immediate future, Adi is coming over for breakfast tomorrow." *And I realized just how much I wanted to see her again and how much I wanted her to meet Jamison.*

Mom's eyebrows went up. "Oh my, we have to clean up. I need to get some more food in, and we'll need to get the good plates out. Will, put Jamison in his bassinet and then the two of you meet me in the kitchen. We have plans to make and chores to do."

I stood up and kissed Jamison on his warm, chubby cheek. I once again noticed how wonderful he smelled. We walked to his bassinet, and I slipped him from my arms into the safety of his bed. "Sleep well champ." I swear he smiled.

CHAPTER 26 – ADI

I TOSSED AND TURNED in bed. Every time I glanced at the clock, it seemed to have advanced only 30 minutes. As I lay in bed, wrapped in cozy winter sheets, the smell of snow still filling my nostrils, I immediately recognized the familiar cycle of the clock. My ten-year-old lizard brain thought Santa was coming and I was going to be opening presents. "This is ridiculous," I said to no one. I rolled back over, adjusted my pillows, and slept for another thirty minutes. *Ok, let's be clear self. If we are too tired to enjoy meeting Jamison, we are not going over.* I immediately felt myself doubt my own thoughts. *I'm serious!* There might have been a click somewhere in the back of my brain. It could also have been just the exhaustion, but this time I slept in until my alarm went off at 6:00 a.m.

I got up and did my morning rituals. I tried not to think too far ahead. My shower might have been longer than normal. Some of my shampoos have an aromatic scent, so I had to find the right one. Then I realized my hair felt dry, so I had to get the right conditioner. Somewhere in there I remembered to shave, and once that was done, I had to put lotion on my legs. It was a process.

When I got out of the shower, I made quick work with the towel, dried my hair with the blow dryer and then started working on my hair. I considered for a moment curling my hair, but put it up in a bun instead. I spun it up and jabbed a couple of deep brown chopsticks into the bun to hold it. My hair seemed acceptable for breakfast. *It looks fine, right?*

I put on eyeliner and some mascara. I then went into the bedroom and turned on the news. As the daily stories played in the background, I started looking through my clothes for the perfect outfit to meet Jamison in. There was a lot to choose from.

Somewhere between outfits, I realized I didn't have a present for Jamison. *Did I need to bring one?* I considered all the unique items I had in my home that were baby safe. Edward and I hadn't purchased too many things when we first tried getting pregnant. One of the few items I had was a Winnie the Pooh frame I saw and fell in love with at a local store. I went into my guest room / nursery / giant closet. I dug around until I found the right box. I pulled it open. I found the frame and retrieved it. I then went into the closet and dug through older boxes until I found the one I was looking for. I carefully opened it and slogged my way through photos until I found the one of Will in high school fishing alongside a river in Leavenworth. I brought both downstairs.

I put the photo in the frame, pausing for just a moment to remember that wonderful day. Whenever I would tell Will I love him, he would reply "me too" or sometimes "I love you too." But he was never the person who seemed to say it first. That day on the river, after taking that photo of Will, he had turned, smiled, and told me how much he loved me. We had made love under the trees. It was a glorious day. I felt flush and I shook the memories from my head. I pulled some wrapping paper out from under my bed and dug through all the Christmas stuff until I found some delicate light blue paper. I wrapped the frame and put a nice blue ribbon on it.

Gift completed, I ran back into the bathroom and finished my makeup and hair. I threw on a blue blouse and a nice pair of slacks and then covered most of it in warm winter clothes. Once my boots were on, I looked at the clock and confirmed it was time. I picked up my gift and headed towards the front door when there was a knock.

"Who is it?"

"Will."

My heart fell. *He's canceling breakfast.* I went to the door and opened it. "Hi."

"Hi." He smiled. "Thought I'd come get you. Breakfast is ready."

"Wonderful." My heartbeat again. I handed him the gift. "For Jamison."

"Thanks." He took the gift. I closed the door, and he took my left hand in his right. "Let's go." We walked across the street, which was plowed. The snow had stopped, which meant the pass would likely be clear sometime today. We got to his parent's front door and he let go of my hand. He opened the door, and we went in.

The smell of freshly baked Christmas cookies, sizzling bacon, and baby powder filled the air as I walked into the house. Their home was warm and welcoming. Will's mother walked around the enormous fir tree decorated with everything Christmas as she headed towards me. Will put the gift at the base of the tree and then took Jamison out of his mother's hands. I stood there, my heart pounding wildly and a tingle of anticipation running through my body.

"Adi, I would like you to meet Jamison."

Jamison was gorgeous. He was chubby, cute, and looked like a little Will. His face seemed to glow with happiness and joy. "May I?" Will passed me Jamison and I took him into my arms. He was warm and smelled...well...perfect. "He's perfect!" I wandered with

Jamison from the entryway into the living room. "He looks so much like you, Will." I sat down on the couch with Jamison in my arms.

"Doesn't he," Will's mother said, "it's like having my little boy back."

"Carol, was Will a chubby baby?" I asked.

"Not immediately. It took him a while to figure out nursing. But once he did, he put on the pounds."

I smiled and looked down at Jamison, who was staring at me with beautiful and alert eyes. I moved to the couch and sat down. "Has he eaten?"

"The bottle!" Carol chirped. "Just a second. I was preparing it." She nearly ran into the kitchen.

Will walked over to us and looked down. "He likes you." He ran his hand gently over the downy hair on Jamison's scalp.

"I hope so." I could feel the truth of that statement in every bone of my body. Carol returned moments later with the bottle and handed it to me. I adjusted our position on the corner of the couch and supported Jamison. As I moved the bottle towards his mouth, Jamison eagerly accepted it.

"He's a good eater," Carol said.

"Talking about eating, where's the grub, mom?"

"Laid out in the kitchen. Adi, I can take Jamison if you'd like."

It took me a second to register that someone had asked me a question. I glanced up at Carol and answered her with a polite, "No, I am doing fine. Thank you for asking." I then focused back on Jamison.

Carol said, "I think Jamison has a big fan."

Will smiled at his mother. "Women seem to love him."

"Hey now," Will's father's voice came from the kitchen, "I'd be mooning over him too, but your mother won't share."

"I know, dad." Will stepped away. "I'll be right back." He then went into the kitchen to join his father.

"I'm going to help the men, or they will devastate my kitchen. Call out if you need anything." Carol walked into the kitchen. I heard her say, "Peter, look at that mess." Then I lost all focus on the adults in the home.

This beautiful baby in my arms was incredible. I was holding Will's baby. But there was something more. I felt so connected to this small human being in my arms. He was a dream come true. He was a true blessing.

"Hello, Jamison." He looked so peaceful. "That milk tastes pretty good, doesn't it?" I smiled at him. He felt wonderful in my arms. He looked into my eyes as I fed him, and he just seemed content. "My name is Adi. I'm incredibly pleased to meet you." My voice dropped to a whisper. "To tell you the truth, I've always wanted to meet someone very much like you." Jamison continued to drink. He ignored my silly banter.

This is strange. How can I feel like this about a baby I just met? What would Will say about how I was feeling? I watched Jamison drink, and I realized I didn't care. This moment wouldn't last forever, but I was going to enjoy every second while it lasted.

Time drifted off and Jamison finished his bottle. I grabbed a towel off the couch and burped him. After two solid burps and a bit of rocking, Jamison drifted off. I stood up and went to the kitchen.

"Hi," I whispered, "where should I put him?" Carol got up faster than Will and guided me down to his bedroom. I hadn't been to his bedroom in this house, but stepping into the recreation of his high school bedroom was a shock. His mother had done a fantastic job recreating her son's old room.

Carol caught me looking around and gawking. "I know, it's silly, but the old house, his room, well, it's all we really had of him since he never came home. I just couldn't give it up when we moved."

I put Jamison in a bassinet. As I stood up, I said, "I like it very much. Brings back a lot of memories." My heart sank as I realized what I had said, and the heat of embarrassment crept up my neck.

"Please, honey, don't you fret." Carol patted my hand. "Peter and I had no misconceptions of why Will cleared out the area below his window. You two did a good job of being quiet, but no one is perfect." My heart felt like it was racing as my cheeks flushed a deep red and my blood pressure skyrocketed and then plummeted. "And I'm no prude, so stop being embarrassed and go out there and get some breakfast." I traveled through the door, followed by Will's mother, and walked to the kitchen.

As I entered the room, my face was still notably hot. I locked eyes with Will as I sat down at the kitchen table. My head was a blustering mix of emotions and confusion. Old memories wrapped with emotions sprung to life. I could feel Carol watching me as I looked at Will. Fresh embarrassment brought more heat to my face.

CHAPTER 27 – WILL

TIME CHANGES A LOT of things, but as Adi came into the room, I recognized the blush in her cheeks immediately. Knowing mom, she had said something straightforward and risqué about us. I couldn't help but smile as I thought about what was probably said and fond memories of my old room came back to me. "It's quite the shrine, isn't it?"

Adi didn't unlock eyes with me. "Your mother was just commenting." Her face showed no signs of blanching.

I turned and looked at my mother. "Really?" She shrugged in response and started making Adi a plate. I knew I had to do something for Adi, so I turned the conversation to Jamison. "What do you think of Jamison?" Her eyes lit up immediately and it was if someone had pulled the red from her cheeks.

"He's amazing!" She paused and asked, "Do you think he looks more like you or his mother?"

"A pleasant blend, I think. Hard to tell since he's so young and chubby, but that nose of his is definitely mine."

"I agree, and the forehead and hairline as well. He has some distinctive William Monroe features."

"Poor kid." I smirked.

"I know, right?"

"Tsk, tsk," my mother said. "Enough of that. He's my miracle grandson."

"Miracle indeed," I replied.

"You would think," my mother continued, "at your age you'd know how to use a condom correctly. You sure had enough practice in high school." She made the statement, then opened the refrigerator and started digging around. I knew with one hundred percent certainty that she was laughing in there.

Adi's face had returned to scarlet, and she was looking down at the table. I was speechless. I wasn't sure what mom was up to, but she was having entirely too much fun at Adi's expense.

"Now, now, Carol," my father said, "give the kids a break. Not everyone is as comfortable with the biological processes as you are." The statement told me way too much about my parents and what had been happening between them over the last twelve years of my absence. That being said, the thought brought up an interesting point and one that my parents were never willing to discuss.

"Actually, now that I'm all grown up, would you all mind talking about why I'm an only child? I always thought it was strange you made that decision." Mom froze in the refrigerator. Any laughter had clearly stopped. My father coughed away discomfort. I followed up quickly with "unless you don't want to, that's ok." Mom closed the refrigerator, went to the table, and sat down. "Are you alright, mom?"

She grabbed my hand and my father's. "It's difficult." Tears welled up in her eyes. "We never told you because we just didn't know how." She paused and looked at my father, who nodded at her. "I guess it's time." She paused again, and then whispered, "I was pregnant twice after you were born. I miscarried both; a daughter and a son." The tears began flowing from my mother's eyes and her grip strengthened. "After the two losses, I couldn't stand trying again. I couldn't lose another child." She bowed her head. *Oh my God, but you did when I left. What if I had known that? Would it have made a difference? I knew I probably hurt them a bit not coming home, but I did not know they had lost a child let alone two.*

My father added, "we thought it best to focus on you, William, and enjoy the life we had." And with that, I suddenly felt like the worst person in the world for being gone the last twelve years.

"You could've told me."

My father said, "We didn't want to burden you with it."

"They were my family too," I heard myself say. A palpable sadness touched me. I thought about prior conversations that touched on this subject and how my parents reacted. It explained the two days a year my mother became melancholy for no reason. *She must have been remembering the days she lost them.*

Adi stood up and hugged me from behind. I heard her whisper into my ear, "Let them have their grief. This isn't about you." I knew she was right. I stood up, gave her a quick hug, and then moved to my mother. Raising her up from her chair, I hugged her for all I was worth.

"Thank you, mom, for giving me such a wonderful life and so many opportunities. I am who I am because of you and dad." She sobbed lightly against my shoulder as she hugged me back. Once we let go, I went over and hugged my father as well. "I love you both."

"We love you too, son."

My mother stepped away and went back into the kitchen.

"Will she be alright?" I asked.

"Give her a minute, son. She'll pull it together." My father turned the conversation to Adi as my mother collected herself in the other room. "So, Adi, how about your brothers? Where are they at these days?"

Adi moved back to her chair and sat down. "They are both still off traveling the world. Joseph works for a tech company in Tokyo and Carl is a banker in London."

"Either married?"

"Joseph has a live-in boyfriend. That took my parents a little while to get accustomed to, but they were getting there. Carl is engaged to an English woman he met in London. We haven't met either of them yet."

My father asked, "So they aren't coming back for Christmas?"

"No plans that I'm aware of."

I started doing math in my head. I realized Carl had left for college the year before I did, and Joseph would've left a couple of years after me. I hadn't realized that so many men in Adi's life had left and hadn't come back. "Well, they should come back home. I have found the experience to be quite amazing." My father and Adi smiled at me, and I reflected on how pleased they were that I was home.

My mother came back into the room. She had fixed her makeup, aside from a bit of puffiness around her eyes, and she seemed to have gotten her emotions under control. "Adi, have you gotten your Christmas tree yet?" When she asked, I realized I hadn't seen a tree in Adi's house.

"No ma'am. I had plans of getting a small Christmas tree from D2 Christmas Trees this year, and then the storm hit."

My mother looked up from her plate. "Will, why don't you take Adi out to the farm and help her get a tree?"

"Sure mom. That's a wonderful idea."

"That would be fun," Adi said. "I wish Jamison was older so he could come with us."

"Little too cold out for him," my mother said before I could, "but next year for sure."

Next year, there would be a next year and a year after that and so on. I was a father with a son who would grow up to be a man. Where did I want him to grow up?

"You ok, son?" my father asked. "You disappeared there for a second."

"Sorry dad. I got lost in my thoughts." I turned to Adi. "So, feel like going out to pick up a tree?"

"Let me finish this fantastic breakfast first." She put more effort into the meal.

I had always enjoyed watching Adi eat. She was a foodie before that label existed. She genuinely enjoyed all aspects of eating. I enjoyed watching her eat. As she dug into my mother's feast in front of her, I couldn't help but think about how much I adored being around her again.

"Lots of daydreaming today, Will," my father pointed out.

"Just enjoying a lovely quiet breakfast, dad," and with those magic words my phone rang. I answered it and went into the other room.

"Slow down, what's going on?" Three different voices on the speaker phone filled my ears with the day's drama. "Ok, stop!" I heard the growing anger in my voice, and I tried to back it off. "I'm not there and that's not going to change today, so get past that." I took a breath. "Now, as far as the issue with the new restaurant app, talk to Linda Sanders. She spotted the possibility of this glitch and I think she has a workaround. As far as Tokyo, tell them the weather is getting better and I'll be home by..." I paused and thought about my next words and then said, "I'll be back in about three days, right after Christmas. Finally, let's give everyone a bit of a break and some holiday spirit. Hand out those bonuses we talked about and give them the next 72 hours off."

There was frantic speaking from someone on the line. With a controlled voice I again said, "stop." I waited for a bit and allowed the quiet to permeate the call. "We've had a fantastic year, folks. Let's let people enjoy their families. Now all of you get in the spirit and relax."

Ana from human resources asked, "Everyone off? No receptionist?"

"Yes, everyone. Put a message on the voice mail and explain the office is closed for the holiday."

"Paid vacation for everyone?"

"Of course, Ana. I want to fill everyone with a bit of Christmas spirit."

Jim asked, "What about the current projects and Tokyo?"

"Everything will still be there after Christmas." *And if it's not, is that the end of the world?* "Everyone, have a Merry Christmas!" I disconnected before they could respond further.

"Nice," Adi said. She was standing in the doorway.

"I can be nice."

"You were being selfish and decorating it with nice Christmas balls, but still it was nice."

"You said balls."

"I did, didn't I." She smirked and a bit of redness reached her cheeks. "It really stinks that I cannot even enjoy a silly joke without making myself blush."

"Just too pure of heart." I grabbed my jacket and threw it on. "Ready to get a tree?"

"Yes, I am."

"Mom," I paused, then added, "Dad, you ok with Jamison?"

"Yes, dear," they said in unison.

CHAPTER 28 – ADI

BEFORE WE LEFT, I STEPPED into Will's room and gazed at Jamison. He was asleep on his back. His face showed only peace and calmness. The room was quiet and I held my breath to listen to him breathe. I brought my ear close to him and listened. A wave of peace washed over me as I stood there, watching and listening to him.

"Ready?" Will's voice broke the spell.

"He's just precious," I whispered, my heart swelling with warmth. "You're one lucky father."

Will smiled. "Still getting used to that idea, but yeah, I do feel lucky." He helped me into my coat, and we made our way to the garage.

As we drove down the street in Will's Highlander, my phone rang. I answered it and heard Clare's voice on the other end. "What's up, Clare?"

"Where you at?"

"Will and I just left his house. We decided to go and pick out a Christmas tree for my house."

"Oh, really!" Clare did not mask the angst in her voice. I realized the phone was loud enough for Will to hear and turned down the volume. "I'm sorry. I forgot you offered to help me pick one out this year."

"No problem at all." I knew that was probably true, but I also knew that I hurt her feelings."

"I really am sorry."

She did not respond. There was silence. Then she asked, "You meet the kid?"

"Yes," I replied softly. "And we'll talk about that later."

"Mhmm. Be careful, Adi. Don't get yourself hurt. Either of these males could break your heart again." Her words stung because I knew she was right. But when it came to Jamison, it was already too late. I knew my heart. I knew the place Jamison already had in it. I recognized it was right next to Will's spot. And I knew and dreaded what would inevitably come to pass.

But I can ignore it for as long as I can. "Always full of good advice, Clare. Talk to you soon." I hung up.

"She worried about you?"

"Perpetually." I shrugged.

Will smiled at me. "Seems to me you take care of yourself just fine."

"Well, thank you Mr. Monroe." He smiled and bowed his head slightly. "So," I asked, "how long has it been since you've bought a real-life Christmas tree?"

"Ha! I got you there. I buy one every year. I may have gone corporate in all other ways, but I refuse to have a fake Christmas tree in my house."

"Good." I turned and smiled at him. "That's the way it should be."

Will fell silent for a bit as we drove to the tree farm. "I'm sorry about your divorce, Adi." He paused, then said, "And everything associated with it." His voice dropped down to almost a whisper. "I know how much you wanted to have a child."

"Want," I corrected him. "It's not like my opportunities are over."

"Fair enough. I wasn't trying to be insulting."

"I know, Will, I didn't take it that way. Seems like plans don't always work out."

"At least not the plans of us mere humans."

"Ahh, leaving Leavenworth didn't drive the faith out of you, either."

"No. I cannot say I'm a churchgoing person, but I have my faith."

"I still attended most Sundays, but I agree I focus more on faith than religion."

"Has it helped?"

"Sometimes." I took a breath and then said, "I think it's easier to hope when you believe there's a plan and it's not just bad luck that your body won't give you the one thing you've always wanted."

"I agree. Even when the challenge is the one thing you never planned for and even tried to avoid."

"Ok, so if we are going to get all metaphysical, how about this weather?"

Will laughed. "Got me there for sure. Something other than my personal choices led me back to Leavenworth."

"But you're pleased you came back, yes?" I turned and looked at him again.

"Definitely! It's hard to figure out what's changed. It might just be me, or maybe it's having a son, but I am so glad I came home."

"Home? Nice to hear you say that." *He felt home, interesting.* "So, you are going to stay for Christmas?"

"Yes, seems like the right thing to do. Jamison deserves his first Christmas to be with his entire family."

"Already sacrificing for your son."

"I guess, though to be honest, it doesn't feel like much of a sacrifice. Work hasn't been the same for me lately. It's felt, I'm not sure..."

"Empty? Lacking? Is there another synonym?"

He laughed and said, "No, that's enough of those, and they aren't quite right. Simpler to say I haven't had a passion for the work in some time. I love the people and for them, I want the company to continue to do well, but my passion has ebbed."

"Well, maybe Leavenworth will help you stir up the old passion." *Oh my God, did I just say that*? Am *I flirting*?

He glanced at me from the corner of his eye, and I could feel the blush begin. He was a gentleman and did not comment on the potential double meaning of my words. "We shall see. Right now, I'm more interested in finding and buying you the perfect Christmas tree."

"You buy? I thought you were just here to help me carry it. I don't need your money, Mr. Monroe."

"Please understand that I'm not implying you must agree," Will began, his tone gentle. "Adi, it would thrill me to buy you an early Christmas gift. This is something I want to do for you. I'm know how much the perfect tree means to you." His eyes implored me, and I noticed a slight pout form on his lips.

"Now, now, Will, don't get all emotional on me. Sure, you can buy me a tree."

"Good." He adjusted his hands on the steering and began drumming his fingers to the music.

"Good."

As we drove, the scenery outside the window became our shared focus, and we enjoyed the silence between us. There was no need for words. We were content. As we arrived at the tree farm, I recognized a sense of balance between us. We were no longer just two people who had once known each other. We were adults with a shared history, rediscovering each other in the present.

Will expertly navigated the unplowed parking lot, clearing a path for us to the farm entrance. "Ready to go?" His eyes were sparkling with excitement.

I zipped up my jacket and pulled my hat down snugly over my ears. "Back into the cold," I said with a smile.

We stepped out of the Highlander and made our way through the thick snow towards the entrance. "I hadn't considered how deep the snow would be here," I said, my breath visible in the chilly air.

"You up for the challenge?" His grin was infectious. He reached out to take my hand.

"Always!" There was determination in my voice. I marched ahead of him into the forest of trees. The crunch of snow under my feet echoed around me. We wove our way through rows of trees. Our trek began in the section with the smaller trees. As we made our way through the lines of trees, they grew in height. Eventually, we reached the towering ten-foot trees I sought. "Big enough?" I looked up at the branches above my head. The smell of the fir trees around me cut through the frigid air of winter with the glorious smell of Christmas.

"Where are you putting it?"

"In the front entryway between the dining room and the living room."

"You have a nice, raised ceiling there, right?" He looked up at the trees surrounding us. "You could go taller if you wanted. What have you done in the past?"

"Smaller, like six feet." I stepped up to a beautiful eleven foot tree. "I didn't have the muscles or the vehicle to bring a bigger one home."

Will flexed his arms playfully and grinned. "I've got you covered," he said with a laugh. "I may not be as strong as I used to be, but I'm pretty sure we can team up." He paused for a moment, then added, "I'm going to run to the farmhouse and ask for a saw."

I watched Will take off at a run. I found my eyes locked on him. Twelve years had not hurt him at all. He was still thin and strong. I let my eyes drop below his waist for a moment and then turned my head as I felt the flush of heat hit my cheeks. *Now that was not embarrassment, but boy, that man could still make me flush.* I wandered through the trees and searched for the perfect one. There were so many, and the farm did a wonderful job on growing straight, full trees. *So many choices.* I looked at two trees, but they just felt too wide. Another tree had a bare spot. I searched through some more. *Where are you?* Then I saw it. A beautiful fir tree with just the right number of branches and the perfect height for my house.

"Find one?" Will's voice boomed from behind me, shattering the quiet and startling me. I jumped and turned to face him, my hands on my hips.

"Sorry," he said with an apologetic smile. "Didn't mean to scare you."

I laughed and was surprised by the nervous edge in my voice. "No, you didn't scare me. Just startled me. I didn't hear you coming."

"You were pretty focused on that tree," His eyes followed mine to the fir tree. "Is it the one?"

"Yes, sir!" I grinned. "Now get to work."

"Yes, ma'am," Will made a mock salute. He sawed at the trunk of the tree for a while. After a couple of pulls on the saw, I reached out and grabbed the trunk of the tree to steady it.

"Thanks," he said from below me. I looked down and saw him working hard, his muscles flexing as he moved the saw back and forth. Will had joked about not being as strong as he was in high school, but he was far from scrawny now. I couldn't help but admire the way his arms and shoulders bulged as he worked.

"Push it away from me a bit, okay?" His words broke my reverie.

I SAID AGAIN, "PUSH it away from me, okay?" I looked up and saw Adi staring down at me. Our eyes met, and for a moment, we were lost in each other's gaze.

"What did you say?" Her voice was soft.

"Can you push it forward and to the right a bit?"

"Yes, sure." She broke our gaze and focused on the tree. I couldn't help but let my eyes travel down her body before I returned my attention to the tree trunk. The last twelve years had been kind to Adi. She was breathtakingly beautiful. Her lean high school body had matured into a stunning figure that even her winter clothes couldn't hide. I hadn't thought of her in that way for so long, but something about the physical activity and Adi standing over me made it hard to focus on anything else. I shook my head to clear my thoughts and then centered my focus on the task at hand.

The tree had a good sized trunk, and the saw was not as sharp as I would have liked. My arm was getting sore as I worked. *You can do this.* All my time behind a desk was showing. I kept at it and a few more minutes into the endeavor I the saw blade neared the end. "Be ready."

Adi slid closer to the tree, placing both hands on the trunk. As she did, her leg brushed against my shoulder and my focus wavered again. And then the saw broke through and the tree wobbled.

"I've got it!" Adi's voice was strained. "But I'm not sure for how long."

I crawled backwards, my shoulder brushing against her leg again. I stood up and wrapped my hands around the trunk of the tree, above and below hers. Together, we lowered it to the ground. I pulled out the twine I had gotten at the farmhouse and began tying up the tree.

Adi walked over and picked up the saw. I caught myself staring at her as she bent over, rather than focusing on what I was doing with the tree. She stood up and looked at me. "What are you doing?" There was a huge smile on her face.

"Just tying up the tree." I refocused on my task.

"Sure, you are." She laughed.

It took me a little longer than I hoped to tie the tree up. I made sure I focused the rest of the time on the tree. It felt like Adi's eyes were on me the whole time, just waiting for me to check her out. *She didn't seem upset. Why would she be?*

When I was finished, Adi came over and picked up the top of the tree. I grabbed the base and together; we carried the tree to the Highlander. The owner came out and looked it over. We haggled over the price for a bit before I paid in cash and handed over the saw. A couple of young men came out to help us load the tree onto the roof of my Highlander.

"Will you need any help at home?" the owner asked.

"I think Adi and I can handle it." I turned to Adi. "We're good, right, lady?"

"We'll be fine." She smiled again.

She is so beautiful. I walked around and opened the Highlander's door for her. Adi got in and as she did, she rested her hand on mine.

"Thank you, Will."

"My pleasure." I closed the door, went around the front of the vehicle, and climbed into the driver's seat. The Highlander came to life and warm air filled the vehicle.

"That feels wonderful." Adi took off her gloves and hat.

"Didn't realize just how cold it was out there until the heat came on."

"I know, right. Thank you again for the tree."

"Merry early Christmas Adi."

We got out of the parking lot and back on to the road to Adi's house.

"So, Will, I have a question," Adi broke the silence.

"Sure, shoot."

She hesitated for a moment before asking, "Were you checking out my butt back there?"

Laughter erupted from me. I felt nervous, embarrassed, and something else. *Wow, what a question.* "I don't know, were you checking me out when I was sawing?"

"I guess it's natural to be curious." She shrugged.

"Right," I agreed. "It would be odd if we weren't still attracted to each other. Wouldn't it?"

Adi looked thoughtful. "I never really thought about it. I kind of never thought I'd see you again." *Her words stung and I realized just how much pain I had caused when I left. It was easy to ignore when I was away from Leavenworth, but now it seemed to be everywhere. What would happen when I took Jamison away from here? What would it do to my parents? Could I do that again?*

"Hey," Adi said softly, interrupting my thoughts. "Sorry, I didn't mean to make you all melancholy."

"Not melancholy," I replied with a small smile. "Just thoughtful. I realized my hope of time with you like this kind of died a long time ago. At some point, it just became too painful to imagine us together again."

"You know you could've come home at any time," I could tell she was trying to be gentle with her words.

"I know." My audible sigh came from deep within me. "But I don't think I was ready for that. So much has changed for me in the last year. It feels like my priorities have shifted and it's resulted in an unfamiliar perspective on things."

"Did Jamison change things that much even before he was born?" Adi's voice was filled with curiosity. I turned and looked at her. Her eyes sparkled with energy.

"Yes. When I found out Koy was pregnant, it made me take a long, hard look at my life and what I wanted out of it. And when I knew for sure she had chosen to keep Jamison, I started to plan for fatherhood. I never planned to move to Spokane, but I still intended to be an active part of my son's life. And then, when it turned out she wasn't going to make it... well, that shook me to my core."

Adi went quiet for a moment. I glimpsed Adi watching me out of the corner of my eye. She broke the silence in a hushed tone. "Do you miss her?"

I shifted in my seat, unsure of how to answer. *How do I answer this? Do I even know the answer? Yes, of course I do. But I'm going to sound like a total ass.* "Adi, I'm afraid to answer. I'm going to sound like an ass."

"You've never let that stop you before." She laughed. "But I'm not here to judge you. Just be honest with me, Will."

"Adi, I am incredibly sad that Jamison will never get to know his mother. From everything I've heard, she was an amazing woman. I enjoyed the short time we spent together, and I miss the opportunity to get to know her better and see her be a mother to Jamison. But I cannot say that I loved her. I cannot even say I really knew her. So, I guess I cannot tell you I miss her." I was quiet for a while and Adi didn't interrupt that. "I guess, until I saw you again, I felt like I missed an opportunity to get to know Koy more and investigate the possibilities. But now, I just don't know. I can't say I miss her."

"Complicated emotions."

"Definitely."

"I would warn you though, that putting it like that makes you sound kind of cold. There are better ways to express how you feel about that experience. As Jamison grows up, I would focus on the positives you know about his mom. Tell him she was a wonderful woman whose last thoughts were to make sure he was safe with his father. Explain how sad you are about the missed opportunity of watching her raise him; that's touching. Answer all his questions and be there for him."

"That is brilliant advice. I'm sorry I didn't mean to come off cold or uncaring. Our relationship was undeveloped. And honestly, it's uncomfortable discussing my relationship with her with you." *This isn't going well.*

"I get how this is difficult to talk about. You will be a wonderful father."

"I hope so. I had two exceptional parents. It's going to be hard being both."

"You'll make it work, and your parent's will be there as exceptional grandparents."

There was another long moment of silence between us. "Alright, so as I continue to be honest, I may have looked at your backside when we cut down the tree. I guess the positive aspect of not having a baby is you kept your figure." I knew my intent, but immediately recognized how flat my words had fallen. The silence grew painful, but I did not know how to undo what I had just said.

Adi turned in her seat and looked at me. I turned a bit and glanced at her. She said, "I'm waiting."

I sighed and nodded my head. "I'm sorry, that was stupid. I was trying to give you a compliment and find something positive about what you've been going through. I failed."

"You could've mentioned being insensitive and a bit of a chauvinist."

"I'll own up to being insensitive, but my comment had nothing to do with being a chauvinist. You are gorgeous Adi, that's just a fact." Her face broke into a bit of a smirk as color raced to her cheeks. "Oh damn, nice, you were just trying to pull a compliment out of me."

She laughed. "For a smart guy, you don't always speak your mind clearly. What you said was insensitive, but I knew it came from a good place." She paused and then lowered her voice. "I would trade my figure for a baby any day of the week and twice on Sunday."

"I know, again, I'm sorry."

"So, you think I'm sexy?" she asked in a joking voice.

"You realize that was never our issue, right?"

She nodded. "It's hard to remember exactly why someone you love leaves. At some point, you doubt yourself. Was I nice enough? Was I pretty enough? You know."

"Adi, we can second guess everything that happened, but I don't think that'll help. I like who I have become. I know I want to change some things now, but I wouldn't have Jamison had I made other choices. I wouldn't have my friends and colleagues at work." I paused and then said, "And now I have you and my parents back in my life, I hope."

"You do, you definitely do. We should've stayed in touch and remained friends. It's my fault as much as yours. I could've asked for your number anytime. But I agree with you, I like myself as I am. I may not love my body and its inability to have a child, but me myself I love very much. It took college, teaching, and even marriage to make me who I am. And I'm extremely glad you and Jamison came to Leavenworth this Christmas. It truly is a bit of a Christmas miracle." She paused, then rested her hand on my right shoulder. "Friends forever?"

"Indeed." I put my left hand on hers and squeezed it. My heart rate jumped. I let go of her hand and locked both of them on the steering wheel.

As we pulled onto her street, I saw that my parents had their drapes open and the Christmas lights were blazing on the outside of the house. Mom was standing in the front window with Jamison in her arms. She gave a little wave as we approached the driveways. I raised my hand in response. I then turned and pulled the Highlander into Adi's driveway.

"Home safe and sound." I put the vehicle in park.

"Well done, sir. Thank you again for driving and for my early Christmas present."

"Ma'am, as always, my pleasure." I got out of the Highlander and walked around to Adi's side. She had already opened the door and was stepping out. I held the door and then her hand. We paused for a moment like that and then time started up again.

We unloaded the tree and I stood with it while she unlocked the door.

"Wait a moment," she said. I stood there until she reappeared. "Ok, I've set up the stand."

We tipped the tree horizontally, and Adi took the top of the tree again. She guided the tree and me into the house. Once inside, she helped me tip the tree vertically and place it in the stand. "It'll need to rest and get some water before we decorate and light it."

I stepped back and looked at the tree, which stood a good twelve feet tall in the stand. "It's a wonderful tree, Adi. You will have a great time decorating it." *Wait a second, did she say "we?"* I turned and looked at her. "Did you say 'we?'"

"Your parents already decorated their tree. It is beautiful, but you and Jamison didn't get to participate in the decorating. What do you think about coming over tomorrow night with Jamison and your folks and helping me decorate? I would love to prepare dinner for everyone."

I turned back and looked at the beautiful tree. I hadn't decorated a tree with family in a very long time. *I want to spend more time with Adi. This could be kind of cool.* I walked over to the door and opened it. "You know what, Adi? That sounds amazing. I'll check with my parents, but I can guarantee you Jamison and I will be here. Thank you for including him and me." I turned to look at her. Her cheeks were warm with happiness. Her smile lit the room. She was gorgeous.

"It will be wonderful. We'll take some photos so he can remember his first Christmas in Leavenworth."

I smiled and started to close the door. "I'm looking forward to it. See you tomorrow." I shut the door behind me and headed for my Highlander. *Tomorrow, I'll get to see her tomorrow. Adi is back in my life.* I got in the vehicle, started it up, and backed it off of Adi's driveway into my parent's garage. I clicked the button on my sun visor and the door closed. *Tomorrow.*

CHAPTER 30 – ADI

I HAD JUST FINISHED writing the last item on my grocery list when my phone rang. I knew who it was before I answered, and my heart leaped with anticipation. "Good morning, Will. What's up?"

"Hey, Adi. Just calling to let you know my parents appreciated the invite and we will all come over for dinner tonight. We are looking forward to decorating your Christmas tree."

"That's great news! Plan to come over at five, all right?"

"Sounds great. You sure that's enough time?"

"Yeah, that's perfect. I'm actually dressed and ready right now. I was just finishing up my list for Dan's. I was thinking of making pork roast. And for dessert, maybe some homemade apple pie?" I said, my mind already whirring with ideas.

"That sounds amazing. My parents are going to love it. Thanks so much for putting in all this effort."

"Of course, it's my pleasure. I cannot wait to see Jamison and your parents."

"See you soon." He hung up.

The dumb smile on my face wouldn't go away as I finished getting ready to leave. Then the phone rang again. I picked it up. I hoped it was Will again.

"Hey kiddo," my mother said. My heart slowed down. "What's your plans today?"

"I just made a list for Dan's. Will Monroe, his son, and his parents plan to come over tonight to help decorate my tree."

"Oh dear," I heard her say in her concerned voice. She paused for a long time and then asked, "would it be alright with you if father and I came as well? You know how much he loves to decorate Christmas trees."

I considered the pork recipe, the potatoes and salad, and the apple pie that I had planned, then I responded, "Sure, I will purchase a larger roast."

"Fantastic! What time?"

"If you want to show up when they are, then five o'clock. If you want to come help me finish things up then sooner."

"We'll be there at two. I assume you haven't gone up in your attic and gotten the Christmas tree lights down?"

"Dad did that when he got the house lights setup a couple weeks ago. They are in the garage."

"Perfect, well he can test those and get them ready, while we clean and cook," my mother said.

"Thanks, mom."

"It'll be fun and your father and I have stayed in contact with the Monroe's all these years, anyway. We'll have a good time."

Mom had never told me that before. I wonder what 'stayed in contact' meant. "Thanks again mom, see you around two." I disconnected and adjusted my list. *I wonder if I should invite Clare.* I picked up the phone and called her.

Clare answered. "Hi, what's up?"

"Impromptu dinner at my house tonight. For the main entertainment we will light and decorate my new Christmas tree. Want to come?"

"Oh, really? Who'd you invite?"

"Will, his son, his parents, and my parents."

"Now that is an interesting group of people. And you thought to add me to that wonderfully stressful dinner party. Thanks!"

I felt the worry start the second she said that. "Do you really think?"

"It has all the makings. Did you tell Will your parents are coming?"

"Not yet."

"Well, good luck with that."

"I thought maybe you'd want to come."

"You thought wrong." She laughed, and then I heard mumbling on the other end of the phone. Finally, she said, "Look, I'll come if you need me, you know that, but this seems like a family thing. I'm not big on babies. And you know my idea of Christmas tree decorating is pulling out my tree from its box and plugging it into the wall."

"Nice."

"It is, saves so much time and looks wonderful. Plus, as I'll remind you, the holiday is not about a fat man, gifts, or trees."

Having heard this speech from Clare for years, I simply agreed with her and then asked, "If I call, you'll come?"

"You know I will. Have fun. No matter what, this should be a memorable dinner." I heard her laughter startup again and then she disconnected.

Our exchange left me feeling anything but ready for the evening's dinner. *I knew I wanted everyone to come over. I knew I wanted Jamison at my home and to be a part of decorating the tree. It just felt, well, exciting. It also just felt so overwhelming.*

I picked up my keys and left the house. The roads were better today and the drive down to Dan's was a breeze. The parking lot was busier than it had been for days, and there were more people around town. I made my way through Dan's and foraged as I went. There were many people to greet and wish a Merry Christmas to, but I didn't stop for conversations.

I targeted my shopping to make it fast. I was in and out in twenty minutes and headed back to my home. Ideally, the roast should've marinated for twenty-four hours, so I needed to get it prepared as quickly as possible. Then I needed to clean the house and prepare everything else. I had a busy day planned and I was eager about it. *I can't stop smiling.*

I exited Dan's and loaded my car. I got into the car and started the engine, which allowed the heater to come on. It might no longer be snowing, but it still was a far distance from warm outside. As the heat filled the car, I took a deep breath and forced myself to slow down. *Alright, let's start with the basics. I'm thrilled about tonight. I know I want to see Jamison, but it's more than that. I want to see Will too. What's going on here?* If there was supposed to be an all-knowing voice that answered that question, they were silent, or I was apparently deaf. I knew I never got over Will completely. Even during my wedding with Edward, infuriating flashbacks of Will kept popping up in my head. I certainly never dreamed two men would propose to me. And the second time was so difficult because I was still contemplating the first time. My feelings towards Edward were real. That didn't change what could've been with Will. "What are you doing to yourself, Adi?" Still no voice answered.

I put the car in drive and headed home. *This is going to be a long day.* The drive was quick and easy as far as the roads were concerned. Navigating through the emotional fog and slippery roads of my thoughts was a struggle. As I pulled into my garage, I realized I needed to figure out what I wanted. However, acknowledging that didn't help. I was flummoxed. It was easy to say I was still in love with Will, but was I? He hurt me, we hurt each other; can love rebuild from that? And then there was Jamison. Were my feelings about him special or was I just wanting to have a baby so badly that I was latching on to Will's son?

I closed the door to the house and tried to leave all those worries and concerns outside. I placed my groceries in the kitchen, grabbed my Joy of Cooking and began dinner prep. I hadn't figured out the answers to my questions, but I could still make a delicious meal.

I worked on the house after I marinated the meat and started some of the preparation. My house was neat and organized, so there wasn't a lot to do. Still, I was determined to ensure that neither my parents nor Will's noticed any dirt or dust. Everything was going well until I started vacuuming. The tempo of the motion and even the sound calmed me. As I became relaxed and worried less about the preparation, other feelings and emotions overcame me.

I turned off the vacuum and pulled my phone out of my back pocket. I searched through my contacts and found the number I was looking for. With just a simple click of my finger, I heard the phone dialing.

"Adi!" the voice hollered on the other end of the phone.

"Megan, how are you? Happy Hanukkah."

"Merry Christmas," she replied. "I figured I'd just get a card this year. Why the call?"

"Always the suspicious one, aren't you?" I replied.

"Adi, I love you to death, but you know you only call me for my amazing psychological skills."

"I apologize for that, but yes, I need your help." Megan had been a confidant in college, but also a counselor. I had met her at the student counseling center when I was still feeling down about Will. She knew the entire story and didn't require me to start from the beginning, so I just filled her in on what had happened with Edward and then the last few days with Will. Her response was silence. "You there? Did we get disconnected?"

"Adi." She paused for about thirty seconds. "What you told me is just, well crazy."

"That's reassuring."

"Not that kind of crazy." I heard the laugh in her voice. "I mean the odds of all these events happening to the two of you are simply astronomical."

"Right. And overwhelming."

"We know you never got over Will. It now seems clear that he never got over you. I think the hiccup in all of this is your obsession with children, which could turn into an obsession over Jamison."

"Don't you think the term obsession is a little extreme?"

"Is it? You have made most of your adult choices based on an interest in having children. You chose a career involving children. By your own admission, the one thing you and Edward really had in common was a desire to have children. What would you call it?"

"Ok, let's say you're right. What do I do with that?"

"There's an old axiom that lunacy is doing the same thing and expecting a different result. You are a beautiful and intelligent woman, Adi. You do not need children to be complete or successful. Whether you ever have children is a different question than obsessing about it. You need to change your focus."

"Easier said than done."

"True self-awareness and change are tough. That's why people *hire* me," she said with a bit too much emphasis on the word hire.

"I understand, and thanks, Megan."

"You are welcome, Adi. I have some family coming up in the spring and they want to see Leavenworth. Can you give us the insider's tour?"

"Sure, just call. We'll have fun."

"I look forward to it. Have a wonderful holiday."

"You too." I disconnected. I sat there and thought for a while about what she said. She wasn't wrong. After a little more introspection, I got back to housework and my dinner preparation.

CHAPTER 31 – WILL

AS WE CROSSED THE STREET to Adi's house, I felt an odd sense of both excitement and dread. I had not seen her parents in twelve years, and they hadn't been big fans of mine in the end. My mother told me she and dad had kept in touch with them, but I hadn't pried about just what that had meant. Now, as the four of us moved across the street to Adi's, I had to wonder just how close both sets of parents had remained. What had they discussed, especially recently? What maturations did they have planned? I knew both families were very interested in us reconnecting.

"Ready, son?" my father asked.

I knocked on the door. "Sure, it's dinner and Christmas tree decorating. What's to be ready for?" He gave me a look that conveyed, *you poor ignorant bastard,* and then looked at my mother and gave her a quick smile. The door opened. Adi's father stood in the doorway. He had a big smile on his face. "Good evening, Mr. Lewis."

"Lee, please Will." He stretched out his hand and when I grabbed it, he pulled me in for a hug. Once he let go, he turned to my father and pulled him into a hug as well. "So good to see you, Peter. You outdid yourself with the Christmas lights this year."

"Thank you, Lee. It was a lot of fun. The new lighting systems are incredible." The two men walked into the house. My mother grabbed Jamison's travel carrier from me and followed them. I turned and closed the door. The house smelled of Christmas and the fantastic feast I knew Adi had prepared.

"You ready to work?" Adi asked as she stepped out of the kitchen and then walked towards me. As I stood there, I felt torn between the desire to hug her and my awareness that everyone was watching us. There were boundaries and protocols, right? My thoughts were a jumble. *Ok, a handshake would be weird. What do I do?* Adi didn't let me suffer. She fixed everything with a small hug, which I returned.

"Thank you," I whispered into her ear.

"You are welcome." She gave me a little squeeze and then let go.

To the room I said, "yes ma'am! Where are all the boxes?"

As we disengaged, she left a hand on my back and guided me into the living room where Jamison held court with the four parents. "In the garage, all stacked up and ready for you."

"I will help," my father said.

Mr. Lewis said, "So will I." And with that, three of the four males in the house headed to the garage.

When we marched back in, we carried the opaque plastic boxes with blue lids. "Adi, where do you want these?"

"In the foyer around the tree and in the dining room."

I headed in that direction. "Will there be room in the dining room for dinner if we do that? This could take a while."

She laughed. "We will eat at the kitchen table family style, of course." She walked back into the kitchen.

The adult men followed directions and transported the boxes to the staging area. When we were done, we rejoined the ladies and Jamison in the living room. As we sat down, Adi came out of the kitchen with a tray of mulled wine. She shared them around the group, discarded the tray, and then sat down on the couch with her own cup of wine.

"Delicious," I said. "Your grandmother's recipe?"

"How do you know about that?" Mrs. Lewis asked.

Adi and I locked eyes and then both broke out laughing. Once the laughter stopped, I said, "The Christmas of our senior year, Adi and I found ourselves alone at your house getting ready for the Christmas party. You had just started the mulled wine when you had to run out and do something. We…"

"Sampled it," Adi interjected.

"Sure, sampled it," I said.

"Define a sample," Mrs. Lewis sounded a bit irked.

"Well, now sampling is a significant responsibility," I replied, "not something you can do based on a limited sample set."

"Right," Adi said, "you need at least two or three, well…"

"Cups," I added and then we both broke into silly little laughs.

Mrs. Lewis' face broke into a smile and then she laughed as well. She asked, "So explain to me why the mulled wine tasted so odd at that party?"

Adi replied, "We drank perhaps too much of it and felt we needed to…"

"Increase the volume," I interjected.

"Yes, increase the volume." Adi was smiling cheek to cheek.

"The problem," she said, "was you had just left to get more red wine and all we had in the house was some rose wine at the back of the fridge."

"Well now," Mrs. Lewis said, "that does explain a few things." She turned to Mr. Lewis, "Lee, sorry about accusing you of drinking my wine."

Mr. Lewis bent his head in recognition, and I heard a small chuckle come from him. "These things happen now and then," he said. He then made a visible sniffing movement with his head and asked, "how's dinner coming, Adi?"

Adi's eyes got wide, and she jumped up and ran to the kitchen.

Mrs. Lewis was holding Jamison, feeding him a bottle. She asked, "William, how are you enjoying being back in Leavenworth?"

I sat in a comfortable leather chair. The room was filled with the love of the people around me. If there was a tangible feeling to Christmas, this was surely it. "I never thought much about coming back, but had I, I don't think I would have imagined it this way. It's great." My mom turned her head, and I knew she was hiding emotions from the room. My dad never hid his emotions, and he had a huge grin on his face with the slightest of tears in his eyes.

"Wonderful. I know that Adi and all of us are happy to have you back." I heard a pan stutter and thump in the kitchen. *Mrs. Lewis is committing a bit much for her daughter.*

"It's great seeing Adi and all of you again. All I hear about is how wonderful a teacher Adi is. It's so wonderful for her and for her students. I remember having some terrible teachers in school."

Mr. Lewis said, "She is an amazing teacher. It is truly her calling."

The slightest of cries started from Jamison and I stood up and took him from Mrs. Lewis. "Diaper changing time." I moved over to where my mother was sitting and picked up the diaper bag. "Adi," I said in a bit of a louder voice, "where's the best room to change Jamison in?"

Adi popped her head out of the kitchen. "Guest room is two doors down. I put a changing pad on the desk in there."

"Thanks," I said and carried my son to the room. She had set up a nice changing station and had a Diaper Genie sitting there waiting to be used. *Amazing,* I thought, and then a bit of dread settled in as I realized why she had the baby equipment handy. I finished changing Jamison and Adi came into the room. "Did the pad work?" she asked.

Jamison was still lying safely on the baby pad with his seat belt on as I was depositing his diaper into the Diaper Genie. "Yes, indeed. That was very thoughtful of you to prepare this."

"I had the stuff in the closet. I figured we might as well use it. In fact, if you need any of it you are welcome to it."

"That's really kind, but my staff should've already bought everything I need. I'm sure the house is already piled high with baby supplies."

"Mind if I hold him?" she asked.

"Sure." I passed Jamison to her and she held him close to her chest and face, making those cooing sounds that babies seem to like.

"Jamison is an incredible baby. I'm glad I could help. And you should know there's always a spot for him when you visit."

"I really appreciate that; we both do. I guess I'll leave the diaper bag in here for now. Should we rejoin everyone?" She didn't answer, instead with Jamison in her arms, she moved out of the room and I followed.

Out in the living area, I discovered everyone had unboxed the Christmas supplies and the fathers were stringing up the lights on the trees with solid direction from the mothers. Adi went over to one box and pulled out a star topper. She then came over to me and handed me the star. "Mind?" she asked.

"Sure." She went over to the couch and sat with Jamison, who was playing with her pinky and smiling. I went over to one of the step stools that someone had brought out and climbed to the top. It took me a couple of minutes to get the star to settle properly. "Look ok?" I asked.

"A bit to your right," my father said. I adjusted the star. "Perfect," my father and Mr. Lewis said. I came down from the step stool and looked up. It looked good and it felt perfect. I became hyperaware of the smile on my face. *When was the last time I felt this happy?*

CHAPTER 32 – ADI

WILL HAD A HUGE SMILE on his face as he got down from the step stool. He seemed so happy. His face was lit up with pure Christmas joy. I thought back about Will from high school and I realized in those days Will was always uptight and stressed. His mind was endlessly racing. He had seemed much the same when he came back to town, but right now, I was seeing a different side of Will. It was a side I liked very much.

I looked down at Jamison, who was still holding my finger. "Such a good boy," I said lightly to him. He seemed to smile at that, and I could feel my heart jump. *Had I fallen in love with this child?*

"Ok, what's next?" my father asked.

"Lights done, let's get the garland up and then the gold and red balls. After that, it's just decorations until there's no room on the tree."

My mother had her phone out. I watched as she made video after video. I caught her eye and she walked over and took photos of me holding Jamison. "He is gorgeous," she said.

"He certainly is," I replied.

I sat there holding love incarnate in my arms as I watched my family and Will's decorate the Christmas tree. I almost felt drunk with the emotions that coursed through me. It was like being in an alternative reality. This wasn't my life, but suddenly it was. I felt complete, but I knew deep down it wouldn't last and that this touch of perfection might just ruin my life.

"You're crying," Will commented.

I looked up at him and as our eyes met, I felt another pulse of joy mixed with fear. "Just happy, Will. It is so nice to have everyone here. It's a perfect Christmas." He didn't let go of my eyes. I saw concern on his face. I felt empathy from him. I knew in that moment he cared about me and that I cared about him. *What is happening?*

"I'm glad you are happy, but you have some family ornaments your father set over on the dining room table that need your attention." Will scooped Jamison out of my arms. Just the slightest hint of one of his knuckles glanced against my breast and for a moment my heart stopped, and the room became somehow smaller. "You alright?" he asked.

I took a deep breath and tried to shut down the sudden and overwhelming desire for Will that flooded my body and mind. Thoughts of Jamison were suddenly replaced totally with his father. "I'm fine," I shuddered, "just tired." I could feel the flush in my face and crossed my arms over my chest. "I'm going to check on dinner and then I'll get to those ornaments."

Once in the kitchen, I drank a glass of cold water. It wasn't enough. So, I moved over to the sink and washed my hands in cold water and then splashed some on my face. My body still tingled from the adrenaline and the memory of when he touched me. "Seriously, Adi, you're not a child. Get a hold of yourself," I said to myself.

"A little inadvertent touch?" Ms. Monroe was standing in my kitchen, smiling at me.

"How in all that is pure did you put that together?"

"I saw how he scooped Jamison up and the blush on your face afterwards," she said.

"Think he noticed?" I asked.

"No," she said and laughed. "Men can be pretty dense about such things." She paused, then asked, "you still have feelings for Will?"

"If you had asked me that a few days ago, I would've have told you decidedly 'no,' but now, I'm uncertain. How can the touch of a man I haven't seen in twelve years make me melt like that?"

Mrs. Monroe put her arms around me and hugged me. "Love is a crazy thing honey, it doesn't care about time, logic, or even what we think we want or need."

I whispered, "you think I love him?"

"Do you? I don't know, but when was the last time you felt that way?"

I thought about Edward and then about Will in high school. "It's been a while."

"Keep an open mind, Adi," she said and then she also whispered, "you two have the support of all your parents." She smiled, let go of me, and grabbed an apron. "So, dear, how can I help get dinner on?"

With Mrs. Monroe's help, we put the finishing touches on dinner. I used some of the time she gave me to go back into the room and carefully hang ornaments on the tree branches. Will sat in the big chair with Jamison asleep on his chest. As I looked at them, my heart doubled its beat and I felt lightheaded again. My father took me by the elbow and steadied me. "Lot going on. Let's not add falling off a step stool."

"Agreed." I steadied myself. I focused on the tree and placed my ornaments where they belonged.

Once the tree was complete, everyone went into the kitchen. "Where would you like young master Jamison to lie down?" Will asked.

"With us, of course." I picked up Jamison's car seat and sat it on the couch. Slipping my hands around Jamison, I picked him up off Will's chest. We locked eyes again and I found myself thinking about the warmth of his chest and his beautiful eyes. I knew I was blushing again, but I ignored it and put Jamison in the car seat. He slept through it all. Nothing could disturb this beautiful child.

"I wish I could still sleep like that," Will said.

"Me too." I picked up the car seat and moved it to a safe, but quieter spot, near the kitchen table. I then began serving dinner.

"The pork roast is beautiful, Adi," said Mrs. Monroe.

"Agreed," my mother said. "Is this Aunt Betty's recipe?"

"Close, but with way more garlic than Aunt Betty uses." I finished serving and we sat down around the table.

My father reached out and took my hand and then hands were grabbed around the table. He said a quick prayer and ended by thanking God for Will's and Jamison's presence at the table and in Leavenworth. Then we ate.

Throughout the meal I listened for Jamison and feeling content when I could hear him breathing. At these times, I would look up and find Will looking at me. *What is he thinking? Is he feeling the same things I am? This is so odd.*

Will said, "Amazing dinner, Adi. Thank you. This has been a wonderful eve of Christmas Eve dinner."

"It has," Will's parent said in unison. They laughed and kissed each other. I turned and looked at Will, who was watching his parents and smiling.

"It has been a while since I've enjoyed such a wonderful home cooked meal and great company," my father said. "You outdid yourself, Adi."

"I agree," my mother said and then asked, "and now who is going to help with dishes?"

Will was the first one up, and his mother joined him. The two of them took charge and suddenly my kitchen was clean. I took Jamison back into the living room and sat him on the couch. I then started a fire and dimmed the lights.

Mrs. Monroe asked, "Adi, mind if I start some coffee?"

"That would be lovely," I replied. As I sat next to Jamison in the fire's warmth, I did not mind someone else in my kitchen. I was happy and content.

"I have a favor to ask." Will sat down on the other side of Jamison.

"Sure, what?"

He lowered his voice and said, "Tomorrow is Christmas Eve and with everything going on, I've been pretty lax with my Christmas shopping."

"Want some help shopping?"

"Yes, please. The weather has improved a lot. I was thinking we could go to the mall in Wenatchee."

I whispered, "This isn't your way of getting me back to that Sunset Highway Motor Inn, is it?"

His face broke into a huge smile, and then he laughed. "That place was both terrible and fantastic, wasn't it?

"It had its charm."

"While that's a wonderful memory, I really need your help. I'm a terrible shopper."

"I remember. If I recall, it's your most hated thing."

"No, that's meatloaf, but shopping is a close second."

"Oh right, meatloaf, I forgot about that."

"How could you?" Will's mother walked out with a tray of coffees. "Don't you remember the fit he would have whenever I made his grandmother's meatloaf?"

I laughed. "Honestly, I had forgotten. There is that great story about how when he was five years old, he stayed in his room a whole day without eating to avoid that meatloaf."

Will coughed. "I guess I should come clean."

"What?" His mother turned to look at Will.

"So, I knew for a week ahead of time that you were going to make that. I stocked my room up with food. I had a great little feast and played computer games all day." She stared at him. There was silence. And then he said, "You knew?"

"Of course, I knew. Suddenly, your favorite cereal, chips, and cookies disappeared from the pantry."

"Why didn't you bust me?"

"Because dear, you were being you. Your father and I respected the planning that went into that at five years old."

We all laughed. And we continued to laugh throughout the night as we enjoyed our coffee, held on to Jamison, and appreciated each other's company. But finally, the night had to end.

"We should get Jamison to bed. This has been wonderful." Will stood up, scooped Jamison from my arms, and put him in his car seat.

"What time tomorrow?" I followed Will to the door.

"Ten work for you?"

"Perfect."

Will's parents gave me enormous hugs, as did my parents. *My house is about to feel very empty.* As the Monroes headed across the street, I watched both Will and Jamison.

My mom wrapped her arms around me. "It's so good to see you happy."

"But how long will it last?"

A tear fell as I closed the door.

CHAPTER 33 – WILL

WE LEFT THE WARMTH of Adi's home and traveled into the cold of the night. Jamison was bundled in his carrier, but I still couldn't stop worrying about whether he was warm enough. I hustled across the street, followed by my parents. By the time I reached the driveway, my father had the garage door open. I entered the warmer air of the garage and then opened the door to the house. The air exiting the house was a wall of warmth. I brought Jamison into the house and let the warm air surround him. I held the door for my parents, who were right behind me. Once they were in the house proper, I let the door close.

"A wonderful night." My mother started to remove her warm clothes.

"Truly." My father helped her off with her coat. "Did you enjoy yourself, Will?"

"I did, Dad. Just a second." I walked through the house and brought Jamison to our room. I transitioned him from his carrier to his basset. Once he was situated and sleeping peacefully in the bassinet, I made sure he was bundled and then slipped out of the room.

I entered the living room. My mother sat on the couch and my father had started a small fire in the fireplace. She patted the spot next to her. "Come sit." I walked over and sat down. "How are you feeling."

"I'm fine, mom. How about you?"

She laughed and her voice cracked a little. "It was such an amazing night." Tears pooled in her eyes. I put my arm around her, and side hugged her. "This is all we've ever wanted, son."

"Even so, this is all a lot of change for you. How are you both doing with it?"

My Dad answered, "Jamison is an amazing son. We cannot be happier to be grandparents. And as your mom and I have told you repeatedly, we are so happy you came home."

"I really wasn't trying to be a jerk, you know. It's not like we didn't talk and write to each other. It wasn't about you guys."

I felt my mother push her weight against me. "We know son. You escaped your average life in Leavenworth and the pain you were feeling about Adi. But we did suffer a bit because of it."

"I know, and I'm sorry mom. I don't feel good about it. The last twelve years have been a whirlwind. But I promise, I'm not avoiding home any longer."

"Nice to hear you call it home," my father said.

My mother asked, "have you finalized plans yet?"

"Still in the works, mom. I do need to get to Edmonds though. There is work I need to do."

"But you are not leaving before Christmas, right?" She faced me with a very serious face.

"Agreed. I'm not leaving before Christmas."

We talked some more and then my parents went to bed. I sat for a bit watching the fire die. The lights were off inside the house, but the colors of Christmas shined in from the outside lights. The embers in the fire burned light red and darkened as they cooled. Eventually, the fire died out completely and I went to my room.

I looked in on Jamison who continued to sleep peacefully in his bassinet. I bent down and gave him the gentlest of kisses on his forehead. His lips puckered a little. The smell of baby floated up. I smiled. *I'm a father. How many times is that going to dawn on me? Why had this always scared me so much? What was I afraid of? Yes, this whole thing was impossible, and I had no idea what I was doing, but the love I felt for Jamison won out over all my concerns, the unknowns, and the need to control my destiny. I was lost in love with this little boy. It was amazing, and I loved every single moment of it.* "I love you, Jamison."

I undressed and dressed quietly and got into bed. Before laying my head on my pillow I plugged in my phone and saw I had missed a text from Adi.

Will: Yes, I'm still up. Sorry wasn't looking at the phone. You awake?

Adi: Just got in bed myself. The tree is beautiful. Thanks for your help.

Will: You're welcome. We had a great time.

Adi: How's Jamison?

Will: Asleep. Barely moved since we left. Little guy stayed up late.

Adi: Sorry.

Will: Not your fault. Nothing wrong with that. We all had a great time and I'm glad he got to be a part of it.

Adi: Me too. It was a pretty special night.

Will: I agree. I haven't had that much fun in a while. It was nice to be around family. And decorating your tree was great. The food was pretty good too.

Adi: LOL, thanks. I appreciate it.

Will: If we don't get some sleep, we're not going to get a good start in the morning.

Adi: True, but I kind of don't want this day to end.

I looked over at the clock, which was approaching midnight. Will: I think time is working against you.

Adi: We still have a couple more minutes.

Will: Sure.

There was a long pause. I could see the three dots, but no writing. Then she wrote back. **Adi: I don't think I'm as angry anymore.**

Will: Me either. Funny how that works.

Adi: I would much rather have you in my life than be angry with you. It was just easier to be angry with you gone.

Will: Makes sense. I've been thinking about it and I think I've felt like you got Leavenworth in the divorce.

Adi: LOL the what?

Will: You know what I mean. You stayed in Leavenworth after we broke up and that plus a thousand other things kept me from coming home. Now I realize how stupid that was.

Adi: Wait what?

Will: It's late and I'm not writing this well. What I am trying to say, is that I was stupid not to come home sooner.

There was another pause. **Adi: Who is this? Do you realize you have William Monroe's phone?**

Will: LOL funny. I can admit to being stupid.

Adi: Since when?

Will: We all grow up Adi, it just takes some of us a bit longer.

Adi: If you say so. Maybe it's just becoming a father.

I paused. *She's not wrong. Where is this conversation going. I'm glad she's not angry anymore. I'm even more glad I'm not. I feel like a huge weight has been lifted.* **Will: I feel like a huge weight is off my shoulders.**

Adi: Me too. Thank you for coming home.

Will: Thank you for having me home.

Adi: It's about to turn 12.

Will: I know.

Adi: Thank you for a wonderful day.

Will: Don't be sad about the day being over.

Adi: I'm trying.

Will: Think about tomorrow. We have a whole day together.

Adi: True.

Will: Dwelling on the past, good and bad, hasn't really been good for us.

Adi: But today isn't the past.

I waited 15 seconds and then wrote back. **Will: It is now.**

Adi: See you in a few hours.

Will: See you then.

Adi: Night, Will.

CHAPTER 34 – ADI

WILL: NIGHT, ADI.

Oh man, what a day that was.

Clare: You up texting Will, or are you actually trying to sleep?

Adi: Neither.

Clare: Sure sure. How was the night?

Adi: Spectacular.

Three dots sat there for a while. **Clare: Adi, love, what are you doing to yourself. He's going to be gone in a few days and he's taking his son with him.**

She probably wasn't wrong. But I sure wished she was. **Adi: I'm very aware, I assure you. But for right now, for Christmas, I'm enjoying my life. OK?**

Clare: Wow, sure, ok. I didn't mean to make you angry.

Adi: LOL, I'm sorry, text was more aggressive than I meant. It was a great night, can we leave it at that?

Clare: Sure! So, give me details.

Adi: Sigh. Like I said it was perfect. Will was there with Jamison. My folks and Will's folks were there.

Clare: Did everyone seem comfortable? Anyone chat about the original break up? Was Will tense around your parents?

Adi: Yes, no, thank God, and no. May I continue with the story?

Clare: Yes, sorry. We are snarky tonight...

Adi: I don't mean to be, but since you asked, let me tell it the best I can. Alright?

Clare: Sure, sorry.

Adi: No problem. So, we're in the house. I have dinner started in the kitchen. And we start working on the tree. The conversation was normal. In fact, it all felt normal. Like it was supposed to be that way. *It was amazing. Why can't it always be like that?*

Clare: And you undoubtedly are wishing it could always be like that.

Adi: Are you sure you're not part of the psychic friend's network or something?

Clare: Nice 80's reference, and no I'm not. But I do know you, Adi Lewis. That's why I'm worried about you.

Adi: Be worried later. Tonight was glorious. We just hung out in my home altogether. And Jamison, oh-my-God, he's the most perfect and amazing baby in the whole wide world.

Clare: Nice to know. Why?

Adi: First, he's a little Will.

Clare: LOL, did you write little Willy?

Adi: I most certainly did not. You know what I wrote. He's a clone of Will. And he's adorable. When he grabbed my finger, he might as well have grabbed my heart. And he's an incredibly well behaved baby. He's just a miracle.

Clare: Sounds like you're more in love with Jamison than Will.

That stopped me in my tracks. *I am in love with Jamison. How did that happen so quickly. And Will, had I ever stopped loving him? Had the anger and resentment just overwhelmed the feelings of love?* **Adi: I know your lawyerly cross-examination tricks Clare,**

I'm not falling for that. I will admit I have strong maternal feelings towards Jamison, but how could I love a child that quickly?

Clare: You? You have to be kidding.

Adi: Well as that may be, as for Will, I'm still very confused.

Clare: A more honest statement has never been texted. And what are you going to do to resolve your confusion.

Adi: Go shopping of course.

Clare: Adi is that you? Since when do you shop your problems away?

Adi: I don't, that's your style, but Will and I are going Christmas present shopping tomorrow.

Clare: Where?

Adi: Wenatchee.

Clare: Oh, going to that old ass motel you two lost your virginities in?

Adi: I'm pretty sure I tell you too much.

Clare: There's no doubt about it. Are you going there? I don't think you can lose that again, though I've heard of people who have tried.

Adi: Sicko. No we aren't going there. Will did not plan to get trapped for Christmas. Now that the snow has slowed we can make it to Wenatchee. He wants to buy Jamison his first Christmas present. He also wants to buy gifts for his parents.

Clare: And you I imagine.

Me? What would he buy me? I hadn't thought about that. *And if he gets me a gift, what am I going to get him?* Adi: Crap, I guess I need to buy him something.

Clare: Why? Your heart is wrapped, tied with a bow, and ready.

Adi: Be nice. I said I was confused. That does not mean I'm giving him my heart.

Clare: It means you are delaying the obvious and inevitable.

Adi: He's going back to Edmonds. I'm not leaving Leavenworth. Nothing has changed.

Clare: Hasn't it? Would you not follow him to Edmonds to be with Jamison and him?

Adi: No.

Clare: Adi?

Adi: No.

Clare: Seriously?

Adi: I have a life here. This is where I want to raise children. This is where our parents live. I'm not leaving Leavenworth. He made his decision before, if he decides the same thing again, well I'll have to live with it.

The three bubbles sat there for a while. **Clare: I think I believe you. I'm shocked, surprised, and maybe even a little stunned, but I believe you.**

Adi: Who's being snarky now? Leavenworth is my home and it always will be.

Clare: Then you are right back where you were 12 years ago.

Adi: Well almost.

Clare: Right, baby Jamison.

Adi: Jamison makes it harder. No child should grow up without a mother.

Clare: Maternal feelings?

Adi: Indeed.

Clare: Enough to leave Leavenworth? *I thought hard about the question. Really hard.* **Clare: You still there? I break you?**

Adi: Close call, but Leavenworth has to win out.

Clare: So, if you aren't leaving what's the plan?

Adi: No plan. Some strong wishes. I'm saying some prayers tonight, but I have to recognize this will likely not work out again.

Clare: And you can live with that?

Adi: I think Will, and even Jamison, will be a part of my life forever now. If it has to be long distance and infrequent, that's better than not at all.

Clare: My little Adi is all grown up.

Adi: Shut up.

Clare: You shut up. I can be proud of you.

Adi: Yes, but you make me feel like I'm ten years old.

Clare: LOL. She paused. I waited. **You going to sleep at all tonight?**

Adi: I have absolutely no idea.

Clare: That's what I figured. You have good night, Adi.

Adi: Sleep well Clare.

Clare: You too, thought I doubt you will. I didn't respond. I waited some more. But, Clare had stopped texting.

I laid in bed for a long time thinking about the evening. I stopped looking at the clock around 2:00 a.m. At some point, I got tired enough that I fell asleep.

CHAPTER 35 – WILL

I PULLED OUT OF THE driveway, onto the street, and into Adi's driveway. It was 10:00 in the morning. The roads were empty, and while the sky was white, there was no snow fall. I tapped my horn and waited.

The door opened. Adi said, "Give me a moment, Mr. Impatient."

I said through my open window, "We have presents to buy lady, let's get going." She came out after less than a minute and locked her door. Adi got into the passenger side of the Highlander. She wore a warm brown coat and tight leggings. I stared, probably a bit too long, at her legs.

"Do my pants look ok?" She smiled and blushed.

"Are they warm enough?"

"I'll be fine, now watch the road." Adi's laughter did nothing to reduce the blush. *I missed that blush.*

We drove down the hill and onto Highway 2. The roads were clearer than they had been in days. As I turned east towards Wenatchee, I could not help thinking about the fact I was driving further away from Edmonds. But it was Christmas Eve and there were presents to buy.

Adi asked, "So, who are we buying for?"

"My parents, Jamison, you of course, and maybe I should get something for Clare, what do you think?"

Adi laughed. "You brought me along to help you purchase a gift for myself?"

"Well, let me ask you something, Ms. Adi."

"Sure."

"What did you get me?" She nodded in recognition. "Neither of us planned for this Christmas."

"True." She was quiet for a moment in thought. "I should probably get something for your parents as well."

"Whatever you'd like. Just try to make this fun. I hate shopping." I focused on the road in front of me, but I could feel the smile on my face.

We talked a lot for the next thirty or so minutes. The conversations were full of reminiscences about our days together, but we also covered the twelve years we had been apart. And then before we knew it, we had crossed into Wenatchee and were approaching the mall.

"Where to first?" She asked.

"I am hungry. I think we should get something to eat first."

"Some things do not change." She kept a straight face for a couple of seconds and then laughed; I joined her.

We stopped at the Wild Huckleberry and had a late breakfast. We scarfed our food down with little conversation. I gave the waitress a thirty percent tip and wrote, *have a wonderful Christmas.* I wanted to pass on the joy I was feeling.

Adi waited for me at the door. "You know, I think I can count on one hand the number of times you have shopped with me."

I opened the door. "It's not personal. I hate to shop." We made our way to Macy's. I wanted to hold her hand but thought better of it. When we got to Macy's, I opened the door and Adi stepped into the store. I paused, took a deep breath, and then followed in behind her. "If Amazon hadn't invented online shopping," I said, "it was on my list of things to do. Once there is an AI that can shop for me without my involvement, then I'll be truly happy."

"You know, it means a lot more when you shop yourself for someone's gift."

"I don't doubt that for a second, but it doesn't change how I feel about being in here right now." She grabbed my hand and pulled me further into the store. Adi's touch changed my focus. *We're holding hands. Now, how did that happen?* I didn't care. Her hand in mine brought back a flood of old memories and old feelings. *But are these feelings old? Or is this something new? I'm so confused.* She dropped my hand, and the loss was palpable. I followed her as she worked her way into the store.

"Who should we shop for first?"

"I think we should start with Jamison." I scanned the store and felt just a little overwhelmed by the magnitude of the store and the shoppers.

She guided us to the escalator. We made our way upstairs to the baby section. "Do you want something practical or memorable?"

I thought for a moment and replied, "how about both?"

"That's a good answer."

We drifted through the shelves, looking at the variety of items. In one section, there was a vast selection of Christmas clothes. Digging through the items, I pulled out a onesie with a cap and showed it to Adi. The outfit was red and the writing on the chest said, "My first Christmas."

"How about this?"

She looked at the size and then switched it to a smaller version. "This is perfect, practical and memorable."

I smiled. I have to admit I felt pleased. *Ok maybe I can shop for Jamison. That's different right?* I watched Adi as she dug through some other outfits looking for the correct size. *Or maybe it's shopping with Adi that makes it ok.*

Adi presented me with another outfit. It was a Ralph Lauren onesie with matching hat and a bib. "Covers a lot of bases."

"He'd be one well-dressed baby, that's for sure."

"Indeed. He must be fashionable, right?" She marched over to another section, and I followed. She picked out a little suit jacket, pants, dress shirt, and a tie. "These are just a tad too big for him, but they should be great for pictures."

Next to the suits was something called a Ralph Lauren Hooded Barn Bunting. "What's this? It looks like a baby space suit."

She laughed. "That is perfect. It'll keep him warm if you want to bring him out for the Christmas lighting ceremony tonight." I had forgotten about that. I wanted him to go to that, so I grabbed the bunting. We went through the store and picked up a few more clothes, sweaters, and a mini-Seahawks wool hat. Then Adi took me over to the ornaments. I watched her as she meticulously went through each ornament.

"What are we looking for?"

"We need an ornament as a reminder of his first Christmas."

I looked through the ornaments until I found a little bear with a Macy's sweater and the year on the hat. "How about this? It recalls the first clothes and gift shopping trip for Jamison."

"That'll work. But we'll need to find a handmade one in Leavenworth as well."

"Of course," I responded.

She gave me a knowing smile then asked, "Who next?"

"Mom and Dad."

We walked into the kitchen area, and I picked out a Nespresso machine for my father.

"Why that?"

"Keurig is fine, but dad has always liked fancy coffees. I figured he'd enjoy this."

"That makes sense. Now, what about your mom?"

"I'm not sure." I paused then asked, "If you don't mind me asking, do you still have those little diamond earrings I gave you senior year?"

Blush shot up into her cheeks, and she looked down. "I lost one in college."

"Nice to know you were still wearing them," I looked around and then headed towards the jewelry section.

"What do you think you are doing?"

"Replacing a lost gift." An employee came over and I pointed at a pair of diamond stud earrings. As Adi came closer, I blocked her from seeing the price and then showed her the earrings. "Like?"

"Of course, I do. I'd be an idiot not to, but you aren't buying those for me."

I slid my credit card to the employee and asked that they wrap the earrings as a Christmas gift. After getting the card back, I told the cashier I'd be back for the wrapped package and then we walked away.

"I cannot believe you did that."

"Did what? It's not nice to peek at your Christmas presents." I smiled.

"I'm not sure I'm comfortable with you spending that much on me."

"Did you peek at the price?"

"No."

"Then maybe they are cheap fakes. Leave it be."

Adi looked at me and then shook her head. "Thank you, but you really didn't need to do that."

"What's important, Adi is that I wanted to do it. I can afford to do it, and you are worth doing it for." I watched as she blushed again. I felt the smile on my face and saw Adi's reaction.

"Stop making me blush!"

"Why?"

"It really isn't fair that you can do that to me, and I cannot do that to you." *She really did not know the effect she was having on me. I was definitely flushing.* Adi pulled at her jacket and looked away from me for a second. "Ok, now your mom, what do you think she would like?"

"I'm not sure how I'm going to top bringing Jamison to Leavenworth." I paused and thought about those words. "The gift she really would want is Jamison living in Leavenworth permanently." The truth of the statement was palpable and left me feeling emotionally vulnerable.

"Are you considering that?"

"I have thought about it. I don't think I have it in me to really consider it. I just have to be aware of the option."

Adi got very thoughtful. I could see her mind at work. She remained quiet as we continued to walk through the store. I thought about my mom, but I also thought about how much I enjoyed buying those earrings for Adi. Until I came home, I hadn't allowed myself to miss her. Now I found I couldn't help but think about her.

CHAPTER 36 – ADI

IT TOOK ME ABACK. The idea of Jamison permanently in Leavenworth was just too much. *Will had thought about it.* Now I found I couldn't stop but think about it as well. We walked through the store and all I could focus on was that Jamison might not leave. But then I realized Will would and I felt old pain and deep emotions come back to the surface.

"You alright?"

"Not sure how to respond to what you just said."

"It's just a thought. A realization of options I need to consider."

Will was putting Jamison before himself. He was thinking about his parents. He might even think about me a little. How should you respond? This is ridiculous. You know how you want to respond, but how should you? I wanted Jamison to remain. I wanted Will to remain. I knew how happy I was as I stood in the middle of Macy's with him. I couldn't remember the last time I felt this happy. *But what to say?* We walked further and Will looked at different things for his mother. The thoughts in my head were a jumble. The emotional side of my mind was in a definite battle with the rational side. I knew what I had to say, but I didn't want to say it. Finally, I just did. "Will." He turned and looked at me. "You cannot leave Jamison. He's already lost his mother; he cannot lose you too."

"He will never lose me; I promise you and him that. Leavenworth would just mean he'd just see less of me." His words expressed his love for Jamison. The pain I saw in his face demonstrated his love for his child even more.

"No, Will, he needs you. You cannot leave him behind."

"But am I even equipped to handle it? And my mom and dad seem so happy. I know I hurt them being gone so long. What happens when I leave with Jamison?"

"Are you going to be gone for twelve years?"

He laughed and replied, "No, of course not."

"So, you'll visit, they'll visit, and everything will be fine. Unless there's something else going on?"

"I'm confused, Adi. I've always had a plan. Now, I just don't know what to do."

"It's alright not to have a plan, Will. You have the luxury of being financially sound. That gives you lots of options. You just need to decide at this point in your life what your priorities are. I think it's clear that Jamison has become your chief priority."

"He has; there's no doubt about that." The smile on Will's face was full of warmth and perhaps just a touch of redness in his cheeks.

"Good. So, for now, we need to pick something out for your mom. Thoughts?"

"I'm at a loss." The frustration of his words was clear in his body language as well.

It is so strange to see Will unsure of himself. "You know your mom's been working out a lot lately?"

"Really?"

"Yes, I see her going to the gym just about every other day. And you are going to be sending her lots of photos of Jamison, right?"

"Of course."

"So, what about an Apple watch?"

"They have them here?"

"I believe so," I turned us around and we headed back towards the jewelry department. An employee greeted us in the department, and we asked about the watch. She directed us to the correct section. Will looked through the options and picked out a new Apple Watch with a blue Silicon Sport Band.

"She loves blue!" Will smiled. It was clear how happy he was. And he seemed to be so relaxed. The sight of his happiness ignited a fire within me. The warmth quickly spread throughout my body. He spotted something and asked, "Clare still single?"

"She is." He picked up the Sharper Image massager. "Great, this is for her."

"You are terrible." The words were mixed in with my laughter.

Once we had purchased everything, we proceeded to a different department to have it wrapped. Will was gone briefly, and I thought he went to get my gift. Even now, I found it hard to believe the gift he had purchased for me. *Oh my God, I haven't bought him anything!* "I will be right back, need to go to the lady's room." He continued to stand in the wrapping department and watched me as I headed away from him. *Ok, what do you buy the guy who proposed to you, the guy who has all the money he'll ever need, and the guy you are crushing on again?*

I walked into the men's department. I looked at the ties and then realized what I was doing and felt like an idiot. I left the ties and moved through the department. At one point, I realized I was staring just a little too long at a mannequin in his underwear. I felt the heat hit my face immediately upon the realization. "Stop it, Adi!" *No ties and no sexy underwear. What should I buy him?*

I went back to the children's section. *Maybe I can get something sentimental.* As I went through the baby's items, I realized I also needed to get something for Jamison. I looked at my watch. Not much time. Will had a stuffed giraffe he slept with for years as a child. He had told me the giraffe had always made him feel safe. I saw a beautiful plush giraffe sitting on the shelf and I picked it up for Jamison. *Perfect. Now what for Will?*

I walked back to the men's department. I had remembered that Will was wearing his father's coat when he was outside. It just dawned on me that Will had not prepared for the weather and didn't have a warm enough coat. He would need something for tonight. I searched through the men's coats until I found a beautiful black parka. It was long enough to cover his upper legs and had enough layers to keep him warm. I headed to the nearest salesperson to make my purchases.

As I was finishing the transaction, my phone rang.

"I'm walking back now."

"Where'd you go?"

"Had to buy a couple of things. Meet me in the men's section."

I finished the purchase and had both items in bags before he appeared carrying multiple bags himself. My plan was to wrap Jamison's gift for tomorrow but give Will his gift tonight.

"Remembered some shopping you needed to do?" There was laughter in his voice.

"Indeed. You ready to head home?"

"Back to Leavenworth? Yes."

Not home for you, right, but Will, it could be.

We walked to the vehicle and loaded up the back with all our bags. The sky was not clear, and the air was cold and it smelled a bit like snow. "Think it's going to snow again?" I asked.

"Let's get back to Leavenworth before it does."

We jumped into the Highlander, and we were off. Will's foot seemed heavier as we got onto the freeway. "Hey now, we don't need an accident or a ticket."

"You're right." He slowed the vehicle to just a few miles over the speed limit.

"That afraid of getting snowed in with me in Wenatchee?"

He laughed and said, "Funny, but no, I just don't want to miss Jamison's first Christmas."

I could almost feel the warmth coming from Will. The love for his son was palpable. In such a brief time, he had become such a, well, father. I felt so proud of him. "You're a good dad."

"I hope so, I really do."

He turned on the music, and we drove mostly in silence. When our song came on the radio, he reached out and held my hand for the duration of it. "Thanks for shopping with me."

"It was my pleasure. Have you figured out what you're going to do?"

He sighed. "You're right. I cannot stand the idea of being away from him. I want to be part of every minute and every moment as he grows up. I need to be there for the good times and the bad times." He paused and then said, "You know how I felt about you in high school, but the love I feel for Jamison is like nothing I've ever experienced."

I knew exactly how he felt. Jamison wasn't my son, but in the short time I had been with him, I felt bonded to him. He was my little William. How could I not love him? "So, home to Edmonds?"

"It would seem so." The car got silent again and he let go of my hand.

You've fallen for him again you stupid girl. Why do you do this to yourself? The answer was simple. There was no choice. *He was my Will.*

There was little conversation on the drive back since our minds were both preoccupied with the thoughts that ran through them. He held my hand a couple times as different songs came on. It was nice, but was also confusing. Eventually, the drive was over, and we reached my house. We parked and I removed my bags from the back of his Highlander. I then walked up to the driver's side door. He rolled down his window. I asked, "shall we go to the lighting ceremony tonight?"

"Yes, I'd like that."

"So, before we go, I want you to have my gift. It'll be useful for tonight."

He thought for a moment. "Instead of exchanging gifts now, how about I come to your house before we leave for the lights?"

"Great idea. See you around 5:30 right after dinner."

"I'll be here. Thanks again for the shopping trip." I had put my hand on his car door and now he lay his hand on mine and gave it a squeeze.

"Don't mention it. Was fun." He let go and rolled up his window. I walked to my door and then turned to look at Will. He had watched me walk to the door. He smiled and I smiled back. My heart did a little flip-flop and a blush rushed to my cheeks. *And this is why you do not play poker for money.* I unlocked the door. Once in the house, I peeked through the peephole. Will just sat there with a smile on his face. *Is he going to come in?* I waited and watched and after a time he backed out and pulled into his parents' garage.

I turned my back to the door, pushed back against it, and slid down to the ground. A couple of tears had made their way down my cheeks. *I feel so damn happy. I don't want this to end.*

I ENTERED THE HOUSE. My mother asked, "How was shopping?" She held Jamison who was very alert and focused on his grandmother.

"Better than expected and successful." I went over to the tree and placed gifts under and around it.

My father said, "nice to see that you can survive shopping, son. We had our doubts." He paused then asked, "and how are you and Ms. Adi doing?"

"What are you asking, dad?"

"We've seen the two of you together son, it appears the old flame hasn't completely gone out."

I walked to the couch and let myself fall into it. My mother brought Jamison to me and I wrapped the two of us up in a warm blanket. The smell of Jamison and the warmth he provided was the best Christmas present I could ask for, but I had to admit Adi would be a close second. "I'm not sure what's there, but I have to go back to Edmonds, and I need Jamison to be with me. Adi has always made it clear she's a Leavenworth girl for life."

I saw tears form in my mother's eyes and she turned away and headed into the kitchen. I said loudly, "I have made some decisions though. I know I'm going to be visiting Leavenworth a lot and I will not take 'no' for an answer when it comes to you both visiting us in Edmonds. Jamison is going to need his family and I want him to know you both extremely well."

My mother turned around, came to the couch, and sat down close to me. I felt the pressure of her side as much as her presence.

"We would love that, Will." Her voice was on the edge of tears. "We've missed you so much. We want to see Jamison grow up. I just wish…" her voice cracked.

My father finished, "We wish you'd consider living here with Jamison. Not in our house of course, though actually we wouldn't object to that either." He smiled and continued, "This week has been amazing for us, son."

"I agree. I never thought I'd feel so at home here. I understand what you're saying, but I have a life and a business in the Puget Sound. I worked hard for all of it."

"We know you have," my father said.

"We just love you both," and with that my mother's tears began to flow. I put my arm around her. "Let's just focus on the lightening ceremony tonight and the Christmas tomorrow, ok?" I switched Jamison into my other arm and gave him a kiss on his pudgy cheek. I turned my attention back to my parents. "If you look in that bag." I pointed with my nose. "You'll find an outfit to keep Jamison warm."

My mother stood up and opened the bag. "Oh, this is perfect. I'll go get it washed."

My father sat down next to me. Jamison's eyes were clearly heavy. I snuggled with him some more to get as much time with him before he fell asleep. "So, what did you buy Adi?"

"Remember those little diamond chip earrings I bought her in high school?"

"I do, I recall you taking a second job to save up for those."

"That's right, the ice cream store. I had forgotten about that." I smiled at the memory. "Well, she apparently lost one in college, so I just bought her a nice pair at Macy's."

"Another pair of nice diamond chips?"

I laughed out loud and answered, "Oh no, these were a pair of their best. If I shopped in Seattle, I would've gone to an actual jewelry store, but I think these will suffice."

"I'm sure they will, son. And how did you feel when you bought them for her?"

"What? What do you mean?"

"How did you feel? How did buying Adi an expensive gift make you feel?"

I thought about it for a moment and replied, "I don't know, it just seemed right. It felt good. What answer do you expect?"

"Money is different for you now than it was in high school, but I remember how important those diamond chip earrings were to you. I don't believe it was because of their intrinsic worth, correct?"

"No, they weren't worth that much. It was because I knew they would make Adi happy. They must have made her happy since she kept wearing them even after we broke up."

"So, again, how'd you feel when you bought the new ones?"

"I felt wonderful, dad. Yes, I want to make her happy. I've always wanted to make her happy. But I've never found a way to make us both happy for the long term."

My father stood up. "You're a smart guy. You'll figure it out."

I sat for a while with Jamison nestled into my arm. He was still awake and appeared to be getting hungry. I told my mother, and she prepared a bottle. While I waited, I texted some Christmas joy to friends and employees. I checked in with my secretary to see how she was doing and to make sure all the gifts she had ordered for me had made it to their recipients. I couldn't very well have had her buy her own gift, so that bit of shopping I had done myself via Amazon. She confirmed it had arrived. I wished her a Merry Christmas and put my phone away.

By the time I had finished my texts and calls, Jamison was enjoying another bottle.

"What's for dinner, mom?"

"Roast with popovers."

"My favorite, thank you."

She laughed. "What would Christmas even be without you eating a pan of popovers?"

I had tried some in restaurants over the last twelve years, but they never were the same as mom's baking.

She announced, "Let's eat!"

"This is amazing, mom," I said through mouthfuls of the fantastic food.

"Slow down," she said and laughed.

We ate in silence for a while.

"Looking forward to the ceremony?" my father asked.

I finished chewing and said, "It will be fun. Has it changed much?"

"No," my mother said, "the same old thing. They'll turn off all the lights that have been on for weeks and then after a speech they'll turn all the lights on and start the caroling."

My father took another serving. "Honey, they added the Christmas tree a couple years ago, remember?"

"Oh, that's right. There's a living Christmas tree they planted next to the gazebo in Front Street Park. They lit it up a few weeks ago, but they've left the star on top unlit. Tonight, they'll light it."

"When do we need to be there?" I pushed myself away from the table.

"Six," they both said and laughed.

I looked down at my watch. It was almost 5:15. "Adi says she has a Christmas present for me for tonight and I need to pop over at 5:30." I picked up my plates and took them into the kitchen.

"We'll clean up and get ready. It's cold out there. Take my jacket," my father said.

"Thanks dad, do you have any extras for tonight?"

He replied, "I'll look around. You should've bought one while you were out."

I was kicking myself for not doing that. "Agreed." I got up, grabbed his jacket where it hung over the couch, and picked up Adi's gift from below the tree. "Be back shortly and we'll drive down in my Highlander."

"No rush," my mother said.

"Have fun."

I opened the door. It was frigid outside. I made my way across the street and when I reached Adi's door, I knocked. I could feel my heart as it beat in my chest. She opened the door. She wore tight leggings and a sweater that hugged her entire body. She looked gorgeous. *Wow!*

"You just going to stand there letting the cold into my house?"

"No," I stammered and walked in. She shut the door, only laughing at me a little.

"I see you're wearing your dad's jacket again."

"Wasn't planning on this weather." We walked into the living room and there was a Macy's bag sitting there with a bow on it.

"I wrapped it simple. Please open it."

I walked over and opened the bag and found an incredible parka waiting for me. "This is perfect." I turned to her and smiled. Then grabbed her up in an enormous hug.

CHAPTER 38 – ADI

THE HUG I RECEIVED from Will was intense. I felt the heat come to my face and I was very conscious of how our bodies meshed during the hug. It felt so good. Eventually, he pulled away a bit, though we still hugged. I looked into his eyes. *My Will.*

"Merry Christmas, Adi."

"You too." I heard the cheer in my voice. The hug continued for a while more, and then he disengaged. I immediately missed his touch. He stood there and stared at me. Flares of heat pulsed into my cheeks. "What?"

"I forgot how truly beautiful you are."

"Shut up." My cheeks got even hotter.

He laughed. "You know, most people don't say that to me."

"All too afraid of the big man?"

"Something like that, I guess." He pulled out a box from his dad's jacket pocket. "Merry Christmas."

"I can wait and open it tomorrow." *No, I can't.*

"No, I opened yours, you open mine."

I unwrapped the beautiful paper and then opened the box to find two huge diamond earrings. "Oh my God," I heard myself say.

"I have to give Macy's credit; they are pretty spectacular. Please put them on."

I went to the table and removed the small crystals I had in my ears. Slowly, and with shaky hands, I put the diamonds in. I turned to him. "How do they look?"

His eyes sparkled. He walked over and gently slid my hair behind my ears. As his finger touched my skin, shivers traveled up my body. *Oh my God.*

"They are beautiful. Almost as beautiful as you."

I went over to a mirror and looked at myself. They were gorgeous and huge. "So, I know it's rude to ask how much a gift costs, but I'm worried about walking around with these in my ears."

"There's no reason to worry. I promise I will never allow you to go without diamonds again."

I looked some more at myself in the mirror and then turned and gave him an enormous hug. My heart did flip-flops at his touch. As we parted from our second hug, I realized just how much I wanted to kiss him. We paused for just a moment, and I thought he was going to kiss me, but then the moment ended.

He asked, "You ready to go to the ceremony?"

No, I want to stay here with you. "Let me grab my stuff." I went into the other room and put on my hat and coat. I made sure my hair wasn't covering my new earrings and then threw a scarf on. Checking my coat pockets, I found my gloves and then joined Will in the living room. When I got out there, I found him in his new parka.

"It's a wonderful coat, thank you again." He picked up his father's jacket and we left the house and went across the street. We entered the Monroe house and found Mrs. Monroe bundling Jamison in his new outfit, getting ready for the cold weather outside.

"This is a wonderful snow suit," Mrs. Monroe said.

I walked over to look at Jamison. "He looks adorable in it."

Mrs. Monroe looked up at me and said, "Lovely earrings Adi."

"Thank you." I felt myself blush once again. "They are a gift from your son."

"I remember the first pair," she smiled.

We all left the house and got into the Highlander. It wasn't snowing, but it felt like it could. Mrs. Monroe sat behind Jamison in his car seat, and I sat to the left of him. The men sat up front, which I had no complaints about. I was sitting behind Will and next to Jamison; it seemed just perfect.

We drove down the hill and headed towards the center of town. Christmas joy illuminated the trees and buildings in Leavenworth. The city sparkled with light. We found a parking spot and then began our hike to Front Street Park. Everyone in Leavenworth was out enjoying the snow and lights. Tourists and residents mingled and participated in the Christmas Eve glory.

"Will, mind if I carry Jamison for a bit?" I asked.

Will handed me the bundled boy and I hugged him tight to add my warmth.

"I don't remember this many lights," he said, "it's so bright."

"New technology, isn't it amazing?" Mr. Monroe turned around and took in the lights of Leavenworth.

We hiked into the hordes of people who milled around the gazebo. There was a stage setup, and the mayor was getting ready for the ceremony. Hidden speakers scattered throughout the park filled the air with music. The choir behind the mayor prepared for the Christmas carols that would follow the mayor's speech.

I saw my parents and waved them over. Will came and stood next to me, and I could feel the heat coming from him, as well as from myself. *He is really getting to me.* Jamison made a gurgling sound, and I bounced him a bit, enjoying having a baby in my arms.

Then the lights went out. Well, not all of them. There were a few streetlights and some lanterns laid out around the stage. But the city went from too bright to very dark in less than a second.

"Hello everyone," the mayor's voice replaced the music in the hidden speakers. "Welcome to this year's Christmas lighting ceremony. I want to welcome all our residents, new friends, guests, and returning family." The mayor seemed to look in Will's direction, but Will was focused on Jamison and me. "We have survived an incredible storm, but we did so in the most beautiful place in the world. Thank you all for joining us this year." He kept going for another five minutes or so, but I lost focus as Will, Jamison, and I stood there just being together.

"And without further ado," I heard the mayor say and I put my hand over Jamison's eyes. Will and I both looked down and then, even through our eyelids, the world lit up. After a second or two, I peered out at the beautiful lights and the giant Christmas tree with the glowing yellow star on top of it. The choir began and Leavenworth was now filled both with Christmas light and Christmas music.

Will scooped Jamison out of my arms. "What do you think, little man?" He hugged him to himself and began singing along with the carols. I slid closer to Will, and he put his free arm around me. "It is a wonderful night," he said.

"It sure is," I agreed. I looked around and saw both sets of parents watching us. The heat hit my cheeks immediately. "What do you want to do now?"

"I was thinking a couple of songs and then get this guy into the house. He seems warm, but it's cold out here."

"I'd like to see Jamison and you tomorrow. I have a gift for him."

"Sure, how about after breakfast? We can have some coffee and enjoy the day."

I paused then asked, "When are you thinking of going home?"

His answer seemed delayed. "Probably the 26th. I need to get some things ready before New Year's."

"It's going to be strange with you gone again."

"I promise it won't be twelve years again. I'm not afraid of coming home anymore. In fact, I want to be here."

"Nice to hear you calling it home again."

He laughed and said, "I'm also very glad it feels like home again."

Three songs in, we said goodbye to my parents and the five of us moved to the Highlander. We drove back to the houses in silence. They dropped me off at my house first.

"Thank you all," I said.

All the adults got out of the car. Both of the Monroes gave me big hugs and wished me a Merry Christmas.

"I'll see you tomorrow, if that's alright?" They both agreed. I went to Jamison in his car seat and gave him a kiss on the cheek. "Get to sleep sir, Santa is coming." When I turned, Will was standing next to me. He reached out for a hug, and I met him halfway.

"It was a wonderful day," he said.

"I agree. It was amazing."

He kissed me on the cheek and I did the same to him. We both wished each other a Merry Christmas and then they loaded up and drove across the street. I waited at my door and waved good night as their garage door closed.

I entered the house, turned on the lights, and closed the door. *I'm in trouble, big, big trouble.* I went into my room and drew a bath. I poured orange Epsom salt into the water and immediately my bathroom became a spa. I turned on Christmas songs on my phone and then turned the sound low. As I entered the water, I felt the shivers of the cold leave me.

I lay there in the warm water and thought, prayed, and maybe cried a little.

I FELT LIKE A CHILD the night before Christmas. I laid in bed, unable to sleep. My mind simply would not settle down. I had done a good job the last few days, blocking out thoughts of work and my responsibilities to my employees and my clients. As I lay there and stared at the ceiling, I could no longer block out the lists of things that needed to be done at work. After running through the list, inevitably my thoughts of returning to work turned into thoughts of leaving Leavenworth and leaving Adi again. *The one that got away. It was always Adi. Every woman I had ever met was compared to the memory of Adi. Jamison's mother was so much like the Adi I remembered. And now that I was with her again, I realized she was even more like the woman Adi was now. With her? You're not with her. You're near her, but you aren't going to be in a couple of days.* Sleep continued to elude me.

I rolled over and then back again. These thoughts weren't getting me anywhere. But I couldn't stop myself from a fall into reminiscence. I remembered my proposal to Adi and how I felt when she turned me down. I remembered what it felt like to leave Leavenworth. I realized now that I was still in shock when I left and I did not handle well the pain I felt.

Could we forgive and forget after twelve years? It seemed like Adi still had feelings for me. It felt amazing when I held her hand. We keep having moments where it seems like we want to kiss. But what if I had come back to Leavenworth before Jamison? Would she have been interested in me then? She said 'no' because I didn't want to have children, but now that I have a child and she does not, is it me she's interested in or Jamison? Or even if it's both, is that enough? And yes, she was always the one, but she said 'no' before. How could she have done that if she truly loved me? I forced thoughts of Adi out of my head and focused again on work.

I must have dozed off because when I woke up, the clock read 3:33 a.m. I rolled back and found I couldn't sleep again. *When I talked with Adi about Jamison, she told me to keep him with me. She could've suggested I leave Jamison with my parents and her, but she didn't. What's that mean? Is she putting me first, or him, or both of us? She puts us above her own desires, right? But then again, what does she want? I have no clue. Have I read too much into our time together? I simply cannot go through this again. I mean, how many times can someone survive a broken heart? And I need to be emotionally sound for Jamison, right?* "This is all screwed up," I said into my pillow, which muffled the sound of my voice and my frustration.

I reached over to my phone and scrolled through my past texts with Adi. I felt myself smiling as I thought about the last few days with her. *Alright, no matter how she's feeling, you know you still have feelings for her. So, what should you do about that?* No answers came to me. *I must think about Jamison. I need to consider work, and I should consider my parents.* I knew that was all true, but in my heart, I wanted to focus on myself and Adi. Twelve years ago, I made choices I believed would keep Adi and me together. I chose a college on that basis. I proposed based on that. Should I make choices like that again? *Probably not, given how badly it ended last time. My choices resulted in my absence from Leavenworth for twelve years.*

It kept me so busy my parents couldn't even visit me. I blocked out everything Leavenworth represented because of my selfish desires. Now, no matter what, I had to think about Jamison first.

It was now almost 4:30 in the morning. I grabbed my phone and texted Demetre, an old friend from college days. He and I stayed in touch by phone, text, and the occasional online game.

Will: Merry Christmas.

There was a momentary pause then he responded. **Demetre: Aren't you up a little early? New baby keeping you from sleeping?**

I had forgotten that I had talked with him while I was at Spokane during the last few days with Jamison's mother. I looked over at Jamison who was sound asleep in his bassinet. **Will: No, he sleeps like a champion. A storm hit and I'm in Leavenworth.**

Demetre: OMG, you doing, ok? Christmas with the parents?

Will: Yes, and I've spent time with Adi.

Demetre: The Adi?

Will: Yes, her.

Demetre: The one that got away?

Will: Yes.

Demetre: And how's that going?

Will: Started out a bit rough, but we talked.

Demetre: One of those cathartic conversations? You both found closure? LOL

Will: You joke, but yes, we did. And after that, well, we've spent a lot of time together.

Demetre: Am I hearing you correctly? You are spending time with the girl who broke your heart and turned you into the world's most insane workaholic?

Will: That's not true.

Demetre: I spent a good portion of my four years in college getting you to have some kind of fun. Do you not remember that?

Will: Maybe.

Demetre: So, I'm guessing you are one huge jumble of emotions at this point.

Will: It's why I'm texting this early in the morning. I can't sleep.

There were three dots on my phone. It sat like that for a while. I realized I'd rather be teased at that moment than have to deal with the silent treatment. I was about to text again, but suddenly his text came through. **Demetre: I remember freshman year buddy, do you want to go down that road again?** I started to respond and then more text appeared. **Demetre: But on the other hand, I've never known you to fall in love with anyone else. Did you ever stop loving her?**

Will: I think that's the heart of the question. I smiled at my own choice of words. **Will: I never stopped loving her. Distance made it easier to kid myself, but now...**

Demetre: So, what's the problem?

Will: Same old problem, not sure how she feels. And there's the added question of how much her feelings are tied into the fact that I now have a child and she doesn't.

There was a pause. **Demetre: that's kind of messed up thinking. Does it really matter?**

Will: I think it does. It feels like it does. I paused again. I thought about Adi being just across the street. I realized that there was no question about how I felt. But I still didn't know what was right for me or for Jamison. I had to think about Jamison, too.

Demetre: When are you going home?

Will: Was planning to leave tomorrow, the 26th.

Demetre: Would distance help clear things up?

Now, that was an interesting idea. I hadn't been home with Jamison. In fact, all of my real Jamison experiences were now wrapped up with Leavenworth. Maybe I just need a bit of space. **Will: That's a damn good idea. See how Jamison and I do in Edmonds and get back to work.**

Demetre: Worth a try. Have a wonderful Christmas buddy. My kids are up. I need to get going.

Will: I appreciate the help as always. Have a wonderful Christmas.

He didn't respond, but I didn't expect him to. Demetre's children were his life and now that they had his attention, I didn't. I slipped out of bed and stood above the bassinet. I looked down at Jamison. The smile that crossed my face paled to the warmth in my chest and heart. *Yes, I may be still in love with Adi Lewis, but my love for this little guy was something entirely different. I had never in my life felt anything so powerful.*

I crawled into bed and found I could sleep a little. I still woke up every time I rolled over, which was annoying. Finally, I started making mental lists. I planned for what I would do when I got to Edmonds to finish getting the house ready for Jamison. I knew my staff would already have the house prepared, but I wanted to finish it all up myself. I planned for work and getting ready for New Years. I planned for my parents and how I could get them to come out to Edmonds soon. And then I thought about how to maintain contact with Adi. I promised myself it would not be another twelve years.

I looked over and the clock was now showing almost six in the morning. I grabbed my phone again. I wanted to reach out to Adi, but I didn't want to wake her up. Would she be awake at this hour? I mean it was Christmas after all. Adi loved Christmas. She loved anything that brought family together and made children happy.

Children. Adi would never leave her school and her students. She loved Leavenworth. "What are you thinking?" I asked myself. Jamison rolled over in his bassinet. Even the best sleeping baby needs to eat, and he would be up shortly. *Are you really thinking of asking Adi to come with you to Edmonds?* I realized I was, but I also realized I wasn't going to. Demetre's advice had been spot on. I needed to get out of Leavenworth. I needed to get away from Adi and my parents. I needed it to be just Jamison and me for a while before I made life-changing choices or worse mistakes.

The plan was simple. We would have a wonderful Christmas with my parents. I would bring Jamison over to spend some time today with Adi. I wanted to spend the day with her. I wanted to talk with her and see how she was feeling. But, most of all, I knew I needed to let her know I had to return to Edmonds. But I also had to make sure this time I didn't hurt her feelings. I needed to return to

Leavenworth without concern. I wanted her in my life, however that looked. And I needed to tell her how much I wanted her in Jamison's life as well.

Jamison moved in his crib. I could tell he was awake. I listened to him for a while until I heard him begin to cry. I scooped him up before his tears woke up anyone in the house. I changed his diaper and then went to the kitchen to prepare his bottle. Mom smiled at me as I came in. She handed me the already prepared bottle. "Thanks." She responded with a little hug and then went back to her room.

I sat down on the couch and fed Jamison. The room was warm, but still I tucked a blanket around us. I looked around the room, spending a fair amount of time examining the Christmas tree. It was an eclectic mix of ornaments from times long before my birth to the present. I recognized many of the ornaments, but others were new to me. It really struck home the mistake I made by being gone twelve years. *I'm so sorry. Never again.* I turned my attention back to Jamison. He was most of the way through his bottle. His eyes were locked on me. I smiled and kissed him. His cheeks were cold, but the rest of him seemed so warm against my body.

Finally, the bottle was done, and I flipped him onto my chest and shoulder to burp him. After a resounding belch, I looked at my content and happy son and smiled. I snuggled him into me and then pulled out my phone. I sent a text to Adi. **Will: When you wake up, let's discuss when we can hang out today.**

I turned on the TV and switched to a radio station playing some soft jazz. Jamison and I sat there on the couch and listened to the music together. We talked for the next hour; well, I talked. I told him about my plans for us. Described what our home in Edmonds was like. Talked about all the new people he would meet. And I promised him we would come back to Leavenworth soon. He would always have his grandparents and Adi in his life. Throughout it all, he listened, made funny faces, and focused all his attention on me. He was so small, but his size did not reflect his importance to me or the people whose lives he had touched. As my mother had said, he was my miracle boy. The very thing I needed to complete my life, even though I hadn't known it.

We snuggled some more on the couch, and then we both drifted off to sleep.

CHAPTER 40 – ADI

IT WAS AFTER 6:00 a.m. when Will texted me, **WILL: WHEN YOU WAKE UP, LET'S DISCUSS WHEN WE CAN HANG OUT TODAY.** I didn't respond. I had been up all night. I couldn't sleep. I admit, I always have difficulty sleeping the night before Christmas, but this time it was worse.

Adi: Clare, you awake? There was no immediate response.

I sat in bed with four pillows behind me. Light music played in the background with the hope it would help me sleep. It hadn't and now I found it annoying, so I turned it off.

Clare: Are you seriously texting me at 6 in the morning? Clare was not an early riser even on Christmas.

Adi: I haven't slept. I'm...I don't know.

Clare: Frustrated?

Adi: Yes. He's going to leave again. Jamison is going to leave. I'll be...

Clare: You won't be alone. You have all of us. And they will not be gone twelve more years.

Adi: Can I call?

Clare: Yes. I called her.

"I know I have all of you," I said when she answered, "but I want them too."

"Of course you do, honey. You never stopped loving Will."

"I loved Edward."

She coughed. "You loved Edward in an Edward way. But you love Will in a first and forever love sort of way." She laughed. "I'm kind of jealous."

"You shouldn't be. From what I can tell, all these feelings are just causing me a lot of pain. He's going to leave again soon."

"Interesting," she responded.

"What's interesting?" I asked.

"You only mentioned Will."

"Well, I'll miss Jamison too, of course."

"Adi, if Will came back without a baby, do you think that would've changed your feelings?"

I thought about the question and realized the answer was no. Jamison was amazing and I felt love for the little child, but that wasn't what kept me up all night. Jamison wasn't what was frustrating me. I didn't want Will to leave me again. *No, that's not right, well it is, but really I don't want to lose Will again.*

"You still there?"

"Yes. I'm not sure I can lose Will again."

"Are you really losing him? I mean, you two aren't 'together.'"

"I'm describing my emotions. You really going to play lawyer?" That got a laugh out of her.

"Sorry. Sounds to me like you two should talk today. You should tell him how you feel."

"I can't do that." *She was right. I should do it. But was I brave enough?*

"Why, why can't you?"

"What if he doesn't feel the same way?"

"So, you are afraid to put your heart out there? Do you remember this is the guy who proposed to you and you said, 'no?' Perhaps it's your turn to take a risk, what do you think?"

"I don't know." I sighed and Clare laughed.

"I wish I had your problems."

"Excuse me?"

"The man of your dreams has returned to Leavenworth days after your divorce from your husband is completed and he brings with him a beautiful baby who needs a mother like you. Now I agree that it is not ideal that he is harboring anger and bitterness over you saying 'no' when he proposed twelve years ago, but it seems like you all got over that." Clare paused, then continued, "And after resolving your twelve years of unsettled feelings, anger, and general unrest, the two of you have spent a few glorious days together. And now, after all of that, you are second guessing it. Boo hoo, what a terrible Christmas!"

"You are making me angry."

"Because I'm right, right?"

I took some deep breaths. "Yes, that and you are making me feel stupid and self-absorbed."

"Maybe a little of the latter, none of the former, I think. It scared you to go off to college, but that worked out. Sometimes we have to get out of our comfort zones."

"What if I tell him how I'm feeling? That doesn't mean he isn't going to leave. It doesn't mean I'm going to follow him. How does it really help?"

"Opening yourself up definitely doesn't mean you won't get hurt. But it will get these emotions out in the open. It allows the two of you to explore the possibilities. Are you 100% certain you wouldn't follow him this time?"

It was a good question. Was there an answer? "No, I'm uncertain about everything."

"Would you leave Leavenworth for him? For Jamison?"

I thought a good long while about her questions. "I've spent my whole life wanting children. Had you asked me the question before I saw Wil again, I would've said I would have done anything to have a child. But, after seeing Will and after being with him. He just..."

"Completes you?" She laughed.

"Sounds cliché, but it's true. I feel more myself with him. I always thought I would be a good mother, but I think I would be a great mother with him as the father. Does that make sense?"

"It does. He's your soulmate."

"Oh, that sounds silly. That doesn't really exist."

"You and Will seem to prove the cliché."

"Do we?"

"Yes, you silly goose you do. I have to tell you though I'm glad your focus is on Will and not Jamison. The baby is three months old. Who knows what he'll be like. But if you plan to follow them to Edmonds, you need to be in love with Will and want him for your partner."

My heart raced as I thought about going to Edmonds with Will. Then I thought about leaving Leavenworth, my family, and my students. "I'm not sure I could leave."

"But would you?"

I paused, then said, "I might." Tears formed in my eyes. A slight burn started in the back of my throat.

"No decisions have to be made yet, Adi. Don't get too worked up and don't count your chickens before they are hatched. But I think you know you need to talk with Will."

"I get it. You are right." I wiped away the tears. "This is going to be an interesting Christmas."

"Which reminds me," she said and then asked, "what'd you get me this year?" We both laughed and let our conversation switch to Christmas presents and our shared past. Once the call was done, I wished her a Merry Christmas and we disconnected.

I texted Will. **Adi: You coming here or am I coming over there?**

Will: Just woke up from a nap. We're going to have breakfast here and open presents. Enjoy your folks. Come over around lunch, ok?

Adi: Ok, Merry Christmas!

Will: You too. Looking forward to seeing you.

Adi: I am too. How'd you sleep?

There was a long pause. **Will: It was a rough night. Mind wouldn't settle down.**

Adi: Me too. I thought a bit about my next question and decided to go for it. **What were you thinking about?**

Will: LOL. Everything. But yes, a lot about Leavenworth and you.

I felt the word "you" down to my toes. He spent the night thinking about me. **Adi: Me too. Sure feels like so much has changed. I'm very glad you came home and we got to talk.**

Will: I am too Adi. And I think we need to talk some more.

Adi: I agree. We will today. Ok?

Will: Yes.

Adi: Ok. I need to go get a shower.

Will: Me too. See you soon.

It felt like I should write something more. But I didn't. I knew what I wanted to write, but it just wasn't appropriate.

I got out of bed and headed for the shower. I sent a quick text to my mom as the shower warmed up. **Adi: Hitting the shower now, will be there in 30 mins.**

Adi's mom: Breakfast is cooking now.

Adi: Ok fast shower, be there in 15.

I jumped in the shower and scrubbed as if my life depended on it. The hot shower helped a lot for my tired body but did nothing for my head. "I'm going to tell him how I'm feeling," I said to myself in the shower. The little voice in the back remained quiet and I felt shivers even through the hot water. *Yes, I'm going to tell him. What's the worst that could happen?* The little voice made a list, but I ignored it. *Sometimes you have to make your own luck.* Nothing *is going to happen between Will and me unless we talk. We need to talk, right?* Silence.

I finished showering, picked up my Santa bag full of presents, left the house, and jumped into my car.

Only once on my way to my parents did I let myself wonder what would happen if he didn't feel the same way. But it was Christmas, a day of miracles, so I pushed those thoughts aside. *It'll all be fine, it'll all work out.*

CHAPTER 41 – WILL

CHRISTMAS MORNING WAS WONDERFUL. Mom made an amazing breakfast and I held Jamison as we opened presents. There were multiple photo moments that clearly ensured that Jamison could look back fondly at his first Christmas.

"I love the watch," my mother said as she gave me and Jamison an enormous hug. "That was very thoughtful of you, son."

Dad was laughing and opening his coffee maker. "We're going to finally have some restaurant quality coffee in this house."

"I know how you like your coffee, dad."

"Yes, indeed." He disappeared into the kitchen with the coffee machine.

My mother was shaking her head. "You've given him a new toy to play with. I'm unlikely to get any sleep for a while all energized on all your father's new coffee drinks." I laughed.

My parents had found some free time themselves to go shopping for us. Jamison was now sporting about every type of Leavenworth baby clothes that existed. His wardrobe would include Leavenworth gear for the next two years easily. I got a beautiful Leavenworth frame that my mother quickly told me she would add a picture of Jamison to. Dad had given me one of his favorite knives. He had been collecting them for years.

Around noon, with Jamison taking a nap and my parents sharing two beautiful cups of coffee, I said, "I'm going over to Adi's for a bit."

My father finished a sip of coffee. "What's the plan, son?"

I paused for a second. I didn't want to rattle the Christmas bliss we were all experiencing. "You all know I need to go home tomorrow, right?" The chill my statement had on the room was palpable.

"Yes," my mother answered for them. She sounded unhappy.

"I want to ensure you both that Jamison and I will visit you a lot and we both want you to come to Edmonds as well, ok?"

My father got up and put his arms around both my mother and me. "We've talked a lot. We should've come out and visited you, son. We were all too stubborn and focused on our own lives and needs. Your mother and I don't want to lose out on any more time with you or Jamison."

"Good, I'm very glad. I love you both." I took a deep breath and continued. "I'll head home tomorrow with Jamison and get settled in. I need to figure out what my life is going to look like with him in Edmonds."

"Who will take care of him?" my mother asked.

"My staff should have hired a nanny by now."

"I could come with you and take care of him until you find the perfect nanny."

I turned and gave mom a big hug. I spoke softly to her. "I appreciate that mom, and love you for it, but I realized this morning I need a little time with Jamison to see what my life with him is going to be like. You and dad are wonderful help and fantastic grandparents, but I need a little time with Jamison, so I can figure things out."

"I get it," my mom said.

Dad added, "We both do. But what about Adi?"

I didn't answer at first.

"Son, what about Adi?"

"I don't know, dad."

Dad replied, "Son, we've lived with Adi in this town for most of the last decade. We saw her with her ex-husband just as we've seen her with you before and after you left. She's a different woman when she's around you."

My mom said, "Her feelings for you are clear, don't you think?"

"I don't know. I cannot even figure out my own feelings, honestly. But are either of you concerned about maybe her feelings for me are based on old feelings, plus the fact that I now have a baby?"

My father laughed and then stopped himself. "Son, I know Adi has always wanted a child, but I'm pretty confident the way she looks at you isn't driven by her maternal instinct."

"Your father knows what he's talking about," my mother said.

Dad said, "I call it the way I see it."

If I was going to get embarrassed by my parents, this would be the moment, but instead they made me feel reassured about my own feelings. I felt supported and loved. "I love you both," I said and then headed to the door with coat in hand. "I'll be back in a bit."

The trek across the street seemed to take forever. About halfway across, I realized I'd forgotten to bring Jamison with me. I thought about going back, but he was asleep, and I really wanted some time with Adi alone. I also realized I was curious about her reaction. Would she be happy to see me without Jamison? Would her focus be on the missing baby? I knew how much I wanted to see her. I noticed the Honda SUV in the driveway, but I admit I didn't think about it much. I got to the door and knocked.

"Just a second," I heard from the other side of the door.

The door opened, and Adi stood there looking beautiful. She had a gorgeous dress on and a bit more makeup than she'd been wearing lately. "I just got home. Come on in."

As I stepped in, I saw the man in her living room drinking a cup of coffee. He was dressed up just like she was and gave me a look that seemed to say, *this is my territory*. "Merry Christmas," I said.

"And to you," she said. I had stopped in the doorway and hadn't moved. "Oh, and this is my ex-husband, Edward. Edward this is William Monroe."

"The one who left you?"

"Sounds like that's a mistake we both made." I stepped into the house and closed the door. I had thought I didn't like the man, but now I knew for certain I was right. "You in town for Christmas?" He stared hard at me and clearly was still processing the last statement. Adi's mouth hadn't literally dropped open, but it was a close call. "Might I get a cup of that coffee?" Adi turned and walked into the kitchen, and I followed.

She whispered, "Really?" as she made the coffee.

"He's a jerk."

"Seems to me you are both being jerks." She handed me my coffee.

"Merry Christmas," I said in a hushed tone. "I'm sorry I didn't bring Jamison with me, he was asleep, but we can go visit him later, ok?"

"That's fine. Edward showed up at my parents to wish them a Merry Christmas. He followed me over here to pick up a couple of things he had left in the house."

"No explanations needed. It's not like we're dating or anything." Her face showed hurt, which surprised me.

"No, of course not." She walked into the other room. I followed her.

"So, you in town long?" Edward asked as if we hadn't just disappeared into the kitchen to obviously talk about him.

"We are leaving tomorrow," I replied, "I have to get ready for a meeting in Tokyo on New Year's Eve."

"Tomorrow," Adi stated quietly.

"Do you live in Leavenworth still?" I asked Edward.

"No, I came back to get some things and got caught in the storm. Since I was here for Christmas, I thought it only polite to stop in and see everyone."

"How nice of you," I said.

"Well, yes," he replied.

Adi asked, "Ed, are you leaving town tomorrow as well?"

He turned to look at Adi. "Yes. I've got everything boxed up and ready to go."

At that moment, Adi looked exhausted. She seemed deflated and maybe even a little lost. I realized that the two "loves" of her life were leaving, which reminded me how much it hurt the first time I lost her. I also realized again just how much I did not like this man, Edward. "Your earrings look wonderful." Adi's right hand went up to her ear and she played absentmindedly with the earring there.

Edward stepped closer and looked at her earrings. "They are beautiful," he said and then turned to me, "a gift from you, I assume."

"Yes, trying to replace an old gift lost."

He asked Adi, "Oh, those were those old diamond studs you used to wear in college, right?"

"Yes." She dipped her head a little.

Before she could say more, Edward said, "I remember you losing one of those on our third date. The camping trip, right? We searched that sleeping bag for hours." He laughed.

It felt like he was laughing at Adi. The flash of anger that erupted in me was a surprise. I wanted to hurt this man, which really was not me. The entire experience was very confusing. I knew I didn't want to get into a fight with this guy, but I so wanted to. "Maybe I should leave." *I needed to get control of myself. What was going on? Why was I feeling this way? Why was I acting like a jealous fool?*

CHAPTER 42 – ADI

I HAD NEVER SEEN WILL this way. They were both making fools of themselves. In a book or television show, this would be some momentous moment where the men in her life decided they loved her and fought for her. In reality, it was annoying testosterone driven madness. They had both left her. They had no right to act this way. I wanted to yell at them both, but all I could think about was that they were both leaving. *I wish Ed would just leave; I need to talk with Will.*

As Will got closer to the door, I said, "Ed, thanks so much for stopping in. If you have everything, Will and I had some plans this morning."

Was the look on Ed's face hurt?

"Sure, Adi," he said. He put on his jacket and picked up his things. "Merry Christmas...to you both."

"And to you," Will said as he opened the door.

Ed left the house with his tail between his legs. In the battle between the two men, I had answered the question of who the winner was. It was all too ridiculous. But it also answered questions about how I felt as well.

Will closed the door.

"You were not being nice," I said.

"He started it."

"Will, what were you thinking? I thought for a moment you were going to get into a physical fight. Why did you behave that way? Since when did you get into petty squabbles?"

"Apparently, since I got back to Leavenworth and was confronted with my ex-girlfriend's ex-husband." He remained straight faced, but I could see the smile in his eyes.

I couldn't help recognizing the jealousy both men exhibited. In some sick part of my brain, I enjoyed it. They both had left, so it was nice to know they both had not gotten over me. But their behavior was ridiculous.

"We should talk."

"I agree." I went into the living room, he followed, and we both sat down on the couch.

"I have to go home tomorrow."

"Yes, you just said as much." The edge to my voice was a bit of a surprise.

He nodded. "Sorry about that. Edward surprised me."

"And your behavior?"

"I guess I was a little jealous. You accepted his proposal."

Damn, I hadn't thought of it from that angle. "Will, I..."

"I get it. We've hashed it out. We are equally to blame. But, when I saw him, it just set me off. I'm sorry."

"I accept your apology." I thought for a moment, then asked, "Will you be gone long?"

"No, I'll come visit soon, but I need to figure out things for Jamison and me. Leavenworth has been wonderful, but we live in Edmonds. I need to get back to work and figure out how I'm going to successfully be both a CEO and a father. I need to get Jamison settled in and figure out the nanny situation. I just need things to normalize."

"A *nanny*?" I heard myself ask.

"Yes, a nanny, I can't very well take Jamison to work every day."

"It just sounds so, I don't know, rich and elitist. I mean don't get me wrong, I think Jamison should be with you, but couldn't your parents go with you or something?"

He sighed, paused, and then said, "I've thought about that. I know my mom would leave to be with him." He looked up and locked eyes with me and said, "This will sound silly, but I'm kind of jealous of the little guy. No one was willing to move for just me." That one statement both hurt and gave me hope.

"I wanted to follow you." Our eyes remained locked and I could see the emotions going through them as if the thoughts and feelings passed through his eyes. "Are you alright?"

"I'll be equally honest. I don't know. It's the craziest thing. I thought Jamison was going to change the path of my life and of course he has, but it feels like coming to Leavenworth has shifted it more. I don't know what I want any more."

"It's hard to know what to do when you don't know what you want."

"Isn't that the truth? You are a wise woman, Adi."

"So, take baby steps. Go slow, figure out what you want."

He nodded his head and looked at me again. As our eyes connected, I felt my heart race and the flush return to my face. "What?"

"I seem to forget how beautiful you are. Either that or you seem to be getting prettier each time I see you."

"You know that's counterproductive," I said as the blush grew in my cheeks.

"Probably," he agreed, "but I thought we were being truthful."

"We are. I'm glad we're friends again. I've missed talking with you."

"I totally agree."

"You need to go home and figure out your life and your nanny." I heard the edge on the word "*nanny*," as much as I tried not to put it there. "Once you're settled in, your parents and I could come out for a visit. You have enough rooms?"

"Yes, and that way you can check out the nanny for me."

"Hmph," was my only response to that.

"What is with you and nannies?"

Because you could choose me, your mom, or both. "Nothing," I said to him.

"Right. You hear the edge in your voice every time you say the word, right? Because I sure do."

Weren't you going to tell him how you feel? Now you can't, right? I mean he's being honest he needs time to figure things out. Telling him how you feel is just going to make things harder.

"Where'd you go?" he asked.

"Oh, just lost in thought about Jamison, you, and Edmonds."

"It's not that far away, right? You all can visit."

"Sure, like we all did a successful job of that the last twelve years."

"I'll take the blame for that. It won't be the same this time."

"Are you sure?" *I know I'm not. What if I return to being angry with you when you leave?*

"Yes, I think. No hard feelings this time, right?"

"Right," I agreed too fast.

This time, he was the one to get lost in thought. After a lengthy and uncomfortable pause, he said, "I'm sorry, Adi."

"For what?"

"For life and us always having terrible timing."

"It seems that way, doesn't it? Perhaps we just want too many different things."

He stood up. "Let's go see Jamison." I stood up and looked at him. He stepped forward and wrapped me in an enormous hug. "If it's alright with you, I don't want to be afraid to hug you like this."

You can do a lot more than that. "No, this is wonderful." I hugged him back and felt our bodies merge. The blush in my face was lost to the rushing heat just about everywhere else.

When the hug finally broke, we were both oddly out of breath. *Did that just happen? That was more than a hug, right?* He wiped something from his eye and turned quickly to get his coat. *Was he crying? No way. Will never cried.* I avoided looking at him as we left the house.

We made our way across the street and entered the Monroe's house without knocking or turning a key. The house smelled of Christmas and cinnamon rolls.

"We're in the kitchen," Mrs. Monroe called out from the kitchen.

We removed our jackets, stamped our feet to get the snow off, and took off our boots. We then made our way into the kitchen. Mrs.

Monroe was frosting cinnamon rolls as Mr. Monroe ate one. Jamison was in his bassinet, which someone had moved to the kitchen. He was awake and looked happy and well fed. I went to him and scooped him up into my arms. "How are you today, little man?"

Will went over and gave his mother a brief hug and then grabbed a couple of plates and fixed us some cinnamon rolls.

"Eat up," Mrs. Monroe said, "they are still warm."

The rolls were wonderful, but the joy I felt was coming from the bundle in my arms. I looked up and found Will smiling at me. "He seems to like you. You are good with him."

"Well, I like him very much," I said with a bit too much of baby talk in my voice. Will laughed at that and then dug back into his cinnamon roll.

Mrs. Monroe said, "I'm going to miss you both so much" and then she disappeared out of the kitchen.

Will looked up and his father said, "She'll be ok, William. She's been waiting so long for you to come home, and she would never have dreamed of a baby like Jamison joining you. She's become extremely attached."

"I know, dad," Will said, "and I'll visit a lot and expect you two to come to Edmonds as well."

"We will," my father said as he got up from his chair. He went out of the kitchen, I presumed, to comfort my mother.

"I guess my leaving tomorrow isn't making this a very Merry Christmas."

I thought hard before I spoke. "We all missed you for a while, but at some point, it was easier to block all those emotions out. Now that you're back, it's kind of a raw nerve, you know."

Will walked up to my side and hugged both Jamison and me. Tears flowed from his eyes. We didn't talk. We just stood there loving Jamison and maybe even loving each other a little.

CHAPTER 43 – WILL

WE HAD ENOUGH GOODBYES on Christmas, and I honestly didn't know if I would have the strength to leave if I saw Adi again. So, like a coward, when I was halfway home on the drive to Edmonds, I spoke to Siri and sent Adi a text telling her how much I enjoyed seeing her and would be back soon.

I didn't get a response right away, which bothered me, but I ignored it as I made my way west on Highway 2. I stopped a couple times, once to feed Jamison and another time to change him. Eventually I got to Interstate 5, which, like a river, guided me down to Edmonds and home.

We arrived at my house a little after noon. I hit the button in the Highlander and the gates opened. I drove up the driveway to find my front door open and Jim standing in it.

As I got out of the vehicle, he said, "Welcome home."

"Thanks, been tracking my phone again?"

"Maybe." He came over to the car and grabbed some of my bags. "You're loaded down."

"Mom sent me home with all of Jamison's stuff. I told her I didn't need it, but she insisted." I pulled Jamison out of the car. He was awake and looking around.

Jim said, "Good looking son. His mother must have been gorgeous to override all your contributions."

"Hey man, I'm the pretty one of the two of us. Don't you forget it."

He moved towards the house with the bags and the few remaining bottles of milk in the cooler. "Speak for yourself. I heard no complaints this morning."

"Well," I said, "at least you know you didn't get him pregnant."

"True," he said and then laughed. "Still cannot get over the fact that you beat the condom odds, but hey, if anyone was going to do it."

We walked into the house. I was home, *but why doesn't it feel like it?* I asked myself. I had two staff people that lived in the house: Lilly and Tom. The two of them were a married couple and were older than me, but younger than my parents. But, as I came into the house, I realized they had been substitute parents for the last five years since they came to work for me.

"He's darling," Lilly said.

"A very strapping young man, sir," Tom said.

"Thank you both."

A middle-aged woman I had not met before stepped into the room. "Sir," Tom said, "this is Ms. Avery. We hired her as Master Jamison's nanny."

"I got the data you sent me. Ms. Avery, very nice to meet you. I hope you have settled in and found your room to be comfortable."

"Yes, Mr. Monroe, it's fine." She walked over and knelt to greet Jamison. He seemed a little unsettled as she picked him up, but there were no tears.

"The rest of the breast milk is in the cooler." I pointed to the bag that Jim was holding. "Could we please get it into the freezer immediately?"

"Yes sir." She grabbed the bag from Jim and disappeared into the kitchen. I felt a lurch inside as I watched a stranger walk away with Jamison. In my head I heard the distinct word, *"nanny,"* in Adi's voice.

"Tom, would you mind dealing with the rest of the bags? I'm sure Jim is beside himself wanting to discuss business."

"Will do, Mr. Monroe."

Jim asked, "You alright? Hello? Where you at, Will?"

I shook the thoughts of Adi and Jamison out of my head and began the walk to my home office. "Been a crazy week."

"You don't know the half of it."

We entered my office and closed the doors. Two hours later, we exited, and I felt completely drained, frustrated, and even a bit angry.

"How the hell did this happen?"

Jim shrugged and said, "We shut down the shop for the holidays like you told us to. A couple of communications got missed."

I moved towards the kitchen. As I entered the modern white kitchen with stainless steel appliances, I realized that in my head I had been envisioning myself walking into my mother's kitchen.

Lilly, who was preparing a bottle, asked, "Do you need anything, Mr. Monroe?"

"A cup of coffee would be nice when you have a moment, Lilly." Jim and I sat down at the kitchen table and looked out at the huge sliding glass doors at the Puget Sound.

"I never tire of this view," Jim said.

"We need to fix this. Make some calls. Let's see if we can do a Zoom conference today and, if not, then early tomorrow."

"Show them the face of the company is back?"

"Something like that. It's all about perceptions, right?"

"As always. Where do you want to do it?"

"Office. Let's make it clear I'm completely back."

He got up and said, "It'll take a couple of hours. It's about 6:00 a.m. there. I'm pretty sure I could get something together for 9:00 a.m. their time."

"4:00 p.m. our time, perfect. Let me check on Jamison and spend some time with him, then I'll shower, suit up, and meet you at work. Text me if the timing changes." I drank the rest of my coffee and stood up.

"He's back!" Jim yelped as he left the room.

I smiled at his excitement. "Lilly, where's Jamison?"

"He's in his room with Ms. Avery. Would you like another cup of coffee or some breakfast?"

"No, thank you. I'm a little too worked up to eat right now." I walked upstairs and to the room Tom and Lilly had prepared for Jamison. I walked in to find the perfect little boy's room with light blue walls, images of dinosaurs, and a shelf full of books. Ms. Avery was in a rocking chair, finishing feeding Jamison.

Ms. Avery asked, "Is he a fussy eater?"

"Not normally. Was he having issues?"

"At first, but eventually he got to it. Lot of changes for this young man. He might just be feeling it all in his little tummy."

Ms. Avery was perfect on paper, and my gut wasn't giving me any negative feelings, but she seemed somehow detached from what she was doing. "I need to go out for a while. Lilly and Tom will be here. If you need me, do you have my number?"

"Yes sir, your staff provided me with a cell phone loaded with all the important numbers, including your direct line and cell phone."

"Wonderful. May I?" *Did I just ask to hold my own child?*

She held Jamison up and I wrapped him in my arms, holding his bottle with my right hand. "Now you be a good boy and I'll be home soon, ok?" Jamison's lips parted from the bottle, and he appeared to smile. "Now finish that bottle and I'll be back the next time you wake up."

I handed Jamison back to Ms. Avery and it felt, well it felt terrible. *I'm not sure this is going to work.*

I hit the shower, got suited up, and then took the Highlander to work in Seattle. I took the elevator from the parking garage and entered our offices through the elevator door. Most people were still enjoying the holiday I had given them, but Jim had brought some staff on board for our Zoom meeting. I greeted them as I made my way to my office.

I sat down at my desk and turned to look out at the Seattle skyline. I remembered sitting here not so long ago thinking about work and the city below us. Now all I could think about was Jamison at home with a *nanny.*

"Ready to go?" Jim asked.

Crap, I hadn't heard him come in. The nanny thing was really bothering me. "What if I said, 'no.'"

Jim sat down in the leather chair in front of my desk. "You're the boss. What do you need?"

"And that's the real question, isn't it?"

"Look, I cannot pretend to understand everything you are going through. My parents were supportive of me when I came out and I certainly didn't leave a woman I proposed to back home when I went off to college." He snickered at his own joke. "But I understand that you've never really dealt with all those emotions. You've put 100% of yourself into work since I've known you." He paused and tapped his fingers on the chair. "Will, is it possible you've awoken something in yourself that you cannot put back to sleep?"

"And if I have, what do I do with that?"

"You deal with it. Just like you deal with everything else; head on. It's not going to do you any good to pretend you don't have feelings for Adi."

"Is it that obvious?"

"I'm pretty sure even the mail room clerks know that, buddy."

I sighed. "Ok, we can all agree, even the mail room apparently, that I have feelings for Adi, but what do I do with those feelings?"

"And that is 100% a Will Monroe decision."

"No help at all?"

"I trust you to make the right decision Will. You have always done so for this company and for me. There's a reason we all hang around, you know."

"I thought it was the great pay and benefits." I smirked.

"Ok that too. But do you have any idea how many recruiters I turn down every year?"

Yes Jim, I'm quite aware. "I have a guess. I appreciate the loyalty."

"You earn it, and that's my point. Just be yourself. You'll make the correct decisions."

"As always, terrific insights, my friend."

"Why you keep me around. Shall we go deal with Tokyo?"

"Sure." I stood up and followed Jim into the conference room.

As the screens came alive, we got down to business.

CHAPTER 44 – ADI

THE DAY AFTER CHRISTMAS was bad, but as I woke up on December 30th, I realized just how bad I had it for William Monroe. *How in the heck had you fallen in love again with the same man?* Of course, he wasn't the same man, in fact. He was older, more mature, and when I watched him with Jamison, he showed an emotional side that made him just so much more attractive.

We had texted every day since he left. The first day, it was limited, but after his meeting with the Tokyo people I started getting pictures of Jamison and texts about him and work. The texts kept me feeling closer to them and reassured me that William Monroe would not disappear again from my life.

I reached over and grabbed my phone.

Adi: Morning

Will: Morning

Adi: What are you doing?

Will: Finished giving Jamison a bath and a bottle. Heading into the office.

Adi: Ms. Avery working out?

Will: She's so damned detached. It's like she doesn't want to make an emotional connection. She goes through the motions, but there's just something off.

Adi: Nannies are hired, Will. It is a job.

Will: I know an awesome teacher who I'm certain connects with all her children. Isn't teaching a job?

I couldn't argue with that. Part of me wanted to drive over to Edmonds on the spot and go meet this Ms. Avery. **Adi: But you're not concerned about her, right?**

Will: She's been very well vetted and Lilly and Tom are always in the house as well. Jamison's safe.

It was still strange to think of Will having household staff. *Staff, what a strange word, what a strange concept, William Monroe mogul and his staff.* **Adi: Good. Will, he has you for his emotional needs. He doesn't need a nanny for that. He just needs someone to feed him, change him, and keep him safe. It's daycare, nothing more.** *Writing that hurt. In Leavenworth, Jamison would have his entire family there to take care of him. He would have me and my family as well.*

Will: But what about when I'm not around?

I had no answer for him there. Well, at least not one that I was willing to text. **Adi: You missing Leavenworth and your mother already?**

Will: LOL, I was missing you all the second Jamison and I left the house.

Adi: Well, that's nice to hear. We all miss you two, too.

Will: Jim just came in. Talk later.

Adi: Ok.

He misses me. I felt the blush in my cheeks. *Oh, Adi, you've got it bad.* I got out of bed and took a colder shower than normal. *How could this work out? Was I willing to leave Leavenworth and join him, and his staff filled house in Edmonds? I was definitely considering it, which was novel for me. I could teach in Edmonds, right?*

"I cannot leave my class," I said out loud. *But was that true anymore?*

Once out of the shower, I dried off and got dressed. I went down to the kitchen and prepared myself an omelet. *He gets to work so he doesn't have to think about all of this, but my classes don't start up until next week. It'll be easier once school starts again.*

Clare: Whatcha doing.

I picked up my phone. **Adi: eating an omelet.**

Clare: And thinking about Will.

Adi: Sure, that too.

Clare: You two still texting?

Adi: Yes.

Clare: Well, that's a good sign, right?

Adi: Sure, isn't a bad one.

Clare: Tell him how you feel yet?

Adi: No! Stop!

There was a knock at the door. I got up and opened it.

Clare said, "Don't tell me to stop. You know how you feel, why haven't you told him?" There was a pause and then she asked, "Could I get one of those omelets? I'm starving."

We walked into the house. She sat down at the kitchen table while I prepared her an omelet. "I'm not saying I don't have feelings, or that I wouldn't consider moving to Edmonds to be with him and Jamison, but I also know I don't want to move."

"You want your cake and eat it too, as they say."

I laughed, "Damn straight."

Clare poured herself a cup of coffee. After a couple of sips, she asked, "Can you have both? I mean, being realistic and all."

"I do not know."

"I think it's incredible you two reconnected after twelve years. I never thought Edward was right for you."

"What?!?"

"Shut up, you knew that. Don't get all drama queen on me. I'm not saying I thought Will was Mr. Right, I'm just saying Edward was Mr. Wrong. And if you want to disagree with me, think about have you missed Edward at all?"

I thought about it. *She was right. Now, to be honest with myself, I missed being a wife and a potential mother, but I didn't miss Edward in particular.* "Why didn't you ever do something with that psychology degree?"

"If you think becoming a teacher doesn't use that degree, you are crazy," she replied.

"Fair enough." I walked over and set the omelet in front of Clare.

"Looks wonderful," she said and dug in.

I sat down. "Will needs time to figure out things in Edmonds. He needs to be with Jamison there. Though I have to say he's not liking the *nanny*."

"You really cannot say 'nanny' without that tone of voice, can you?" Clare asked through mouthfuls of omelet.

"I've met some *nannies* as a teacher. I'm not a big fan."

"Clearly, but is that really what's going on here?"

"What do you mean?"

"One could also interpret your tone to mean you think you'd be a better person to take care of Jamison than any *nanny*." She put even more emphasis on the word than I did.

I thought about what she said. *There's no doubt I would be a better mother, but that's not it, right*? "I'm not a big fan of *nannies*, but I agree I'd rather have Jamison at home in Leavenworth with his family."

"And you."

"I could do a passible job taking care of him," I said and felt the smirk cross my face.

"And you," she said again a bit louder.

"And me, yes and me, alright? I would do an amazing job. We both know it. Everyone knows it. Will knows it too."

"Ah ha!"

"Ah ha, what?"

"Will knows it too."

"What are you getting at?" I was feeling both sad and mad suddenly, and I wasn't sure if I wanted to cry or hit Clare.

"I think, Adi, that you are unsure of yourself." I started to interrupt but she shushed me with a gesture of her hand and continued. "You realize you are still in love with Will or maybe in love again with Will, I don't know, but either way he chose to have his son be raised by a *nanny* rather than you and that's making you question everything. I think you need to get past what you perceive as a slight and focus on the real question."

"And what, may I ask, is the real question?" The words barely came out my jaw was so tight.

"Do you love him enough to leave Leavenworth?" I didn't respond. I just sat there staring at her for a couple minutes. Finally, she asked, "Well, do you?"

"I would hate it. I would really hate it. But yes, I would leave. I don't know if I screwed up twelve years ago. I don't know what our lives would've been like. But I don't want to screw it up again. Though it doesn't really matter now does it?"

"Why not?" she asked.

"Because he didn't propose to me this time. He didn't even ask me to go with him. He didn't suggest we date or anything else. I hurt him last time, I'll admit it, so I don't think there's going to be another chance."

"Have you told him you love him, and you'd move to Edmonds?"

"Of course not." *Because I only became sure of that fact just now. I screwed up again. I shouldn't have let Will leave without telling him.*

"I think you should." She held out her hand. "That'll be a $1,000.00. You can pay me now or I can put it on your tab."

I slapped her hand.

"Good enough, on your tab." Clare wiped her mouth, got up, and headed for the door. "See you at South for lunch." She left, closing the door behind her. I sat and thought after that for a very long time.

CHAPTER 45 – WILL

I SAT ON MY BED AND stared at myself in the mirror. Tom had packed my suitcase and it sat by my bedroom door, waiting for me to leave. Jim had arranged the flight and my ticket was in my phone waiting for me to use it. There was a car waiting for me outside to take me to the Sea-Tac airport where I would catch an international flight to Japan. It was December 30th, but with the time change I would land just before New Year's Eve with plenty of time to make the party.

Tom stepped into the room and asked, "Do you have everything, sir?"

"I believe so. Where are Avery and Jamison?"

"They are in the nursery, sir."

I went silent.

Tom walked farther into the room. "William, is everything alright?"

"Tom, you and Lilly have been watching Avery with Jamison, right?"

"Yes sir, we would've anyway, but you asked us to do so many times." He smiled.

"I did, didn't I? I'm nervous Tom. I trust your opinion, what do you think about Ms. Avery?"

Tom pulled a chair from the corner of the bedroom over in front of me and sat down. "William, I will guard Master Jamison with my life. Both Lilly and I will."

"I know that. But it's Ms. Avery who is with him. Who should provide him, I don't know, I guess love and attention. How is she with him?"

"She does an exceptional job sir. Jamison is well taken care of."

"Has she warmed up at all?"

He paused and then said, "She seems most businesslike."

"That was my assessment, too."

"And you believe that is not sufficient?"

"I don't know." *Part of me wishes his mother had not died, but then I wouldn't have gone back to Leavenworth. How could such a terrible tragedy have resulted in such a personal miracle? I wanted Jamison to be surrounded by the love I felt for him, for the love my parents showed him, and yes, for the way Adi connected with Jamison. That was love. Ms. Avery was just businesslike.* "I really don't want to leave Jamison for a week."

"Work and duty sir, you have responsibilities other than your son."

"I do, so long as I choose to have them. My responsibilities to my son are not a choice, they are bigger than that, but I feel like by leaving him for a week, I'm already failing him."

"If I may?"

"Sure, of course Tom."

"William, you did not choose to become a father, but you have accepted the responsibility completely. That says a lot about you. You want to succeed at being a father and, like everything else you do, you aspire to be perfect at it. Having been a son and a father, I can tell you it is impossible to be perfect at either."

"I never demand perfection, Tom, not even of myself. At least not the way you mean it. My parents always told me that being perfect meant doing the best job I could do. Didn't mean I'd be perfect, or everything would work out, but I had to give it my best shot."

"And going to Tokyo is what?"

I thought about that for a moment and replied, "It's the best shot for my company to get the deal."

He asked, "But?"

"But I don't think it's the best thing for Jamison."

"Why?"

"He's only three months old, his mother has died, the grandparents he seemed to flourish with were left behind in Leavenworth, and his *nanny* is 'businesslike.'" *I just said the word nanny the way Adi does.*

"And does Ms. Lewis factor into this, William?"

"She'd be a damn better *nanny* than Avery," I said.

"Is that how you think of her, sir, as a nanny?"

No, I don't think of her as a nanny. I think of her as my friend, the woman I used to love...the woman I still love, have always loved. "Adi is my Adi."

"William, I've worked for you for many years now. I've never known you to be indecisive. You are obsessive, a workaholic, and usually harder on yourself than you should be. What is making you unsure about going to Tokyo?"

"I haven't stopped moving since I originally left Leavenworth. It was easy to focus on work because that was it. Now I have work and Jamison. How can I do both successfully?"

"Many people manage it."

"Do they? How many stories are there of workaholic parents whose kids don't really know them? I don't want that for Jamison. And I don't want that for me. But I also don't want to leave the company I created or the projects that we have coming up. Work still excites me. It's not that I hate my job, that would make it so much simpler."

"So, what are you going to do?"

I stood up. "Long term, not a clue." He stood up as well. "But, in the short term, I guess I'm going to Tokyo. Please have my bag put in the car. I'm going to go say goodbye to Jamison and Avery."

"Yes, sir."

I left the room and walked down the hall to Jamison's room. When I walked in, I found Avery preparing his bottle. "Well timed, Mr. Monroe. Would you like to feed him?"

"I would." I picked Jamison up, threw a blanket over the shoulder of my dress shirt, and sat down in the rocking chair. Avery brought me the bottle.

Jamison took the bottle and immediately began feeding.

"He's hungry," I said.

"I have been scheduling his meals, as we discussed. He's a growing baby; he seems always ravenous."

"Is that normal?"

"He is a very healthy baby, Mr. Monroe. Nothing to worry about." Avery stood stiff like a soldier. Her face was stoic. Her voice was honest, but businesslike.

"Do you find in this line of work that you get attached to the children you care for?"

"If the job goes on long enough, yes, it has happened."

"No immediately falling in love with a baby?"

She made just the slightest sigh. "Mr. Monroe, my experience has taught me that new parents, especially single parents, don't know what they want out of the parenting experience. They might initially think that having a nanny or using daycare is the best for their family and child, but after a time, that changes." She paced a bit, making circles on the carpet as I fed Jamison. "Also, while there are some parents who are comfortable with the bond between a child and a nanny, there are others who discover they are not. You cannot know which one you'll be until you've experienced it."

"So, everything is businesslike and unemotional until you size up the parents?"

She nodded. "A fair assessment. It's easier to be guarded at the beginning. See where things progress. It's difficult to control. I've had my heart broken more than once."

I thought of my parents and Adi. I was fairly sure they all became emotionally attached to Jamison instantly, just as I had. "I'm concerned that not showing emotional connection skews your theory. How do the parents know if they are uncomfortable or not?"

"They figure it out. Some faster than others. But in the end, a decision is always made."

"And how long does this usually take?"

She laughed, which surprised me. "For some a day or a week. Most others no more than a month or two. And then there are some where it does not show itself until the child begins to demonstrate a bond with me."

"That must be difficult."

"I have had my heart broken more than once. It's an unfortunate aspect of my chosen career."

"That much pain, and you still choose to be a nanny?"

"I could never have children of my own and honestly never really wanted to get married, anyway. I loved watching Mary Poppins as a child. I liked to think of myself as her. I appear and help until I'm no longer needed. Leaving can be hard, but I can feel good about my service to the family and the child or children. I'm still in touch with the families and the children, especially those I got close to. It's not perfect, but it's the way I've chosen to live my life."

"I like that. Though that places me in the role of Mr. Banks. I've always thought of myself more as Bert."

"Many men are either or both. Being Mr. Banks or Bert isn't the issue, right? It's how the Banks and Berts of the world decide to father their children. It all comes down to choices made or not made."

"Two roads diverged in a wood, and I took the one less traveled by, and that has made all the difference."

"The Road Not Taken by Robert Frost. I enjoy that poem as well," she said.

"Is it really that simple?"

"No, neither path is simple, and it's even harder when you tried to jump back and forth between both paths."

"And so, the answer is?"

"To find the path that works best for you. It won't be perfect; it will just be best."

"So, for some, the road less traveled and for others, the busy road."

"I would think there are probably many paths and byways between those two. Life is not a poem after all. But like the character in The Road Not Taken, everyone one must ultimately choose a path to walk on."

Jamison had finished his bottle. I gave him a hug and a big kiss on the top of his head and then handed him to Avery.

"Have a pleasant trip to Tokyo. Everything will be fine."

I left and turned to look back at Jamison in Avery's arms. *My son!*

CHAPTER 46 – ADI

IT WAS NEW YEAR'S EVE. We had gotten a bit of snow, but nothing like what had fallen just before Christmas. I had just cleaned the dishes from breakfast when the doorbell rang. *Well, at least this time Clare wasn't playing games on the telephone.* I wondered if I had enough eggs for another omelet.

"Coming, Clare."

I opened the door and found Will standing there with Jamison in his arms. "Hi."

"Hi." He just kept on standing there.

"Come in."

Once in the house, Will passed Jamison to me and then removed his and Jamison's coats.

"What are you doing here?" He stopped and then started putting his coat back on. I realized how that sounded and said, "No, take your coat off. I'm so happy that you are both here."

He took his coat off again. "Good, you scared me there for a second."

We went over to the couch and sat down. I cradled Jamison, who was half asleep in my arms.

"He seems so content with you," Will said.

"He's a beautiful baby."

"He is, and you are a beautiful woman, Adi." I felt the blush in my cheeks as I looked down and focused on Jamison. "I think we need to talk."

"I agree. I've been thinking a lot about the past and the recent present."

"I have too."

"It's crazy, but I realized when you were here that I wish I had said yes when you proposed."

"Don't say that. Never say that." He stood up and walked away from the couch. "The paths we took were appropriate for the time. If you had married me, you might never have gone to college or become a teacher. And if we had married, then Jamison would never have been born. The paths we chose were necessary to get us here."

I looked down into Jamison's sleepy face and realized how right he was. "You are right, any choices that would've prevented the birth of this angel would've been incorrect. But Will, you being back home, I just realized at some point, I still, you know…"

"Love me?"

"Yes, yes, I still love you, though perhaps I love you more and differently. As a woman loves a man, not high school love. You are just so much more than you were."

He knelt in front of me and rested his forehead on my knee. His arms wrapped around my legs. "I've never stopped loving you." I could hear the tears in his voice. "There was never anyone else. Once I left Leavenworth, I always feared coming back because I knew seeing you would crush me. You have always been my one true love."

"And how do you feel now?"

Will raised up, moved forward, and kissed me. It was a passionate kiss that made me very aware of the baby I had in my arms. I wanted to reach around and hold Will. But I had nothing to complain about. I was with the two men I loved.

The kiss broke and he said, "I love you, Adi Lewis."

"And I love you. But aren't you supposed to be in Japan?"

"I was about to get into the car to go to the airport for Tokyo and all I could think about was the plane was going to take me even farther away from you and Jamison. I kept coming back to both of you. I couldn't do it. It hurt too badly. I've been missing you every day since I left Leavenworth again. Feeling that, and then leaving Jamison as well, was just too much. I knew I had to take the path less traveled. I needed to come home to Leavenworth."

"You are coming here to stay?"

"Yes, I want Jamison to be raised here. I want him to know his grandparents. I want him to know you. I want him to know what it's like to be loved and to see two parents that love each other and him."

"Parents?" My voice cracked.

He smiled and said, "Yes, parents. You rejected my proposal once before, Adi Lewis, if I ask you again, what will be your answer?"

"William Monroe, we can live here in Leavenworth, in Edmonds, or even Tokyo. I don't want to lose you again. I love you and my answer would be 'yes.'" I laid Jamison, who was asleep, on the couch, using pillows to keep him safe from the edge. I stood up, as did Will. I hugged him and kissed him, and in that moment my life was complete.

He knelt and pulled a small blue box with light blue trim from his pocket. I had not seen that little blue box in twelve years. "Is it the same ring?"

"Yes, I've been holding onto it." He smiled. Opened the box and turned it towards me. "Adalynn Jane Lewis, will you make me the happiest man in the world and be my wife?"

"Yes!" He removed the ring and put it on my left ring finger. My hand was shaking. My heart was pumping hard. Tears of happiness were flowing down my face. We kissed and kissed.

When we stopped kissing, we started to both laugh. "Who are we telling first?"

"Jamison is going to be asleep for a couple more hours. Let's wait to tell anyone for now," and then he kissed me again and again.

The kissing went on for some time. We eventually told everyone. Will passed on many of his duties to other people in the company and bought a beautiful house in Leavenworth. Lilly and Tom came to live with us. Avery found work elsewhere. The wedding was in July, and it felt like all of Leavenworth came out for it. I was content. And then the strangest thing happened, I got pregnant. But that's a story for another time.